The Moon at Noon

Book Three in the

House Next Door

Trilogy

By

Jule Owen

First published in 2015 by Mean Time Books

Text and Illustration Copyright © 2015 Jule Owen

ISBN 13: 978-0-9934097-6-9

www.juleowen.com

www.meantimebooks.co.uk

THE MOON AT NOON

For my dad, John Owen

1 THE END

DAY TWENTY-THREE: Tuesday 14th December 2055, London

Mathew stands by the dragon Yinglong's massive head. She might be sleeping. Her eyes are closed, her neck rests across one foreleg, her long tail curls around her body like a sleeping cat. Though she has been dead many years in the time of this world, she still looks whole. Untouched, her scales will not easily decay, but if he pushes at her with any force, she will crumble to dust. Her mate, Shen, lies ten feet away, resting less peacefully, splayed out on the ground, a broken leg awkwardly angled away from his body.

They rampaged through their world, eating whatever they found, destroying anything they couldn't eat, until there was nothing left. Then, starving, they turned on one another. At the end of their last battle, Shen came crashing down to earth with Yinglong hurtling after him. Finding him already dead, broken on the ground, she was too weak and exhausted to eat him. Instead, she curled up at his side, nursing her own wounds, and went to sleep forever.

Mathew walks around their bodies until he can no

longer stand looking at them. He kicks at the ground, stony and cindered, black with charcoal from thousands of incinerated trees. It crunches under foot. As he steps back, he puts his hands behind his head, and looks about. The whole world is burned.

On the mountain in the distance a line of black tree stumps rears against the sky. Fog rolls down between the bare rocks. Now there are no trees, no living things at all. There is nothing to stop the wind blowing across the hills and the mountains and howling between valleys. The forest that once grew lush and green is all gone to ashes. Behind him, the hunting lodge Eva built for him is reduced to its stone foundations; the carcasses of armchairs stand forlornly by the charred stone fireplace. Everything is burnt. Everything is destroyed. He surveys the world Eva left in his care with dry, hard eyes and thinks, bitterly, *how appropriate*. There is a flat low rock nearby. He goes and sits on it and contemplates the things he made, neglected, and through neglect, destroyed.

Eva has not come. She knows when to leave him alone. He does not want company.

He waits for a long time until it starts to rain, hard driving icy rain numbing the skin on his face, and then he stands and walks back to the lodge, stepping over broken glass, stooping beneath the felled charred beams of the roof, heading to the back of the house and the door out of this world, standing oddly untouched in its frame. He steps through and closes it behind, knowing he will never return.

Then he is sitting in a chair in the Darkroom in his house at Pickervance Road.

It really is my house now.

Initiating the program managing Eva's world, he finds the delete option and selects it. A prompt is thrown up, "

```
Please enter administration password.
```

He enters the password and submits it.

```
Proceeding will delete all files. Do you wish to
continue?
```

"Yes," he says.

```
Deleting…
```

And he watches the dead world disintegrate, crumbling into sand until finally there is nothing left, just a bare black room with some cameras and technical equipment.

In the kitchen, the robot HomeAngel, Leibniz, is making lunch. When his food is ready, Mathew sits and eats in silence. The Canvas is off. He doesn't care about the news now. He finishes, and lets the HomeAngel take his plates and cup, stack them in the dishwasher, switch on the thirty-second wash cycle and then put away the clean, dry dishes. As Leibniz finishes, Mathew says, "Leibniz, go and fetch your docking station and then follow me."

Without questioning, Leibniz goes over to the wall where it normally recharges, bends and picks up the wireless power pack from the floor. Then it follows Mathew out into the hall, carrying its charger.

O'Malley is asleep on the sofa in the front room. Mathew picks him up, and holds him, kissing his head. "Come on, old friend. Come and see your new home."

The three of them make a strange little caravan, out of the front door, down the short pathway, through the gate, onto the pavement in the street, along and around into Gen's front garden. She opens the door almost immediately.

"That was quick," he says.

"I was watching for you in the window. I didn't want you to have to wait outside with O'Malley. Come in." She observes curiously as the robot lifts its legs high over the unfamiliar step and she stands back against the wall as it moves inside.

"Go to the kitchen, Leibniz," Mathew says. "Straight ahead."

"Yes Mathew," the robot replies, and it does as it is instructed.

Gen shuts the front door and Mathew puts O'Malley down. The cat walks about on short cautious legs, sniffing. "You've been here before, old fella. Remember?" he says to the cat. But O'Malley seems to have no such memory.

"Shall I keep him in one room for the time being?" Gen suggests.

"Great idea. Front room okay?"

"Perhaps if I put the lid of the piano down," Gen rushes over and covers the grand piano up.

"I'll get his bowl and litter tray just now. Leibniz deals with it all, feeds him, cleans his box. He even brushes him and administers basic vet care. The robot will order anything the cat needs."

They shut the door on O'Malley and go into the kitchen.

"I'm sorry you have to leave your cat, Mathew."

"It's only for a while, until I'm settled. I'll send for him."

Gen nods. "I'll take good care of him in the meantime. Don't worry."

"I know you will. Thanks Gen."

In the last few weeks, Mathew has come to understand what his mother had meant when she said Gen was kind. He doesn't know how he would have survived without her. He wants to tell her this, but no longer trusts himself with any conversation involving emotion.

They shut the door on O'Malley and go into the kitchen. Leibniz is standing in the centre of the room, still holding its power pack.

"Where's good for it to put its charger?"

"What about over here?" Gen asks, walking over to the far wall and indicating a gap between the fireplace and the fridge. "Will it fit?"

Mathew walks over. "Yes, I think this is fine. Leibniz, your new charging station is here. You can put down your power pack."

Leibniz walks over and does as it is told.

Mathew says to the robot, "You will stay in this house now and look after Gen Lacey. Normal duties apply here and once a fortnight I want you to go next door and dust and do any maintenance necessary to keep number nineteen running. Do you understand?"

"Yes Mathew."

"Is there anything I need to know in order to look after him?" Gen asks. "Any instruction manual?"

"It is self-maintaining. Unless there's a chronic system failure, you shouldn't have to do anything. There's an emergency number and its model and individual serial number on a panel on its back, here. To instruct it, you speak to it normally. It takes instruction in plain English, although you can't have a philosophical conversation with it. It'll crash if you try. If it crashes, it will automatically reboot. It's nothing to worry about. It's currently set to clean the house, do household maintenance, all of the grocery shopping, and look after the cat. It will ask you about your shopping preferences the first time it makes a shopping list. After that, it will adjust only if you specifically request it to do so, but it's hardwired to your bio-chip so it will automatically adjust meal planning to best suit your personal nutritional requirements. It can also do gardening. If you don't want it to do something or you want to change what it is doing, tell it."

"It?"

"It's a machine, not a person."

"I see."

"You'll find out." Mathew says.

Gen says, "Do you want a coffee? Something to eat?"

Mathew shakes his head. "I've eaten. Thanks." They stand together awkwardly in silence for a few moments. "Anyway," he says. "There's a few things I have to finish before they come. I need to get O'Malley's things."

Mathew nips back next door, collects O'Malley's litter tray, his blanket and basket and takes them to Gen's house.

"Where should I put them?"

"Leave them here for now. I'll figure it out later."

"There's some cat food and litter too. Leibniz can go and fetch it if you ask him."

"Okay," Gen says. "You will keep in touch, won't you?"

"Of course."

"Right then."

She shows him to the door.

"Say 'Hi' to Clara for me and tell her I'm sorry I missed her today. Tell her I'll write to her."

"I will." Gen holds the door and watches him walk away.

Mathew's travelling bags are by the front door. There are boxes in the front room, things he wants to take with him to his grandmother's house. They will be sent by courier and so will follow after him later. Everything has been arranged by Panacea.

On a table in the front room there's a tall shrilk jar, about the size of a vase, with a lid. It is very plain, very ordinary-looking. Beside the table, Mathew has laid out some package tape, some scissors and a roll of bubble-wrap. He tapes the lid of the jar as securely as possible, laying down strip after strip. Then he cuts a length of bubble wrap and rolls the jar in it, securing it with tape. When he's finished, he puts the package in a small blue rucksack, zips it up and puts it by the door in the hall with the other bags he's taking with him in the car.

Ju Shen, his grandmother, calls while he is tidying the

front room.

"I wanted to check you were alright," she says.

"I'm okay," he replies.

"When are they coming for you?"

"Soon. Two o'clock, they said."

"Do they still think you'll be here by tomorrow morning?"

"Yes, we're stopping in a motel tonight."

"You'll call if anything happens, won't you?"

"Nothing will happen."

"But you will call?"

He understands her anxiety. He hadn't called her about Hoshi. Panacea had. He says, "Yes," and feels again the sickening guilt and anger. It is like black treacle inside of him. He can't breathe for it.

"You're bringing her ashes?"

"I said I would. I've wrapped them up." He doesn't know why he tells her. Perhaps it's to make himself feel better about the fact he's wrapped his mother up in bubble plastic.

"I still can't believe what they did. I've been talking to a lawyer friend about suing."

He sighs.

"We can't let it go. They cremated your mother, my daughter, without our permission, without us being present. What they did is not only highly immoral, it is against the law."

"I know," Mathew says. But he doesn't want to hear it. He simply cannot deal with anything more. Not one more thing. "They said it was because of the nature of her disease. It was a matter of public safety."

"It's a cover-up. They wanted to destroy the evidence as quickly as possible."

"Evidence of what?"

"That she was killed by something from one of their own labs."

He knows this is true, but the thought overwhelms

him. "I can't…" is all he says.

"Okay Mat," she says, immediately sorry. "We'll talk about it when you get here."

But he doesn't want to talk about it. Ever. He dreads his grandmother's questions, the interrogation of the lawyers and political people she has around her who will be looking for a way to take on the multinational, Panacea.

He wants – he *needs* – peace.

It is ten to two. He takes one last walk around the house, checking everything is as it should be, saying goodbye. He goes into his mother's room.

It is exactly how she left it, how they left it, the day she was taken into hospital. Leibniz has straightened the bedcovers. Her clothes are still in the wardrobe, her makeup and perfume on the dressing table, her shoes arranged underneath.

The room smells of her.

He picks up a brush from the table. It has her hair in it.

He goes to the window. It is a cold December day; wind blows and bends the trees, clouds pile on clouds and slowly roll in the low sky.

Down below, Mr. Lestrange's conservatory is as it ever was; unbroken, undisturbed, empty.

2 TIME TO GO

It's five past two. Dr Assaf and Mr. Truville are sitting with Mathew in his front room. Truville is wearing an expensive grey suit made of shiny material that slides noisily on the fake leather sofa. There are two strangers with them: a man and a woman. Dr Assaf is introducing them.

She indicates the woman first, a tall, broad-shouldered, square-jawed and serious-looking person. Her head is shaved. She has a nose stud and a tattoo, visible under the cuff of her uniform shirt. Assaf says, "This is Ali Falkous. She's one of our most senior security officers."

Falkous nods at Mathew. Assaf indicates the man, slighter than the woman, wiry, smooth-skinned, clean-shaven, swarthy. "This is Christian Vidyapin."

"Call me Vid," the man says. He smiles slightly. He has large warm brown eyes.

Truville says, "These are the best people we have, Mathew. We wanted you to know that we take what has happened seriously and we intend to continue to look after you."

Mathew notes the word 'continue'. Anger bubbles in him. He looks at Dr Assaf. A few days ago she had come alone to bring his mother's ashes. He suspects she did it without asking anyone. He suspects she shouldn't have done it. Now, on the day he is scheduled to leave London, she is here again with Truville.

Truville doesn't leave him thinking for long. He pulls a small portfolio onto his lap from where it has been resting at the end of the sofa by his immaculately shod feet. He opens the wallet and takes out a Paper. Leaning forward, he hands it to Mathew.

"Before you go, we'd like you to sign this."

Mathew watches Assaf glance at Truville, her eyes narrow, her mouth pulled down at the corners. She looks uncomfortable. There are dark circles under her eyes.

Mathew stares at the Paper. It is displaying an electronic document, legal in nature, he notes, from the type and the language.

"Here," Truville says, leaning across again. "You can use my electronic pen. It can verify the writer by biochip."

Mathew ignores Truville's outstretched arm. He doesn't take the pen. Truville stretches some more, as if Mathew hasn't seen it, waggling the pen around. Mathew still doesn't move. He is staring at the document. "What is it?" he asks.

"Just a formality," Truville says, as if that explains everything.

Mathew offers it back to Truville.

Truville smiles, "No, no. I want you to sign it."

"What is it?" Mathew asks again. He scans the adults in the room with wary eyes. Assaf looks distressed; Falkous and Vid look embarrassed. "What does it say? You want me to sign something without knowing what is in the document?"

Truville smiles indulgently. "It's a document acknowledging receipt of your mother's ashes."

"It waives your right to sue Panacea," Assaf says.

Truville glances daggers at her, but she continues to stare ahead at Mathew. Mathew holds her gaze. Whatever her part in his mother's death, she's trying to put it right now, probably at her own expense.

"It's a precaution, that's all. A formality," Truville says quickly.

"I'm sixteen," Mathew says. "I can't sign this." As Truville won't take it back, he puts it on the floor between them, making Truville bend down to pick it up.

"Ah. Yes you can. You are next of kin and there is a precedent. A case involving Britannia Utilities five years ago. It changes the age of majority for certain types of contract law. There is a sum mentioned in the document. It would mean you wouldn't have to worry about money for a long time." Truville is smiling again. "As I said, we would like to look after you."

"I'm not signing anything," Mathew says. "Not until my grandmother has seen it."

"Your grandmother is Ju Shen, isn't she?" Truville says, frowning. "She is known for having some strong views. Following her advice might not be in your best interests."

Mathew sniffs, "You care about me more than my grandmother, do you?"

Truville stiffens. Mathew thinks he catches a slight smile on Assaf's face.

"Right, well. You should think about it. I will send you an electronic version."

Falkous shifts in her seat and then stands, "We should be making a move."

"Of course," Truville says, also standing.

They go out into the hallway. "Is this what you're bringing?" Vid asks.

"Yep," Mathew says.

Vid and Falkous grab some of the bags. Vid reaches for the small blue rucksack.

"No," Mathew says. "I'll take that one myself."

"Is this all of it?" Falkous asks.

"There're some boxes in the front room, the ones by the table. Dr Assaf said they could be sent up."

"Yes, it's fine," Assaf says, stepping forward. "There's a courier coming shortly. You go now. I'll wait here to make sure they go securely. They will be with you in a few days."

Falkous and Vid load Mathew's travel luggage into the boot of the car. "Ready?" Falkous asks Mathew.

He nods and steps out into the road. As he gets into the car, he looks back at the house, his home for sixteen years. He glances at Mr. Lestrange's house. There is no one at the window. He looks at Gen's house. Gen is standing on her front doorstep. She holds up her hand when he looks at her.

"You take care of yourself!" she shouts across.

"I will," Mathew says. "You too."

Falkous shuts the door on him and the two guards get into the front of the car. Slowly they glide away. Mathew turns his head and watches Gen wave. Assaf is standing on the steps of his house. Truville is climbing into a second car. He waves at Gen one last time and they turn out of Pickervance Road.

In the back of the car there are two fake leather sofas and a digital table. The bottom of the table levers so it can be watched like a Canvas as well as used as a Paper surface or as an ordinary table when flat. The sofas can be flattened to form a bed. There are cupboards behind the back sofa containing a mini fridge, nuts and fruit. Mathew takes a Coke from the mini fridge and reclines his seat slightly. He switches on the news and watches the hyper-partisan coverage of the war, footage of US and allied robot soldiers and drones in battle in Poland and human soldiers helping refugees at the border. The news is on a loop and, thirty seconds into the first repeat, he turns it off, searching the library of documentaries, drama, films and table-top hologames. But his heart isn't in it. He switches the table off, flattens it, puts his Coke on the top and looks out of the window. They are on an A road heading towards the motorway. It is going to be a long journey to Elgol.

He sends a brief message to his grandmother, telling her that he has left, and then initiates the Dictaphone program in his Lenz.

"New file," he says to the program. "Title: Letter to Clara. New line:

"Dear Clara, I haven't seen you since that first awful night at the hospital." He pauses and breathes. "You've left me lots of messages. I'm sorry I haven't responded. I know you will understand. You will have heard from Gen that my mother is dead. She may also have told you I am heading north to be with my grandmother. I don't know how long for. I don't know what will happen to our house. My mother's lawyer called me the other day to tell me my mother left everything to me. The house is on a mortgage and will have to be sold, but there will be some money from the sale and she had some savings. I don't know whether I will be able to come home or not. A bureaucrat from Panacea, I think he was my Mum's boss, visited me today to try and get me to sign some contract to let his company off the hook about what happened to Mum. I think he was offering me lots of money, but I handed the contract back to him. I hate them and I don't want their money.

"I still don't know what happened to Mum. A friend of mine managed to hack into the Panacea network and found some of Mum's documents. I think she was working on biological weapons and she was exposed to some kind of man-made virus.

"I feel so exhausted. I don't seem to be able to focus on anything.

"I left O'Malley and Leibniz with Gen, so they will both be there when you go round later today for your lesson."

The car is accelerating to join the motorway. Mathew looks out of his window as the vehicle slots seamlessly into the computer-controlled flow of traffic, all cars travelling at ideal stopping distance from one another and optimal speed.

It is a long time since he's been on the M25. The height of the fence shocks him. Fifty feet high, two lines of electrified steel and wire to keep out the undesirable and the unwanted, hugging the perimeter of London on the outside of the ring road motorway. Somewhere beyond the fence are the thousands of acres of refugee camps he's seen on Psychopomp, but never on the news on the Nexus.

He continues, "I had another one of those dreams, like the one I told you about. In the dream, I broke into Mr. Lestrange's house. I actually stamped on his conservatory roof this time, to break it. The book was in the dream, the one with my name on the cover. I put it on the table in his front room, opened towards the end. I'd decided that the older me could help me cure my mother. Lestrange's Darkroom let me into the future. I travelled with a huge army called the Accountants. They were the people the government had excluded from the cities. They marched north to this amazing new city called Silverwood, named after Cadmus Silverwood. It was the city he wanted to build, an Adaptation city. It had a huge dome growing over it. There was a building a mile high called the Cadmus Tower. On the way to Silverwood, I met Mr. Lestrange. He told me I was in a game, which I was ruining and he needed me to leave. We went looking for the door to come home through. Then I heard someone call the name 'Hoshi' and I broke out of the room where we were hiding and I saw someone who looked like my mother, but it was not my mother and I watched as she was shot. I was shot too. Then I saw my older self. I had grey hair and I'd gotten fat. You were there, but you were older, and there were other people I didn't know. While I was looking at him, my older self was killed. Then I woke up."

The car is slowing again; they are exiting the motorway, driving around a long bend, ahead a series of toll gates.

They pull up to one. In the front of the car, Vid winds down the window and talks to a man in uniform. Vid opens his door and he and Falkous get out. The uniformed official scans them with a biochip reader. The official then points at Mathew. Vid opens the car door.

"He wants to scan you," Vid says.

Mathew nods and climbs out of the car.

The official is stone-faced. "Turn around, please," he says.

Mathew does as he's told. The official bows Mathew's head with his hand and Mathew feels the scanner run across the back of his neck. The scanner beeps.

"Okay. Thank you," the guard says, looking at Mathew a bit more respectfully.

The official walks away to scan the occupants of the car behind them.

"What was that about?" Mathew asks Vid as they get back in their car.

"He just found out you're a homeowner."

Vid shuts the door on Mathew. The barrier in front of them lifts. They drive on.

3 NORTHWARD

Mathew and the guards, Christian Vidyapin and Ali Falkous, are on another motorway. They pass a blue road sign reading, "The North." Here the land on either side of the road is covered by a sheet of water as far as the eye can see. Many years before, the motorway had been raised so that it couldn't flood and now it is a bridge cutting through an inland sea. They pass a small hamlet, a gaggle of houses huddled together in the midst of the lake, submerged to their top windows. Later on, a half-drowned forest, the tops of leafless winter branches like arms stretching out for rescue. They stop for a comfort break at a service station, the car auto-docking for electricity while they all visit the bathroom.

Back on the road, it grows dark. Mathew closes his eyes and falls asleep.

He is woken by the stillness. Then a light comes on. Vid has opened the door and is peering in at him, grinning.

"Don't tell me," Vid says. "You were resting your eyes."

Mathew smiles, embarrassed. "What's happening?" he asks.

"We're stopping for the night. Dinner and then a

proper bed."

Mathew grabs his blue rucksack, takes out his overnight bag from the boot and follows Falkous and Vid out of the car park, towards the motel.

They are parked on a kind of island. Tall streetlights pick out the edges of the land above water, and cast reflections on the flooded land beyond, rippled by wind.

"Bit of a breeze," Vid says to Falkous, gathering his coat closer around him. "I hope it's not a storm brewing up."

"Forecast is good for tomorrow. We'll be fine. A straight run through."

They check in and are assigned three rooms in a row. Mathew drops his bag in his room, a plain, basic but clean place, with its own bathroom and a double bed. He joins Vid and Falkous in the corridor, bringing his blue rucksack with him, and they head off to the motel restaurant. There are only two other guests eating.

"This place is buzzing, hey?" Vid says, grinning at Falkous.

She scans around and smiles ruefully. "It's probably busier when the country isn't half under water and there's not a war on."

Vid accesses the tabletop menu and flicks through the options. "Food looks alright."

Falkous, who is also reading the menu, says, "Not exactly health food, but at least we won't go to bed hungry."

Mathew selects a burger and chips, a Coke and an apple pie and ice cream for pudding. Vid leans across and looks at Mathew's selection. "Boy after my own heart," he says, grinning.

They place their orders. Vid leans back in his chair with his arms behind his back. "What's in that blue bag, anyway?" he asks.

"My mother," Mathew says.

Vid laughs.

Mathew stares at him.

"I think he means his mother's ashes," Falkous says.

"Shit. I'm sorry."

"Idiot," Falkous says.

There's a long awkward silence. "I'm sorry," Vid says.

Falkous looks at Vid.

"What?" he says. "I am sorry. How was I to know? Who carries their mother's ashes around with them in a rucksack?"

Falkous sighs, "Someone who is sixteen, recently bereaved, and is travelling north so he can have a proper funeral with his grandmother present?"

"Shit," Vid says again. "Shit. Sorry."

"Can you be quiet?" Falkous says.

"Hey, no one else is going to keep the conversation going."

"You call this conversation?"

"Better than silence."

"No," Falkous says. "It isn't."

Mathew shifts in his seat. The robot waiter comes with his Coke and drinks for Falkous and Vid.

"Is your grandma a radical, then?"

"For frack's sake, can't you shut up?" Falkous says.

"What? Truville said so."

"Oh, Truville said! *Jeeze.*"

"Is she, then?" Vid asks Mathew.

Mathew shrugs and drinks his Coke. He doesn't care about Vid. Or anyone. Or anything.

The robot comes back with their food and lays it out in front of them. "Will there be anything else?" it asks.

"No," Falkous says.

"Enjoy your meal," the robot says as it retreats.

"The reason I'm asking about your grandma is I want to know what we'll face when we get there."

Falkous says, "I swear, if you won't be quiet I will make you."

"There may be a hostile reception for us. Those

Edenists are extreme."

"She is Garden Party, not Edenist. And she's not extreme. She doesn't carry guns. She doesn't kill people with biological weapons," Mathew says.

"Whoa! Boy's a radical!"

"Will you please shut the frack up?" Falkous says, slamming her hand down on the table.

The other two guests turn around to look at them disapprovingly.

Vid sulks. They eat in silence for a few minutes. "Pass the ketchup," he says to Mathew. Mathew hands him the ketchup.

"No hard feelings?"

"Hush!" says Falkous. "Not a peep."

"What time do we start tomorrow?" Mathew asks Falkous.

"Seven-thirty," Falkous says. "Straight after breakfast. Okay?"

Mathew nods.

"We should have you with your grandma by nightfall, so long as there're no holdups on the road."

"What kind of holdups? Is the road flooded?"

"The motorway won't be flooded," Falkous says. "Although some of the smaller roads we have to go on as we get further north may be. We've had a good report though, so I'm not expecting anything untoward."

"Do you know Truville?" Mathew asks her.

She shakes her head, "No, not really. We're from central security. We can be assigned to any department across Panacea."

The robot returns to clear away their plates, "Have you finished?" it asks, swiping Vid's plate. He grabs his burger away. "Hey!"

"I will return with your pudding shortly," the robot says.

"It's insane," Vid says, watching the robot retreat across the restaurant and through the double doors of the kitchen.

Falkous shakes her head.

In his room, Mathew checks his messages. Clara has responded to his note, asking if they can talk when he has time. He sits for a while, thinking, and then calls her. An image of her appears, sitting on her bed, sheets pulled around her.

"Did I wake you?" he asks.

"No," she says. "I was reading. It's good to hear your voice."

He sighs, "I'm sorry I haven't called."

She shakes her head. "Don't even say it. I can't even begin to imagine what you must have been through."

"It's not been good," Mathew says. "It feels like it will never be good again."

"It will," she says. "Where are you?"

"In a hotel on the motorway."

"What's it like?"

"It's fine. I have a double bed."

Clara smiles.

"Do you have a guard with you?"

"Two of them. The woman's alright, but the man's a dick. He started saying my grandmother is a radical."

"Well, she is, isn't she?"

He is sitting on the edge of his bed; he shuffles backwards and props himself against a pillow. "No more than your parents were. But to be honest, I don't know what to believe any more."

"You'll feel better when you're with your grandmother."

He sniffs, "She usually tells me what I should think. I told you about Truville, the bureaucrat, didn't I?"

"The one that wanted you to sign the contract? I can't believe it."

"I can. My Dad's company was the same after he died. They have whole teams of lawyers dedicated to shutting down trouble."

"You were right not to sign. You should get a lawyer to look at it."

"My grandmother knows a lawyer. I told Truville I wanted my grandmother to look at it, which I think frightened him a bit. I'm never going to sign it, not unless they tell me what actually happened."

"Do you think they ever will?"

"No. But a friend of mine might be able to find out." Mathew is thinking of Lich King.

"It is good to hear your voice. I've been so worried about you," Clara says.

"I'm okay."

"Yeah." She pauses. "Your dreams are weird."

"I know."

"Still feel real?"

"Nothing feels real to me right now. The whole universe may be a giant hologram for all I know."

"Isn't there a theory saying it is?"

Mathew laughs, "Yes, there is."

"What do you think?"

"I'd like to ask Lestrange."

"Mr. Lestrange?"

"Yeah. If I wasn't on the way to Elgol, I would knock on his door and ask him what's going on. I bet he knows."

"You're joking, right?"

"Nope. I'm not joking. But I'd never get to ask him because he's never there. He never answers his door."

"Now you're worrying me again."

"I'm tired."

"I should let you sleep. What time do you start tomorrow?"

"Seven-thirty, so up at six."

"Yuck."

"Exactly."

"Night, Mat," she says.

"Night, Clara."

"Let me know when you get there."
"I will for sure."

4 ROADBLOCK

DAY TWENTY-FOUR: Wednesday 15th December 2055

In the daylight, in the car park of the hotel, Mathew can see the surrounding landscape clearly for the first time. The flooded fields are like quicksilver under the low grey skies.

Vid seems more subdued, perhaps from a dressing down from Falkous.

They are quickly on the road, joining the steady stream of traffic. Mathew is alone again in the back of the car. He feels better for having spoken to Clara. Now he doesn't know why he avoided her, but in the days following his mother's death, he didn't want to speak to anyone.

Setting the table at an angle, he calls the news to view footage of hypersonic warplane attacks across Russia and China. The big announcement is wireless power has been switched on for the Allied soldiers fighting in Poland, and funding has been signed off by Congress and the EU for an accelerated programme of development for new Battlestars. Mathew absently watches some commentary, and then switches to a tabletop holofilm. It's been ages since he's watched one, the characters and scenery appearing before him like a minute version of the world, real enough to reach out and touch. The story is engrossing and he is grateful to lose himself.

A few hours later, the film has finished. He looks out of the window to see the motorway now bordering a camp. High barbed-wire-topped chain-link fencing runs along a ditch on the other side of the hard shoulder. Beyond the fence there are hundreds of tents and makeshift shelters, separated by straight muddy pathways. No one is about. The rain is lashing down. The fence seems to go on for miles, then suddenly it ends, and there are fields, actual fields with soil and trees. There are grassy hills with sad-looking cattle and sheep huddled together against the weather. The road ahead is empty and they are speeding along, making good time. In spite of himself, Mathew feels a flicker of the old excitement he used to experience when, as a boy, he would be taken north to stay with his grandmother.

Then the car starts to slow.

They crawl to a halt, joining the back of a line of traffic. This is unknown. He immediately feels alarmed. Through the glass plate separating him from the front of the car, he can see Vid and Falkous talking. Their body language tells Mathew he's right to be afraid. Falkous notices Mathew staring at them and opens one of the glass windows that separates them.

"Nothing to worry about," she says. "Must be a crash."

"A crash?" Autonomous cars don't crash.

"It happens." It doesn't.

"Vid is going to take a look and I'm going to check in with our intelligence team and find out if they know anything."

Mathew frowns.

"Don't worry," Falkous says. "Okay?"

Mathew nods, but he knows something is wrong.

Vid gets out of the car, edges between the other

vehicles stationary on the road, and walks over to the hard shoulder, disappearing behind an autonomous delivery truck. Falkous is deep in Nexus conversation. She looks worried now. She hangs up and immediately makes another call, still speaking as she gets out of the car. Vid comes jogging back. Mathew opens his door and steps out into the road.

Mathew hears Falkous saying to Vid, "We need to turn around."

Vid says, "How, for frack's sake?" He indicates to the cars and trucks now queuing behind them.

"We can use the hard shoulder."

"We're in the middle lane."

"Let's ask this truck here to move."

"There's no human in it," Vid says, peering in through the glass.

"Even better. We can get our on-board computer to talk to its on-board computer."

Falkous sees Mathew and barks at him, "Get back in the car until I tell you to get out!"

Other passengers are getting out onto the road. "What's going on?" a man in a suit shouts over.

Falkous watches Vid return to the car out of the corner of her eye. She says to the man, "There's a roadblock ahead. Potentially a hold-up. The motorway is blocked with articulated lorries."

"You've got to be joking!" says the suit. He's irritated about being late for his meeting.

Vid is back inside the car, talking to the on-board computer.

Falkous sees Mathew, still standing there, hesitating. "In the car!" she yells. He opens the door and gets in.

Vid has his door open. He leans out and shouts to Falkous, "Hey, Falkous, back here! I think it worked."

Falkous strides back and gets in the car, as the delivery truck starts and moves on the hard shoulder. "What worked?" She looks across at the truck blocking the lane next to them, her mouth open. "It's trying to turn," she says.

"Yes, it's what you asked."

"No. I want it to pull up there ahead on the hard shoulder," she points, "so we can get through. If it tries to turn it will get stuck; there isn't enough room. Like that." She thumps the dashboard. "Frack!"

"You didn't tell me that."

"Wasn't it obvious?" She puts a hand to her forehead. "We're sitting ducks here," she says.

"The car is bullet-proof," Vid says. "Secure. Whoever is out there won't be able to get in."

"Do you want to stake your life on it? And the boy's?"

"But where do we go? The fields are flooded and there's not even a ruin out there to take shelter in."

"The further from the front of the queue we get, the better. We can walk back to the service station."

"That's miles back."

"There's bound to be something. I saw a camp." She looks at Mathew. "We need to go."

Mathew nods.

"Leave your stuff."

Mathew grabs his rucksack. Falkous catches his eye, holds it for a moment and then nods. "Okay," she says. "But just the one." She checks inside her jacket for her handgun, takes it out, takes something from an inside pocket and fits a silencer. She notices Mathew watching her. "Don't want to attract attention, do we?" she says.

Then she gets out, goes round to the boot and pulls out two automatic weapons, handing one to Vid. Opening the door for Mathew, she bundles him between her and Vid, keeping him close, and they start to walk away between the cars.

More people emerge now on the road. The man in the suit follows them. "Where are you going?" he asks.

Falkous says, "Away from here." She doesn't look back.

There's ten of them walking now, but many passengers stay locked in their cars. Their fearful eyes follow them as they pass. "They're smart," Vid says.

Then suddenly there are no more cars. They come to the end of the queue. Instructions have been broadcast to all vehicles travelling north to exit at the preceding junction. They are unlucky to be amongst the last cars that passed the junction before the warning was issued.

"Help must be on its way," Falkous says. "They've closed the motorway. The authorities know what's going on."

"What should we do?" the suit asks. "Should we go back to our cars?"

"Your guess is as good as mine."

"Who do you think they are?"

"I would bet whoever is doing this is working their way down the line, taking whatever they can get. I doubt they're friendly," Falkous replies. She is looking out across the field. "There's a house over there."

Vid says, "What? Do you want us to swim?"

"It might be surface water. We could wade. Why don't you go and see?" Vid looks at Falkous. "Go on."

Vid walks uncertainly over to the hard shoulder and slides down the muddy, raised embankment of the motorway onto the field. He wades out a few feet. "It's shallow," he says. "Bit slippy, though."

"What about further out?"

He turns and walks out a few metres. "Same," he says. He is smiling as he turns back towards them. "I think it's fine."

The first shot hits him in the arm, making him drop his automatic weapon. Instinctively, he moves with his other arm to pull his handgun from its holster, but the second shot hits him in the head. Mathew is standing mesmerized by the look of surprise on Vid's face as he hovers where he stands for a moment before collapsing to the ground with a splash.

"Crap!" Falkous says, pulling Mathew back with her towards the shelter of the cars. "Crap. Crap." She pushes his head down, "Keep down, for God's sake!"

"We should have stayed in the car," Falkous says. "The idiot was right. The one time he was *ever* right and I didn't listen to him!"

They are crouched by the side of a lorry with large wheels. Falkous starts taking off her jacket.

"What are you doing?" Mathew whispers, alarmed.

"Put it on. Now," she says to Mathew, thrusting it at him. "It's bullet-proof."

He watches her check her gun strapped to her body in a cross body holster. She takes the gun out, takes off and throws away the holster, then puts the gun inside her shirt in a special pocket with a strap.

"Can you see it?" she asks.

"You'd have to be looking."

She helps Mathew do up the bullet proof vest.

She says, "There."

"What about you?" he asks.

"I got you into this, didn't I?" She peers out from behind the wheel. "It's okay. We are going to be alright." She seems to be talking to herself as much as to him. "I think they took a long shot at Vid. I don't think they are close yet. Let's go."

She pulls Mathew after her. "But we're going towards them," he says.

"I want to get back to our car."

"Why?"

"Because there's a large box in the back. Did you see it? The one with the fridge in?" Mathew nods. "Good. If you pull the fridge out and get in, there's an emergency button to shut the door. It's a mini-panic room. A bit tight but you should be fine," she says, sizing him up.

"Where will you be?" Mathew asks.

"I'm going to try and ram our car into that truck to push it out of the way and get out onto the hard shoulder.

If it doesn't work, I'm going to sit tight, hope help arrives soon, and pray that Vid was right about the car being bullet-proof. Let's keep moving."

"Where are you going?" the man with the suit asks. He is standing above them, bowed slightly.

"You should get down," Falkous says.

"Right," he says. Some of the other people on the road come over. "You should get down," the man in the suit says to the others. They all crouch down, looking at each other for validation.

"Jeeze," Falkous says. These people are a complication she doesn't want.

"What's the plan?" another man asks. He is wearing casual clothes and is in his early twenties. A student, most likely, Falkous thinks.

"The best option we have now is to go back to our vehicles, lock the doors and hope that they, whoever 'they' are, don't get in."

"They'll shoot us through the glass," a third man says. He's middle-aged and balding and sweating heavily through his shirt, in spite of the cold air.

"It depends on your car."

A gunshot makes them all jump.

"Oh God!" says the first man in the suit.

Falkous looks at Mathew, "Come on, let's go."

"I'm coming with you," the man in the suit says.

Falkous stops and turns to the man. "I'm a security guard. I'm not police or army. And I'm responsible for this boy. You're a grown man."

"You have a gun and I bet your car is armoured," the student says. "Isn't it?"

"We could probably all fit in your car," the balding man says.

"No you won't," Falkous says, responding irritably to the aggression of the men. Then she relents, "Look, I'll try and see you all back to your cars, but you are on your own from there."

"Why can't we come in your car?"

Falkous looks at the man hard, "Do you want to stand about chatting right now?" There's more gunfire. "It's getting closer," she says. They hear shouting. Falkous grabs Mathew by the lapel of the jacket she made him wear and urges him forward. They move quickly. "Come on, come on," she whispers sharply to the others. "And keep down."

They stop to take breath by a Techno Food delivery truck.

Falkous peers through the line of cars ahead. "I can see our car," she whispers to Mathew. "Stay close to me." She is thinking *Thank God for the curfew*! Otherwise the whole road would be crawling with people. Those travelling today must have a good reason. Whoever is blocking the road knows that and perhaps it's good news. Perhaps they are looking for someone in particular.

Falkous starts to move again and then ducks down. "Shit," she says.

"What's wrong?" asks the suit.

"There are people over there," she says, indicating with her thumb.

"They could be like us, people in the jam getting out for a stroll."

"I don't think they are," she says.

Then they hear gunshots, one gun firing again and again. Someone shouts, "Come out! On the floor. Spread your arms."

Falkous catches the man's eyes. She shakes her head and peers around the truck again and sees their car. *So close.* She is thinking of making a run for it when the voices get closer.

Someone says, "Look, Scott, there's a food truck here."

"Jackpot!" another voice says.

The sounds of boots.

"Hey, Scott, I've found something else too." The speaker is a tall boy-man, seventeen, maybe eighteen years old, lanky, slumped and hunched at the shoulders. "Drop your gun," he says to Falkous.

She drops her automatic weapon.

5 PANIC ROOM

"Kick it to me," the boy says.

Falkous kicks the weapon away from her.

Scott, his companion, comes from around the truck, much shorter, fair-haired, though not much older, with a soft baby beard that covers his cheeks. He raises his gun as soon as he sees them, pointing it at each of them in turn, bouncing nervously on his feet. He's clearly on something.

"Have you checked them for weapons, Nigel?"

"Only this one," he says, indicating Falkous.

The blond boy goes round the group, searching them. He's carrying a bag; he swings it off his back and opens it up. It contains boxes, containers for Lenzes.

He opens one and shoves it at the man in the suit. "Drop your Lenz in here," he says. He hands out boxes to the rest of them. The tall boy trains his gun on them all, while Scott, his friend, works.

"Bingo!" says the tall boy, excitedly. "Must be thousands in cash here, once we've off-loaded this stuff."

Mathew takes out his Lenz and puts them carefully in the Lenz tray. It is awkward to do without a mirror. The balding man in the suit drops one of his.

"Clumsy bastard," Scott says. "Pick it up." The man

bends down to find the Lenz on the road. He finds it and puts it in the tray, closes the box and hands it to the boy. The boy strikes him across the head, making the man, who is still crouched on the floor, fall. "Leach," he spits, his voice full of hatred. "Now your e-Pinz," the boy says. He looks around the group. "All of you!" He waits as his prisoners take out their e-Pinz, holding out his palm to receive them. Then he carefully empties his hoard into a pocket in his bag, zips the bag and hefts it onto his shoulder.

"What should we do with them?" Scott says.

"We'll ask Ran. Watch 'em a sec, will you?" The tall man shoots at the back of the food truck to break the lock and yanks open the door. "Would you look at this?!"

Falkous takes them out with two neat shots to the head, using her hand gun. The silencer dulls the noise the a whip-crack. They fall to the ground where they are standing. No one had body-checked her. She smiles slightly as she pulls their weapons from under their bodies.

"Can you use a gun?" she asks the man in the suit.

He nods. She passes him one of the boy's weapons.

"You?" she asks the student.

"No," he says.

"Anyone else?" She looks around the group at blank faces. She thrusts the gun at the student. "You'd better learn quickly," she says, bending and retrieving her own automatic. As she stands, she spots someone, another boy, another one of the gang. He sees her, turns and runs. She shoots at him, but misses.

"Frack!" she says.

Falkous drags a dazed Mathew along by the arm. "Come on, come on," she growls. They run at full pace, not even bothering to duck. Then she pulls him down with her.

There's a gaggle of people around their car. They crawl under the belly of the vehicle they've landed by.

They hear a nasal voice saying, "This is a pretty nifty

one. Military vehicle, I reckon. Almost certainly comes with guards."

"Where are they? There's no one in here," says a deeper voice with a strong northern accent.

Someone pulls repeatedly at a car door handle. "Locked," the nasal voice says.

"Of course it's locked."

"What if it's booby-trapped?" This is a third voice, less confident.

"Booby-trapped?" the nasal voice says mockingly.

Someone runs up to the group. An out-of-breath voice gasps, "Nigel and Scott have been shot!"

"What the…?" begins the deep northern voice.

Falkous can only see boots, but she can tell that these are boys or teenagers, not men, from their voices.

"Who shot him?" the nasal voice asks.

"There's a group back there. They were armed."

"How many?"

"I dunno, I ran."

"Your comrade is down and you run?" the deep northern voice says, with disgust.

"It was probably one of the guards from this," the nasal voice says, kicking at a tyre.

"Where're Nigel and Scott?" the deep voice asks.

"Down there, by the food truck." The out-of-breath voice is getting steadier, catching its breath again. It shares the same accent as the northerner, but the timbre is not as deep.

"Is it a Techno Food truck?" asks the deep voice.

"Yeah, why?"

"It will be full of food."

"For frack's sake, man, Nigel and Scott are dead!" snaps the nasal voice.

"We don't know they're dead. He didn't say so."

"Are they dead?" the nasal voice asks.

"I don't know," says the out-of-breath northerner.

"There you are, you see," says the northerner.

"Where's the truck? Show us," says the nasal voice.

The boots start to move away. Falkous starts to move. Then there's a gunshot and the boots halt.

"What the frack, man?!"

"Was that one of ours?"

"It came from the Techno truck."

"I saw someone. Over there."

"C'mon."

The boots move off again and Falkous edges forward, indicating that Mathew does the same. She can see the wheels of their car. They are almost there.

Then they hear raised voices, "I didn't kill him. I don't even know how to use this!" There is another shot. Silence. Then more raised voices.

"For God's sake. It was a woman. I don't know who she is!"

"Is she armed?"

"Does she have a gun?"

"Yes!"

"Where is she? Show me!"

Falkous and Mathew watch the boots return.

The nasal voice says, "Come out."

Falkous turns to Mathew, puts her finger to her lips and indicates with her hand, a flat palm, and then points to the ground. *Be quiet. Stay here.* She leaves her handgun next to him and looks him in the eye, meaningfully. *Use this.*

She slides out her automatic weapon, which someone grabs, and then crawls out from under the car. She is on her hands and knees, starting to get to her feet when someone kicks her... then kicks her again and again. She falls to the floor. Her eyes are open. She smiles slightly at Mathew.

"Get up!" the nasal voice screams. He is hysterical.

Someone else bends down and grabs at her. "Get up, he said!" It is the deep voice.

She is forced to her feet. Mathew can only see her boots now. She staggers.

"Did you shoot our friend?" the deep voice asks.

"Of course she shot him!" the nasal voice almost screams. "Let's finish her. I'll do it myself."

"Is that your car?" the northern voice asks. "That car over there, the black one. Is that your car?!"

Falkous is silent. Then suddenly there is a scuffle, grunts, shouts. Someone lands heavily on the floor. Mathew scoots back into the shadows. It isn't Falkous. It is one of her assailants, a boy not much older than Mathew. He lies winded for a second and then gets unsteadily back up. Then there is another gunshot, followed quickly by more. Bodies fall to the floor. Thud. Thud. Thud. Thud.

After a long moment, Falkous' face appears. "Come out," she says.

Mathew crawls towards her and she helps him up. She is clutching her side. "Flesh wound," she says, but her face is drawn.

There are four bodies on the floor, all young men and boys. The first man in a suit is standing several yards away. At his feet is the body of the student. He steps over him, coming forward. Falkous looks at him, "Frack off," she says, waving her gun at him. "Fracking traitor."

"They were going to shoot me," he says. "Look what they did to him."

"C'mon Mat." They head for the car.

The two men and the woman follow.

"You've got to let us in," the balding man says, aggressively moving forward. "It would be murder not to."

The car doors open for Falkous. She holds the door open for Mathew and slams it on him.

She points to the wound in her ribs, "This is murder," she says. "Betraying that boy is murder. That is murder too," she points to the dead boys on the ground. "So we're all murderers."

The man steps forward and tries to get in the car. She shoots at his leg. He screams and rolls onto the ground.

Then she gets in the car, throwing the gun on Vid's empty seat.

"Car," she says. "Safety over-ride off."

"Please submit emergency code for that command."

"Wet weekend," Falkous says.

"Thank you. What are your instructions?"

"I need you to turn and ram the vehicle directly to our left out of the way so we can access that hard shoulder and drive the wrong way along it."

"Acknowledged." The car starts to drive forward.

"You're wounded," Mathew says. "Were you shot?"

"No. Stabbed."

"I was wearing your jacket. You'd be fine if you hadn't given it to me."

"Probably. Difficult to make all good decisions in these situations. Might have gone differently."

"Is it bad?"

"Feels it. Not sure. Medibots are going to town. Hold on."

The car rams the truck. It doesn't budge. "Car, can you instruct the truck to take its handbrake off and cooperate in any way it can? Explain what we're trying to do."

"Acknowledged."

There is a moment's pause and then the car rams again. They are both thrown forwards and then backwards in their seats.

"Put your seat belt on," Falkous says. She pulls hers across and clips it in as the car accelerates. This time the truck moves forward a few feet.

"Who were those people you shot?"

"According to central security, a local gang, probably being run by a more organised criminal group."

"Why hasn't anyone come to help us?"

"Now, that I don't know. Perhaps the police and army have lost control here. It's happened elsewhere. Hold on."

The car rams the truck again. There is a noticeable gap now. Alarms are going off on the dashboard.

Mathew looks out through his window. The two men and the woman are standing watching. "Shouldn't we take them with us?"

"If we still have a working car at the end of this, we will take them. If we don't, you crawl into the panic room and lock yourself in for the night. Okay?"

"Okay," Mathew says. "There are some other people with guns coming," Mathew says.

"Shit," Falkous says, turning her head.

There are four of them, young men, but older than the others. They examine the dead boys. The man in the suit points at the car. They run over.

The car rams the truck again. One of the young men opens fire at the car. Mathew dives down as bullets splatter like rain at the window.

"I guess Vid was right about that too. Bloody car is bullet-proof."

The car pushes the truck forward several yards with a great lurch.

The men with the guns have stopped firing. They are standing watching.

The car tries to reverse, but its wheels spin. Its bumper is caught firm on a broken panel on the side of the truck. The truck is pushed far onto the hard shoulder and topples down the bank, dragging the car after it.

"Get into the panic room," Falkous says. "Do it."

Shaking, Mathew undoes his belt; his fingers feel thick. The belt comes off; he pulls his seat forward and opens the cupboard, the momentum of the car lurching slowly after the truck down the bank making it easy to pull out the fridge. Mathew slides into the box. He has to brace with his feet and one hand, gripping the plates that held the fridge to stop himself from falling out. He reaches and grabs his rucksack and pulls at the door.

"Hit the button!" Falkous yells.

Mathew searches around and then sees the red button. He hits it with the side of his fist. The door starts to close.

THE MOON AT NOON

It locks. An emergency light comes on. He is thrown about in the box as the car crashes down the bank after the truck. For a few dizzying moments, there is silence.

"Falkous?" he says. "Ali?"

There is silence.

Then there is a faraway muffled noise outside. Some voices, but too indistinct for him to hear anything. There's a dull thud, possibly gunfire, but the box muffles sound. More noises. Someone is outside his box, scratching and banging around. More muffled voices. Is that laughter? He holds his breath until it bubbles and burns within him. There's a final muffled bang and then silence.

6 THE BOY

Falkous said to wait, but it's been hours now. Hours in this tiny box the size of a coffin, smaller than a coffin. He can't fully stretch out his legs. There's a dim blue light, which he is grateful for because he can at least see the edges of his confines. He has enough space to turn over, but not to sit, and the box is angled awkwardly so that he is constantly rolling down to the door. It is not a comfortable place to be. The blue rucksack is wedged in by his feet. He has no water and his bladder is ready to burst. They, whoever 'they' are, have taken his Lenz and his e-Pin. He has no means of contacting Falkous or anyone else besides.

He listens.

Silence. But he doesn't know if that is because the box is soundproof, or if it means it is safe to come out. The worry that it is not, keeps him there.

Then it occurs to him that he is not sure how to unlock the door, and the sudden overwhelming fear of being trapped drives him out. In a panel by his head there is a flap and a switch and a button. He flips the switch and hits the button and the door swings open, spilling him onto the floor of the car and into the back of the car seat. The car is almost sitting on its nose, the front of it ploughed into the back of the truck they had been ramming. The digital table is broken. He tries to wake it, but there is no response.

The glass partition separating the guards' seats from the back is shattered. He can't see Falkous. He tries to open the back doors but both are locked tight.

With his feet, he clears the remaining broken glass from the partition and slides through into the front of the car, pushing his rucksack before him. The on-board computer is gone, ripped out, wires dangling. The door beside him is open, buckled and hanging on one hinge. Tumbling out, he sees Falkous fifteen feet away, lying in the water at the bottom of the slope.

He scrambles down and then stops. She isn't moving and her face is in the water.

"Falkous?" he says, somehow already knowing there will be no response. He doesn't want to go down, but he finds his feet leading him there. Five feet from Falkous' body, he squats, hugging the rucksack to him. "Falkous," he says again.

The wind blows wavelets over her and her hand moves slightly. His heart leaps in hope, thinking for a second that she's actually moving, that she's alive, but it is just the water. After a while, he stands and edges further down. He puts the rucksack on the dry ground above her body, leans down and shakes her gently. No response. He needs to turn her over. The idea fills him with dread but he grips one of her shoulders with both hands and levers her awkwardly onto her side and she falls back with a splash.

Her eyes are open, staring blankly. There is a dark neat hole in her forehead.

He staggers to the dry bank, wiping his hands on his trousers, horrified. Grabbing his bag, he runs up the bank and stops at the top, glancing back at Falkous one last time. Then he steps onto the road, half-expecting to be shot or ambushed. But there is no one there. He scans about. Some of the vehicles are gone. He wanders aimlessly amongst the cars, until he comes across the body of the student and the boys and young men Falkous shot. He reaches the end of the queue of cars and sees Vid's body in the field. The house stands alone on the horizon in a lake of sunset water.

Mathew is standing alone amongst forty or so abandoned cars the gang had not wanted, or did not have the means to take away.

And still no help. There is no sign of the army or police to help them, or at least to come and clear the road. The sun is dying, the sky a raspberry and vanilla smudge. He has no means of contacting anyone. He wonders if any of the on-board computers in the vehicles left on the road work. The cars have all been broken into, the locks blasted away, the doors yanked off with crowbars. He checks several. Everything that can be taken has been taken, including all communication devices. He thinks again about walking to the house in the flooded field. But first he wants to grab a few of his own things from the back of the wrecked Panacea car.

In spite of everything, his bladder is still bursting and he finds a place, against the wheel of an empty, looted van, to obey the call of nature.

Remarkably, no one has broken into the boot of the Panacea car, but it is locked tight and with the car computer stolen he has no way of getting in. Then he remembers Falkous' handgun. He slipped it in his rucksack when he hid under the car. He pulls it out now. It is cold and heavy. He's never held a real gun before, but he's handled similar weapons in hologames he's played. He taps the bottom of the magazine, looks for and releases the slide on the side of the gun, then points and shoots. The first time he fires, the gun kicks back hard and flips towards his face. The gun, even with the silencer, cracks in the peace of the day. Near the lonely house, large black birds take flight. Mathew sees their silhouettes in the distance and hears the flapping of their wings and their caws. The next shot he takes is with a firmer grip. He makes a mess of the boot, but after a few rounds, the lock is obliterated. He slides the safety back on and puts the gun carefully back in his rucksack.

In his bags, in the boot, are the waterproof clothes packed for outdoors life in Elgol, a pair of boots and a coat. He pulls them out, as well as a dry pair of socks and trousers. He stuffs the clean clothes around the bubble-wrapped package in his blue rucksack and retrieves some cans of Coke, a bottle of water and nuts and fruit from the back of the car. Then he sets out back over the bank and weaves his way through the cars, heading in the direction of the house.

There is someone else left alive. A small figure, silhouetted against the sunset in the dimming light, staggering, hands reaching out, feeling wildly in front. Mathew considers changing direction, skirting around the new threat. He hesitates. Stops. Then cautiously he steps towards the stranger.

"Hello?" Mathew says, finally. "Are you okay?"

The figure spins around, hearing his voice. It is a child,. The boy turns his head from the shadow cast by the truck he is standing beside, Mathew's eyes widen in horror. There is blood all over the front of his clothes. His left eyeball is hanging from its socket by a flesh thread. Bile floods Mathew's mouth.

"No. No. I'm not okay. Where are you?" the boy asks.

"Here," Mathew says, moving forward, in spite of his impulse to back away, pity overriding revulsion. He takes hold of the boy's outstretched hands. "I'm here."

The relief and gratitude on the boy's face is extraordinary.

"What happened to you?" Mathew asks, his voice sounding strange and strangled to himself.

The boy is swaying. Mathew opens the door of a nearby car and helps the boy to sit down on a seat. The sight of his face is too much. Mathew stares at the boy's jeans, stained with blood to the knees. He can hardly believe the boy is conscious or at least not writhing around in pain.

"I couldn't get my Lenzes out. I was taking too long. So they pinned me down on the floor took them themselves," the boy says. "I can't see anything. Is there something wrong with my eyes?"

Mathew doesn't know what to say. He says, not believing it himself, "You'll be okay. We'll get you help."

"Are the police coming?"

"No," Mathew says, "I don't think they are."

"Why not?"

"I don't know."

Mathew looks behind him. It is getting dark.

"We need to go," he says. "We can't stay here."

"My parents," the boy says. "I can't leave them."

"Where are they?"

"In our car."

Mathew wants to ask why they aren't with him and then stops himself. "Which is your car?" he says; then, realising immediately the boy won't be able to point it out, he asks, "What does it look like?"

"It's a taxi."

"What colour?"

"Yellow."

That is easy. There is only one yellow car in the huddle still on the motorway. "Do you have anything with you? Clothes? A coat?" The boy is wearing jeans and a sweatshirt and it is getting cold.

"My suitcase is in the boot."

Mathew walks towards the car. A man and a woman are slumped awkwardly inside. He doesn't look too closely. It is obvious they are dead. The boot is open. There are three suitcases. Mathew tries each of them until he finds the one belonging to the boy, full of boy's things. He can't carry the suitcase, his rucksack and help the boy and there's little room in his own rucksack for more clothes.

He chooses a jacket, a clean pair of trousers, t-shirt and a jumper and closes the boot, then rolls them and stuffs them as best he can into his own bag. He ties a spare pair of shoes by their shoelaces to one of the straps of his bag and swings the whole lot on his back. There's no point in getting the boy to change until after they have waded through the water, but he helps him into his coat.

"Did you find my parents?"

"Yes," Mathew says. "We'll come back for them tomorrow." He knows this is a lie. They both know it. The boy nods. "Can you walk?" Mathew asks.

"Of course I can."

"Here," Mathew says. "Take my hands." The boy grasps at him. Mathew helps him to his feet. "Now take my arm. Try and let me lead you."

They step forward haltingly as they learn to walk with one another. It's slow progress. They get to the bank where Vid's body lies at the bottom. The boy doesn't know it's there. "There's a slope," Mathew says. "It's quite steep. I'll walk in front and hold your hands to guide you. Come down after me slowly." The boy shuffles down haltingly. They reach the bottom. "The field is flooded. We're going to have to be careful. Take my arm again." The boy does as he's told. They set off. The light has all but faded, but there is a moon casting a pale light. The house, their target, is a square black silhouette on the horizon. The water is inky. They make silver ripples in it as they walk.

"My feet are cold," the boy says.

"We'll be there soon," Mathew says. "I have a spare dry pair of shoes for you."

"Thank you," the boy says. "I don't know your name."

"It's Mathew. What is yours?"

"Isaac."

The boy is more than a foot shorter than Mathew. He has fine blond, almost white, hair. Mathew is conscious all the time of the boy's face, which he can't bring himself to look at. Staring resolutely ahead or at his feet, he tells himself he needs to concentrate.

The water is coming over the top of Mathew's boots; it's over the boy's knees. The ground underneath is slippy. Mathew is worried about the boy falling, of what will happen to him if water gets into his wound. But they stay upright. The house gets closer. The stars are incredibly bright, magically splattered across the black sky. He has to stop himself from telling the boy to look up.

"How did you escape?" the boy asks.

"I hid in a box in our car."

"Were you with your parents?"

"No," Mathew says. "I was with some security people. They were both shot."

"Dead?"

"Yes."

"What did they do to my eyes?" Isaac asks.

Mathew doesn't know what to say.

"It's bad, isn't it?"

"You need a doctor."

They are close to the house. It's a square red-brick building with a tiled roof; an old farmhouse, built on a bank, but only a foot or so out of the water. They start to climb to it. Mathew's heart sinks when he sees the windows are dark.

"I don't feel so good," Isaac says. Mathew feels him swaying, sinking at the knees.

"No!" Mathew says, grabbing at him. He gets his wrists under the boy's forearms and manages to drag him up, but he's not strong enough to carry him. The boy lolls, semi-conscious. Mathew hauls him through the water, up the bank of mud, slipping and struggling to keep his balance. They make it to the top, onto dry ground, and Mathew and the boy collapse. Mathew allows himself to rest for a moment, then gets to his feet and makes for the house. He walks around the darkened building, looking for the front door. There's a porch, but the light is out and the bell doesn't work. He hammers on the door.

"Help!" he yells. "Please. Help us." He keeps hammering.

The house remains dark and still.

"Mathew! Where are you? Mathew!" the boy calls to him in panic.

Mathew goes back to the boy, crouches down and takes his hands.

"I'm here," he says. "I'm here. It's okay."

"Where did you go?"

"I went to try and find help. There's a house here. Can you stand?" Mathew gets Isaac to his feet. "We can shelter in the porch."

They find their way back to the front door. Mathew helps the boy to sit with his back against the wall. He finds a place opposite him as the rain starts to come down hard, spitting off the flagstones. It is cold, but at least they are dry. There's a pathway leading away from the front door of the house. It passes between a hedge into the darkness, but it must go somewhere. This can't be the only house here. Even if it is, he should make sure. If he can break into the house and get Isaac into dry clothes, he can go and find help. Maybe inside the house there's a Paper or a Canvas or some means of connecting to the outside world. Then he can tell someone what has happened and summon help.

"Isaac," Mathew says. "I'm going to try and find a way into the house. I won't be long."

"Don't leave me here," Isaac says.

"I'm not leaving you, I promise. We need to get out of the rain. I will be back in a few minutes."

Mathew pulls the hood of his jacket over his head, steps out into the rain and takes the path to the gate. The street beyond is in darkness. The houses have been abandoned. He looks back to the garden. There's a shed. He goes to it and pushes open the door. It's pitch dark but he manages to fumble his way to a spade. He grabs it and walks back to the house, finds the nearest window and smashes it. Pulling the sleeve of his jacket over his hand, he picks the remaining blades of glass out of the window frame and then climbs in, falling onto the floor noisily. He's in a living room. There's a rug on a wooden floor, an old battered sofa, a fireplace, a coffee table, a bookcase. He stands and dusts himself off, walks into the hallway and opens the front door.

"Isaac," he says. The boy is huddled into a ball, shaking. "Come on. Let's get you up." Mathew hefts the boy to his feet, grabbing under his armpits, and drags him back into the house, into the hallway.

"What do you think you're doing?" says a man's voice in the darkness.

Mathew freezes and turns his head, still holding Isaac.

There's a man on the stairs holding a candle in a candle holder. In his other hand he grips a long sharp kitchen knife.

7 EYEBALL

The man walks down the stairs holding a knife. The candle flickers and shadows dance on the high wall by the staircase.

"Get out," the man says. "Get out of my house."

"I banged on the door. No one answered. We didn't think anyone was here." Weakening under the weight of Isaac, Mathew shuffles slightly towards the man, who is standing at the bottom of the stairs.

"Stay back!" the man says.

Mathew says, "Please. My friend is badly hurt. He needs to see a doctor. We need help."

The man glances at the boy slumped in Mathew's arms. Isaac's face is in shadow. A woman comes down the stairs and stops behind the man. "Jack?" she says.

"Go upstairs," Jack tells her, brusquely.

"I will not. What is going on?"

"Please," Mathew says. "My friend is hurt. You have to help us."

The man holds out the candle and he and the woman both see Isaac's face.

"Oh my God!"

The woman comes down the stairs, pushing past her

husband. "Let's get him to the sofa." She helps Mathew lift Isaac. The man follows them into the front room.

"What on earth happened?"

"We were on the motorway. The road was blocked. A gang attacked us. Kids with guns. They shot the people I was with. They shot his parents." Mathew looks at Isaac, unsure if he can hear. "I didn't see what happened to him, but Isaac told me they tried to take his Lenzes and…" Mathew stops. "I found him like this. There was no one left on the motorway. All the others had been killed or taken away. No one came to help. I saw your house and headed here. I knocked. I did knock pretty hard."

"I know. We heard you. I'm sorry, we didn't realise. We thought you had come to harm us."

Mathew nods. "Is there a doctor in the village?"

The man, who is standing in the hallway still holding the knife, says, "I'll go and get her." He puts the knife down, staring at it, as if surprised it is there, and brings the candle in the holder to the woman, who reaches and takes it from him. Then he goes back into the hall, grabs a coat hanging on a hook behind the door and pulls it on.

"Be quick," she says.

"I will."

The woman puts the candle on the floor and sits down beside it. She is in her forties, brown-skinned, small and thin, dressed in a print dress. She offers her hand to Mathew, "My name is Elia. My husband's name is Jack."

Mathew shakes her hand, "I'm Mathew. This is Isaac."

She reaches out to Isaac, who is very still, and strokes his hair. Mathew does not know how she can bear to touch his face. "What monsters would do this?"

Mathew shrugs. "They killed the others."

"They don't normally come this close to town."

"Who are *they*?"

"They call themselves the Reapers. A large gang of boys and young men. They rob, loot, kidnap and worse. There is no money, no work, no food, no law and order since the floods, so they take what they need from others. But they usually leave us alone. They are scared of the village. You should have been too."

"Scared?"

The front door opens again. Jack returns with an older woman, grey-haired and stocky.

"That was quick," Elia says.

"I was on my way back from Gerrard's."

"Mathew, this is Dr Russell."

The elderly doctor nods at Mathew. "Who's the patient?"

"Isaac."

The older woman hands her coat to Jack, and hurries into the room, putting her bag on the table. She stops short when she sees Isaac's face. "Dear me," she says.

"Can you help him?" Mathew asks.

"I will try. How long has his eye been like that?"

Mathew says, "I don't know. A few hours, maybe?"

The doctor leans over Isaac, "His eyeball is pretty shrivelled up. Can we get him onto your kitchen table, Jack?"

Mathew, Jack and the doctor carry Isaac from the sofa in the living room into the kitchen. Elia clears the table and they place Isaac flat on his back. Jack holds the candle for the doctor as she leans over the boy. "I need more light," she says, exasperated.

Elia, hovering by the door, says, "I'll get some more candles."

"And what happens to us when we burn through them all?" Jack says.

"The doctor needs light."

"So do we."

"Oh, for god's sake! I'll give you my bloody candles to replace them the next time I come," Dr Russell says as Elia lights candles around Isaac's head. "Thank you, my dear," she says to Elia.

She examines Isaac. After a few minutes she says,

"There's nothing I can do with this," the doctor says, "but cut it off."

"You're going to cut off his eyeball?"

"It's dried out. If we were in a hospital with the right facilities I might be able to do something, but here…" she looks around helplessly. "It will be all I can do to stop infection."

"What about his other eye? He said he couldn't see at all."

The doctor takes an instrument from her bag, peels open Isaac's closed lid and peers into his eye. "Looks okay. Did he say he could see out of it?"

Mathew says, "He can't see anything. He's totally blind."

"It may be scratched… If he's lucky, it will heal."

"So he's not blind?"

"I have no idea. I need to work on this other eye. I'm not sure how squeamish you all are, but I'd like some space to work." She looks around at everyone. "Would you vacate the room please?" She indicates the door.

"Of course," Elia says, shepherding Mathew and Jack out of the room.

Mathew goes with Jack and Elia into the living room, following the dim light of Jack's one candle. Jack indicates to the sofa and Mathew sits down. Elia sits next to him and Jack takes a seat on one of the two armchairs, putting the candle holder on the coffee table. The back of the sofa is wet where the rain has blown in through the broken window. There are shards of glass on the floor.

"Sorry about the window," Mathew says.

Jack lifts his chin slightly in acknowledgement, but not necessarily acceptance of his apology.

"Could I use your Nexus connection? I have people I should call. The gang, the Reapers, they stole my Lenz and my e-Pin. I have a Paper, though," he says, taking a small square out of his pocket and unfolding it.

"We don't have a connection," Elia says. "We don't

have power. Nothing is working here."

"But the Nexus is wireless. That shouldn't be affected by the floods."

"They shut it down," Jack says. "You shouldn't have come here," Jack says.

Elia glances at Jack, "What else could they have done?"

"They could have walked down the motorway."

"We were the nearest house. They weren't to know. We don't exactly have a sign outside telling people to keep out."

"Perhaps we should put one up. Normally, it isn't an issue. The patrol keep people out, but they must have scarpered when the Reapers moved in. Bloody cowards."

"They're not here to protect us."

"No, they're not."

"I don't know what you're talking about," Mathew says.

"Of course you don't."

There is a sound in the kitchen, something metallic being dropped on the stone floor. Dr Russell swearing. They all look towards the kitchen door. "Poor boy," Elia says.

"We're all poor people, these days," says Jack.

"Is there a village nearby, where I can connect to the Nexus?" Mathew asks.

Jack laughs. "Perhaps, if you go now, you might get out, if you don't expect to come back. The patrol will be there again in the morning. They may be out there now."

"What are they patrolling?"

"This town. Us. Keeping us in."

"Why?"

"They're frightened of us. They're worried they'll catch what we have."

"What is it you have?"

Jack and Elia glance at one another. Elia hesitates and then says, "We don't know."

"Are you ill?"

"Not exactly," Jack says.

Elia looks at Mathew. "We're in quarantine. That is why the soldiers patrol our village. That is why we can't leave. There's sickness in the village."

"You don't look sick," Mathew says.

"Jack was, a few months back."

Jack shifts in his seat and turns to Mathew, "I fell asleep and couldn't wake up."

"That doesn't sound so bad," Mathew says, smiling.

Elia and Jack don't smile back. Jack says, "I was riding my bike at the time."

Mathew's eyes widen, "How is that even possible?"

Jack shrugs, "Luckily, there was nothing else on the road. I simply drove off the road onto a verge, hit a wall and toppled over."

"Well, it must have woken you up."

Jack shakes his head. "Actually, it didn't."

Elia says, "He was asleep for ten days. That was three months ago, before any of us understood what was going on."

"Not that we know now," Jack says.

Elia says, "We initially thought he'd had a stroke, but his medibot didn't record anything. As far as the hospital was concerned, there was nothing wrong with him. They sent him home."

"An anomaly, they said."

"Then it started happening to others."

"In the last three months, half the village has had it, whatever *it* is. Mr. Mackey fell asleep sitting outside his house in the sunshine and no one could wake him up. Mo Sadat went out cold with his head in his soup. Vic Nafzger didn't wake in the morning when his wife brought his morning cup of coffee.

"It took us a couple of months to persuade the authorities something was wrong. It was a mistake to try. When they did take us seriously, there were a few weeks of them running tests, and then suddenly they shut down the town. No one could come in. No one could leave. And they shut down the Nexus."

"How can they do that?"

"They have signal blockers ranged about the town."

"We haven't spoken to our family and friends for over six weeks. They may have tried to come here. If they have, they will have been turned away at gunpoint."

"Has there been anything on the news about us?" Elia asks.

Mathew says, "No. Nothing on the Blackweb either. If anyone knew about it, it would be all over Psychopomp, even if the main news wasn't covering it." Elia raises an eyebrow but Jack smiles slightly. Mathew continues, "There's nothing but stuff about the war, and the floods."

"We knew it had flooded again, but a war? What is this about a war?"

"We're at war. Did you not know?"

They both shake their heads, "The patrol keep their distance. They won't talk to us. They're frightened they may catch something, although Dr Russell doesn't think it's airborne contagious. She doesn't think anything was wrong with our water either. Her best guess is it was something in our food, or something sprayed over us, pesticides perhaps."

"Or biological weapons," Mathew says. Elia and Jack stare at Mathew. "We *are* at war," Mathew says.

"When did the war start?" Elia asks.

Mathew thinks, "Three weeks ago."

"We've been sick for months."

"The war officially started on 25th November with the destruction of the Battlestars, but perhaps the war had already started, and only the government knew about it. Perhaps that's why you're sick."

"Who destroyed the Battlestars?"

"Russia and China."

"We're at war with Russia and China?"

Mathew nods.

"The boy might have a point about why we're sick."

"Biological weapons are illegal."

Mathew says, "Maybe, but our government has some kind of bioweapons programme. I know it for a fact."

"How do you know?"

Mathew shrugs. "I just do."

Dr Russell comes into the room, wiping her hands on a cloth. "I've done what I can. I'm afraid I couldn't save his eye. If you can get him to the right kind of hospital and the right kind of doctor, they may be able to rebuild one for him."

"How is he going to get to a hospital?" Jack asks.

The doctor shakes her head. "I don't have a clue, but right now Isaac needs to rest and recover. I wouldn't suggest moving him for a couple of days."

"Where's he going to stay? We're on meagre rations as it is."

"Well, if it's an issue for you," Dr Russell says, "I'll take the boys home with me, but I only have one bedroom."

Elia says, looking at her husband, "They will stay here, of course they will. Won't they, Jack?"

Jack sighs.

"Thank you both. That is generous," Dr Russell says. "Isn't it, Mathew?"

"It is. But I want to leave tomorrow."

"What about your friend?"

"He's not my friend. I found him on the road. I don't know him."

"You do now."

"I need to get word to my grandmother. She'll be crazy worried."

"We all want to get word to our families, Mathew."

"I will get word to them. I will get out of here and tell everyone what is going on. I will contact your families and tell them you are okay."

Jack and Elia look at one another. "You would do that?"

"Of course I will."

"And Isaac's parents?" Dr Russell says.

"Isaac's parents are dead. The Reapers shot them. I saw them in the back of a car on the motorway."

"Oh God, the poor boy!" Elia says.

Mathew is silent. Dr Russell says, "So he is blind and totally alone."

"I am alone too."

"So you should understand why that is not a good thing. You said you have your grandmother."

"*He* might have a grandmother."

"He might," Dr Russell agrees, continuing to study Mathew's face.

"He will slow me down. It will be harder to get away with him along."

Jack says, "He's right. If we can get him out, we should do it now, while the patrol is hiding from the Reapers." He gets up and goes to the window. There are no patrol lights. "I think they are still keeping clear. He could walk back the way he came along the motorway. Shevinton isn't far. I could even give him my bike. He could cycle on the hard shoulder."

"Is that what you want?" Dr Russell asks, looking at Mathew.

The thought of going out into the rain and the dark alone, passing the bodies of Vid and Falkous and potentially running into the Reapers again, makes Mathew's heart sink. But he says, "Yes."

"It's too dangerous," Elia says. "The reason the patrol hasn't come back is because the Reapers are still out there. Look what they did to the boy."

"He wants to go!" Jack says. "He just said. We can't keep him here against his will."

Dr Russell sighs and turns to Mathew, "Jack is right. Go if you want. Isaac will need to stay here and I will look after him." She turns to Elia. "He's heavily sedated. He needs somewhere to sleep it off."

"Upstairs," Elia says.

"Can you help me carry him? He's not heavy."

"I'll do it," Jack says and he follows Dr Russell into the kitchen, reappearing with Isaac folded limp in his arms, a surgical dressing over his eye. Elia follows Jack and Isaac upstairs with one of the candles from the kitchen.

Dr Russell takes a seat next to Mathew, slumping down heavily, rubbing her face. She looks exhausted. She says, "Don't let us keep you. The door isn't locked." Mathew doesn't move. She watches him for a moment and then nods, as if satisfied. Then she asks, "What happened today?"

"I don't know. A gang blocked the motorway. Jack and Elia said they're called the Reapers."

"Yes, Jack said as much. I meant to you?"

Mathew shrugs, "My guards were killed."

"Did you see it happen?"

"I saw one of them shot. I saw the body of the other one. She saved my life."

"They are paid to."

"Not like she did."

"How do you feel?"

Mathew is surprised, as if the question is irrelevant. He says, "Numb. Tired."

Dr Russell nods, standing up. Elia and Jack come down the stairs again. "I'm going to go home," she says. "I will come first thing in the morning. We can make a plan then. Thank you both for being so generous in helping the boys."

Jack holds the door open for the doctor, as she grabs her coat, pulling the collar around her neck, and she steps out into the rain.

After she has gone, Jack and Elia have gone to bed and he is settled under a blanket on the sofa, occasionally sprayed with fine rain from the broken window, Mathew thinks about why it was that Dr Russell had thanked Elia and Jack, when it was she who had helped Isaac and himself. He falls asleep still thinking about it.

8 JACKDAW

The bird wakes him. He opens his eyes and lies still, his breath steaming. A frost came overnight and the broken window funnels in the cold. It is morning. Pale winter light spills into the room. His eye catches movement over his shoulder. Without turning his head, he looks out of the corner of his eye. A large black bird with a grey feathered hood and small blue eyes is sitting on the back of the sofa. Its head is cocked and one beady eye is looking down at him, trying to figure out if he's dead or not and therefore whether or not he is food. A moment later Jack comes heavy-footed down the stairs and straight into the living room. The bird tries to fly off, hits the ceiling and then proceeds to flap around the room.

"Bloody hell!" Jack says, chasing after it. "That bloody broken window. These birds are horrible. Horrible."

Mathew scrambles to his feet, grabbing his blanket and cornering the bird; he throws the rug over it. It immediately becomes still. Mathew bundles the blanket all the way around the bird, picks it up and goes through the front door, into the garden. Away from the house, he

60

kneels on the gravel pathway leading down to the road, opens the blanket and lets the bird go. It half-hops, half-flies away, skittering down the garden towards the wet fields beyond. Then it takes a perch on the low branch of a tree, shaking its feathers and preening, trying to restore some of its bruised dignity.

There is a shed at the bottom of the garden. Jack walks towards it, "Come on," he says, tapping Mathew on the shoulder. "As you broke the bloody window, the least you can do is help me fix it."

The grass is soft and waterlogged. Mathew is still in his bare feet. The water is freezing. He stops to roll his trouser legs and then trots on after Jack, wishing he'd pulled on his boots. Jack stops him and points through a gap in the hedge.

Across the watery field, there's an armoured military vehicle on the motorway, which is otherwise now clear. There is no sign of the cars, vans and trucks Mathew left behind the night before. "Our brave friends are back," Jack says grimly, indicating the camouflaged truck. "You missed your chance to escape."

They retrieve tools and some plywood and return to the house, Jack nailing the board, as Mathew holds it in place. "That will do for now," Jack says. "It will have to, I suppose. There are no glaziers in the town."

Mathew is sorry, but decides there is no point in saying so again. He helps Jack put away the tools and returns to the house, where Elia is in the kitchen. She sees Mathew's feet.

"What are you letting the boy go out in the garden in his bare feet for? Apart from the fact that he'll probably catch his death, he's trailing mud into my living room. As are you." Jack looks at her dumbly. She says, "Take off your boots, for heaven's sake!"

"Sorry, sorry," Jack says, sitting down on the nearest chair and removing a pair of beaten old walking boots.

Elia hands Mathew a towel and he dries his feet. "Put

some socks on, at least," she says and Mathew goes off to the living room to dig his socks out of his boots. When he returns, Elia is toasting some bread.

"It's only a slice each," she says. "We have to be careful with food. We don't know how long we will be here and we only have what was in our local village store, in our food cupboards in the house and what the replicator can make."

Mathew takes a seat at the old battered farmhouse table where Isaac had been operated on the night before.

"I hope Dr Russell sterilised this," Jack says, which is what Mathew is thinking as Elia places a mug of tea and a plate of toast in front of him.

"She said she did," Elia says.

"Did you check on the boy?" Jacks asks.

"Still asleep," Elia passes Mathew a plate and a mug. He eats and drinks greedily. "I hope he's alright."

"What time is Russell coming?"

"She said first thing."

"Good, because we'll need her support to figure out what to do about these boys. Many in the village won't like them being here."

"Not as broadminded as you, eh?" Elia glances at Mathew and he smiles from behind his cup. "They'll be helpful when they find out Mathew wants to leave and take our news with him. Just like you were."

Jack grunts and says, "The patrol's back. No drones, though. The Reapers must have shot them down last night. We may have a few days' grace if they have to order some more."

"That's good news," Elia says. She says to Mathew, "We're being 'looked after'," she does air speech marks, "by the security forces. They don't have enough men to patrol the perimeter of the entire village, so they're using drones. They can't use robot soldiers safely on the ground because of the flooding, although they do have a robotic hound that can go through shallow water. One of the men from the village got out. It tracked him down and shot him."

"They're not messing around," Jack says. "You should have gone last night when you had the chance."

"I'm glad he didn't. I'd rather he had to deal with the patrol than the Reapers," Elia says.

"There's not much in it, though," Jack says.

The sound of feet on the floorboards in the hallway makes them all turn towards the door. "Hello?" a voice says. Dr Russell pokes her head around the door. "Door was open," she says. "Hope you don't mind? I let myself in."

"No, no. Of course," Elia says, standing and kissing Dr Russell 'hello'. Jack does the same.

"Do you want some tea?"

"No thanks, had some. How are you this morning, Mathew?"

"Okay," Mathew says.

"He was woken by a crow," Jack says.

"It was a jackdaw," Elia says. "The birds that live in the tree in the garden are jackdaws."

"A jackdaw?" Jack shakes his head as if this makes it even more remarkable. "Whatever it was, it got in through the broken window. It was sitting over him like he was a corpse. The boy here wrapped it in a blanket and put it outside." Dr Russell raises her eyebrows, but Mathew can tell she's thinking of something else. She says, "I'll go and see the patient if you don't mind. I have quite a full appointment card this morning."

"Yes of course, I'll come with you," Elia says, sucking the jam and butter off her fingers and pushing her chair back as she stands.

Dr Russell digs around in her bag, "Oh and before I forget, Jack, here's the candles I promised."

Jack holds up his hand, "I can't take those."

"I insist," Dr Russell says, bundling them into his arms. "Mathew, will you come with us, please? He may not remember us from the night before and if he wakes it would be better to see someone he recognises, or at least someone nearer his own age."

Mathew follows Elia and the doctor through the old house. Pictures in frames line the wall by the staircase. At the top of the stairs the landing separates. Elia leads them through to the back of the house, to a small box room. Isaac is lying under a duvet on a single bed pushed against a wall. Dr Russell kneels down beside the bed and takes his hand. She says, "Isaac? Isaac, are you awake?"

The boy moves. Dr Russell turns her head over her shoulder and says to Mathew and Elia, "The sedative I gave him was strong. I'm going to take a look at his eye to see how it looks this morning." She removes the dressing. Mathew stares, unable to look away. There is a red bloody hole where Isaac's eye should be. The doctor works quickly, cleaning the wound and redressing it. Mathew watches. Isaac suddenly cries out and hits out at the doctor. "It's okay. It's okay," she says. She holds onto his wrists tightly. "Isaac. Isaac," she says. "You are safe. I am a doctor. Mathew is here. Mathew, say something."

Mathew steps forwards. He hesitates and then speaks. "I am here, Isaac. It's as Dr Russell says. We are safe now. We are in that house, the one we walked to last night, remember? It was raining. We were in the porch. Then I think you passed out."

Isaac says, "I thought it might be a dream."

"It wasn't a dream," Mathew says. "I'm sorry."

"I can't see anything. Am I blind?"

Mathew catches Dr Russell's glance as she says, "In one eye, yes. We'll have to see about the other one. But there are doctors who can help you with your blind eye. There is medicine now that can fix it. You need to go to a hospital."

"Why aren't I in a hospital now?"

"Because this was the nearest house Mathew could find last night."

"My parents are dead," Isaac says, wonderingly. It doesn't seem real to him yet.

"I know. I'm sorry." She hovers for a moment, looking at Isaac, and then steps back, putting things into her bag. "I have to go to see another patient. I will be back as soon as I can, to see you. Elia, could you get Isaac something to drink and eat now he is awake? Mathew, would you sit with him a while?"

Mathew nods.

The doctor says to Elia, "I've got to see Jim, Carl and Rena. I'll swing by here when I've finished."

Elia and Dr Russell leave the room, pulling the door closed behind them.

"Are you still there?" Isaac asks.

"Yes I am."

"Where are we?"

"A house in a village called Amach," Mathew had found this out from Elia, "just off the motorway. The house is owned by Jack and Elia. Elia's nice. Jack's not pleased with me because I broke a window last night when I tried to get in."

"You broke his window?"

"I didn't think there was anyone here."

"Have you called your parents?" Isaac says.

"My parents are dead," Mathew says. "I live with my grandmother. Or I will do. I was on the way to her house when we were attacked."

Isaac takes this in. "Both your parents are dead?"

"Yes," Mathew says. "My dad died two years ago. My mum died last week."

"Last week?" Isaac takes this in and then says, "What did she die of?"

"Some kind of virus. They don't know."

"So have you called your grandmother?"

"I can't. The Nexus isn't working here."

"The Nexus always works."

"The government's blocking it. Don't worry about it

now. We'll get out of here and then we can tell people what has happened and get help. Do you have any other family? Grandparents? Uncles or aunts?"

"I have two uncles; one uncle fell out with my father. He won't want me. My mother's brother went to America two years ago. I don't know him. My grandparents are dead."

"Brothers or sisters?"

"No. You?"

"I'm an only child. My parents tried but they couldn't have any more."

"Same with me."

There's a gentle knock at the door and Elia comes into the room carrying a mug and a plate of toast. She puts the mug on the bedside table next to Isaac. "I have some toast for you," she says to Isaac. "I'm going to help you get hold of it, okay?" She guides the plate into Isaac's hands. Looking at Mathew, she says, "Can you help him with the tea?"

Mathew nods. He sits down on the bed.

"I'll be downstairs if you need anything," Elia says, pulling the door behind her as she leaves.

"You're right. She is nice."

"Yeah."

"The people who did this to me weren't."

"No," Mathew says thoughtfully. "What happened? Or don't you want to talk about it?"

Isaac finishes his toast. Mathew leans across the bed and takes the plate, putting it on the bedside table. "Do you want a drink? It's tea."

"Yes. Please." Mathew passes the drink to Isaac, guiding his hands around the mug.

Isaac carefully takes a sip of the drink and then says, "We were driving along. The traffic stopped. We waited for it to start again. We didn't know what to do. Dad and Mum didn't want to leave the taxi without completing the journey as it can double-charge you if you get in again.

66

Eventually, a gang of boys came along with guns. They didn't even speak to them, they just shot them through the windows of the car. They took their Lenzes from their eyes while they sat there shot. One of the boys yelled at me, told me to give him my Lenzes. I tried to get them out, but I was crying and shaking so much I couldn't, so he dragged me from the car and pinned me to the ground to take them out himself. He got one out but my other eye kept closing. He pressed and pressed on my eye. The others were standing around laughing. Then I couldn't see anything. They went quiet, then one of them said, "That's gross, man." He got off me. Another one of them said, 'Shoot him.' Another said, 'Nah, he's a boy.' There was some shouting elsewhere. Then there was silence. They left me. I was there ages. And then you found me."

"Where were you going, when we were attacked?" Mathew asks.

"Newcastle. My Dad got a job there. We're from London. Dad lost his job because of the floods in London. We lost our house and lived in a camp for months. Then he got offered a proper job in the North, where we could afford a place of our own." He falls silent for a minute, thinking about this and then asks, "Where were you going?"

"Scotland. A place called Elgol."

"It's a kind of alternative community. It belongs to Cadmus Silverwood."

"I've heard of him. Isn't he a politician?"

"He's the leader of the Garden Party."

"I don't know anything about politics."

"It's the opposition party."

"Oh. What does that mean?"

"The second biggest party in parliament." Issac's face is blank. Mathew says, "My grandmother's house has a grass roof. I helped make it."

"Doesn't it leak?"

"No, not at all. The walls of her house are made of

straw bales. She grows her own real vegetables outdoors. The community has animals, goats, cows and chickens and they drink real milk and eat real cheese and butter."

"Sounds cool."

"It is. You can come with me if you like."

"Me?"

"Yes. If you want to."

"Won't your grandma mind?"

Mathew laughs. "No. She'd like it. The community is welcoming."

"Isn't Scotland a long way away? How will we get there?"

"I don't know," Mathew says. "But we will. I promise."

For the first time since Mathew had met him, Isaac smiles.

9 THE SLEEPING TOWN

"Just when you thought things couldn't get any worse," Jack says, heaving another sandbag against the back door of the house. Mathew passes another one to Elia, who passes it to Jack. They are forming a line to the house from the garage, where their store of sandbags is kept.

"We won't die of dehydration, at least," Elia says, nodding at the water butts that sit underneath the guttering, now flushing with water.

The rain is coming heavily, steadily, straight down without a wind. Mathew peers out from underneath the hood of his waterproof coat. A large pool has already formed on the sodden lawn.

"Last one here," Jack says.

They stop and trudge back around the front of the house, where they have already built a wall of sandbags to protect the front door. There's a large yellow inflatable dinghy on the lawn outside.

"Help me get this down to the road will you, Mathew?" Jack says.

They drag the boat down to the edge of the lawn and then have to put it on its side to squeeze it through the gap in the hedge to get it onto the street. At the edge of Jack and Elia's property, the road falls away at a gradient and a foot of water runs mud-brown along the road. A short bulky figure in Wellingtons and a waterproof coat comes steadfastly wading towards them, head bowed against the driving rain. The figure raises their hand. It is Doctor Russell.

Mathew and Jack get the boat into the water and tie it to a lamppost with a rope.

"I see you have transport arranged. Just as well; the river has burst its banks and the high street is flooded."

"Thought as much," Jack says.

"How's the boy?"

"Still awake. Want to see him?"

"Yes. Better had."

"I don't want to be left alone," Isaac says.

Elia is trying to get him to go back to his room. He has made his way down the passage, sliding his hands against the wall and falls down the two steps at the top of the landing. "You'll hurt yourself," Elia says, rushing towards him.

Dr Russell goes up the stairs. "Hello Isaac. Dr Russell here."

Isaac blurts, "I don't want to be left here. I want to come with you."

"I told him to go back to bed," Elia says.

"How are you feeling?"

"Fine," he says stubbornly.

Mathew is at the bottom of the stairs looking at them. Dr Russell sees him and says, "Can you help Isaac get dressed?" Issac is wearing a pair of Jack's pyjamas, rolled up at the sleeves and ankles and tied at the waist.

Mathew goes into the living room, retrieves his rucksack and climbs the stairs. At the top, he says to Isaac, "Come on." He takes his arm and leads him back to his room.

"Can I come with you?" he says.

"Yes," Mathew says. "But you have to get dressed."

Several minutes later, Mathew and Isaac reappear with Isaac wearing the clean clothes Mathew had taken from Isaac's suitcase in the boot of the taxi. Mathew and Dr Russell guide Isaac down the stairs and outside. Jack holds the boat as they all get in, then unties it from the lamp-post, pushes off and clambers in himself. He slides the oars out from under the seat and starts to row.

They float down the street past half-flooded, sandbagged houses. At a T-junction they turn right onto the high street. There's an old church, shops, trees, people wading about carrying things. A woman in a canoe paddles past them. Then, where the street meets the village green and further on, where normally a visitor would find the banks of the river, there is just a flowing expanse of brown water. A little further still is the village hall. It is dry, positioned on top of a slope. There are other boats outside. Jack jumps out, steadies the boat as they get out and then pulls it out of the water with Mathew's help. They walk to the hall together. It is a green wood-clad building on stilts with steps to an open door. Inside, there is a large gabled-roofed room with a rough wooden floor, laid out with chairs. About thirty people are already seated. They turn around in their chairs when Jack, Elia, Dr Russell, and the two boys enter. Mathew feels many eyes staring at him and Isaac. Whispers and murmurs rise around them as they take their seats. Dr Russell goes to the front of the room, where a middle-aged man and a woman stand.

The woman says, "As most of you will know, the vicar and I spent the last two days doing an inventory of all of the food left in the village. We have about three weeks before the food situation becomes dire. The flood wasn't unexpected and we managed to move most of our supplies from the store. Cynthia went house to house yesterday afternoon telling everyone to move their food upstairs. If we go on at the current burn rate we will run out of candles and oil lamps by the end of next week. We advise people only use what they have in the evening to cook or make hot drinks and to try and navigate their houses in the dark. As you know, we are asking for donations of furniture to burn to keep the sleeping victims warm at the infirmary. Brian has the update on infrastructure."

The man standing beside her says, "The bloody sewers flooded last night, so take care when wading through water and please, please tell your children and young people not to play in it or drink it. It's filthy. We're looking for volunteers to take in people whose houses have been flooded. Dr Russell will update us on health."

The doctor says, "We currently have twenty sleepers. Last week, Kit Flemming and Will Cosgrove woke and we had no new people falling asleep. As of today the number of people who have been affected by the sleeping sickness is seventy. As always, I would advise you be careful when operating machinery or doing anything dangerous and be aware of how you feel before you undertake any tasks that could prove fatal if you fall asleep while performing them. Please pay attention to this advice even if you haven't slept yet. Most people report feeling nauseous and dizzy before they sleep.

"Now, I also have some other news. Last night there was a raid on the motorway, we think by the Reapers. You will have seen I came in with two boys, two strangers. The Carters have kindly offered their home to them. The boys found their way to us across the fields. They managed to escape. One of the boys is seriously injured. I would like you to show kindness to them."

A large man with curly black hair pipes up, "We have barely enough food and water for those of us who were already here."

Dr Russell nods, "Thanks for your honesty, Phil. It's true. We are running out of food. The government hasn't brought aid recently. We have no reason to think they will, and we have no way of getting the word out to our friends and family elsewhere. Everyone who has tried to leave has been shot." Dr Russell turns to Mathew and says, "Could you stand, please?" Awkwardly, Mathew gets to his feet. Dr Russell says, "We are prisoners here, yet this boy brought his sick friend here last night. They just walked in. The motorway was blocked by Reapers, the cars on it attacked, and the government patrol made themselves scarce. We all could have walked out of here last night if we had wanted to." There are murmurs around the room. "If we can help this boy escape, he can get word out about us."

"The patrol will never let them through," the man with the curly hair says.

"Who knows," Dr Russell says, "I know someone who works for the BBC. Maybe, if I can get news to them, they will report on it."

Someone says scornfully, "The BBC won't cover it. There's a government blackout on us."

Mathew says, "The Blackweb will definitely pick it up."

"What difference will that make?" the curly-haired man says.

Dr Russell says, "The word will be out. And our friends and family can at least bring supplies. The patrol won't stop them leaving food and water in no man's land, surely? It's better than carrying on as we are."

"But how do we get the boy out?"

"We need a plan."

In the afternoon, it is still raining. Elia takes Isaac back to the house. Mathew and Jack go on to Dr Russell's to help her secure her house against the steadily rising waters. In the evening they make a meagre meal. Mathew's empty stomach feels like it is eating itself, and he thinks wistfully of the abundance in the kitchen at Pickervance Road. He remembers the nuts he had pilfered from the mini bar in the car and fetches his rucksack, offering to share them with Jack, Elia and Isaac. Elia says, "You should keep them for your journey. We will have nothing to offer you, and we don't know when you will find food when you are away from the village."

Mathew nods and tucks the nuts away in the bag once again, placing the bag on the floor between his feet.

Jack asks, "What is in that bag? I picked it up before. It's heavy."

Mathew stares at Jack. He doesn't like the idea of anyone touching his rucksack.

"Alright," Jack says, pulling a face. But he doesn't pursue it.

They go to bed early in order to save the candles. Mathew sleeps on the couch again, warmer and dryer now the window is patched. It is odd to be without a Nexus connection. It reminds him of being in the hospital. Or in one of Mr. Lestrange's worlds, in his dreams. He hasn't dreamt anything so colourful since his mother died. But he has nightmares that turn out to be true when he wakes.

DAY TWENTY-SIX: Friday 17th December 2055

The next day, Isaac is stronger and insists on trying to walk about the house, using his hands to guide him. Elia goes around nervously before him, putting things out of his way that he might knock over. In the afternoon, Dr Russell comes to examine him. She removes the patch on his remaining eye, the one that was scratched. "I can see!" Isaac shouts excitedly.

DAY TWENTY-SEVEN: Saturday 18th December 2055

Low cloud covers the stars and the moon. An unmanned boat goes floating out into the darkness across the water on the fields. A quarter of mile out, after the engine cuts out, the boat rocks gently to a stop, and then bursts into flames. Within minutes the patrol comes out to investigate with their strong-beamed lights casting into the night. As it gets close, close enough for one of the patrolmen to need to shield himself from the heat, the boat explodes.

Dr Russell, who is in the centre of the village, standing alone in the clock tower holding a pair of binoculars to her eyes, says, to no one in particular, "One down." Then she grabs the rope hanging by her head, and rings the church bell. One after the other, fires go off all around the village, with the exception of the place where Mathew and Isaac are.

Jack nods to Mathew. Elia whispers, "Goodbye. Good luck." And Mathew and Isaac head off into the night, with nothing but an old-fashioned compass to guide them.

They follow the direction Jack has told them to go in, and Isaac grasps Mathew's arm, thinking he has gone blind again. "I can't see," Isaac says, the panic rising in him.

"Neither can I," replies Mathew.

The ground is solid under their feet at least. They are walking along a gravel path by a tall chain link fence overhung with trees. They find their way by feeling along the fence. Isaac, overcoming his initial panic, having had a few days' training moving around by touch, is more confident now than Mathew. Nevertheless, it is slow-going to the end of the path. Here, in the open, there is some limited visibility. The land is flat and the clouds, dimly backlit by the thin-cloaked moon, reflect some small light down upon the earth. Mathew doesn't like the idea of stepping out into such an exposed place, but Jack was adamant that they follow the compass and the compass is telling them this is the way they must go.

They are about to make their move when Isaac says, "What is that?"

"What?"

"Over there," he points.

Mathew doesn't know how he's spotted it with his one not particularly good eye, but there is something moving towards them, a dark shape, barely visible, a swift kinetic smudge in the still greys and the blacks. It isn't tall enough to be a man, and it isn't a drone. A chill runs down Mathew's spine.

It is the hound.

For some reason Mathew thinks about what Jack had said to him over dinner about the weight of his rucksack and he realises the bag isn't only heavy because of the jar with his mother's ashes. It also contains the gun that Falkous gave him.

With a speed and efficiency he is surprised he possesses, he pulls out the gun now. He pushes Isaac into the cover of the trees and shrubs growing on the edge of the end of the path where they now stand.

I need height.

He looks up; there is a twisting hardwood with a fork in its branches.

I know how to climb trees.

And he is in the fork of the tree before he's given it a second thought, but as he releases the safety catch and aims the gun, it passes through his mind that he's only ever climbed trees in his dreams.

His naked eyes frantically scan the open land for the killer machine. If he had his Lenzes he'd be able to use night and telefocus to find what he is looking for. He feels at a disadvantage, especially as he knows the hound will be sniffing out their body heat using infrared sensors. They only have a few minutes before it locks on to them and shoots. If he shoots now and misses, the hound will retaliate. He takes a deep breath. There is no more time to think. The red dot sight of his gun casts out its beam and miraculously, suddenly finds its target. He squeezes the trigger. The gun kicks back and knocks Mathew in the head. He falls out of the tree onto the ground below, his leg snagging painfully in the branches.

Isaac scrambles over to him. "Are you okay?"

"Did I get it?" Mathew asks, getting to his feet.

Isaac peers out across the land and says, "Well, it isn't coming."

There is no movement. Mathew reloads the gun and walks cautiously out. Five hundred yards away, there is something lying in the dirt. With the gun still trained on it, they approach. There's a mangled chunk of material on its side; angular and utilitarian, grey metal. No attempt has been made to make it look like a real dog. At the front, on the "head", there is a gun.

"Do you think it's dead?" Isaac asks.

"It can't be dead," Mathew says. "It's a robot. The question is, is it broken enough, so it can't kill us?" Mathew kicks at it with his boot. The machine suddenly shudders and something whirrs inside. Mathew quickly raises his gun and shoots again, aiming first at the head and then at the body, having no idea where its 'brain' is supposed to be.

"That should do it," he says, turning around to look for Isaac, who has run back several metres.

"You're insane," Isaac says.

"We're alive, aren't we?" Mathew worries the noise from the gun, silenced as it was, will have attracted attention. He says, "So far. Now let's go."

10 CLARA PAYS A VISIT

Clara Barculo gets out of the Aegis car on Pickervance Road and glances at Mathew's window, searching for his pale face, the aquiline nose she likes so much, his still, watchful eyes, knowing full well that he won't be there. She is still smarting from the fact that he hasn't called as he said he would. He must be in Elgol now. Telling herself he has other things to deal with doesn't quite dampen the hurt she feels. She thanks her guard, turns towards Gen's house and sees her teacher waiting. Gen stands back to let Clara past and shuts the door. They go into the front room. Clara takes her seat at the piano, then she turns and looks at Gen. Gen's face is drawn and pale. She doesn't look herself at all.

"Are you okay?" Clara asks.

"I had some bad news this morning."

It doesn't feel appropriate for Clara to pry into her teacher's life. Finally, she says lamely, "I'm sorry to hear that." Clara waits to see if Gen will volunteer more and when she doesn't, and the silence grows awkward, she says, "Should we cancel? I can call back my car. It won't have got far."

Gen says, "No."

"Should I start, then?" she points at the piano.

Gen says, "Clara, you and Mathew have become good friends, haven't you?"

Clara reddens slightly, "Yes... before his mother died. We haven't spoken much since."

Gen nods, but she is distracted; she only seems to be half-listening. "Clara, the bad news I've had is about Mathew."

Clara's mind is racing. "He's in Scotland with his grandmother."

Gen shakes her head, "He never made it. His grandmother called me this morning. His car was attacked on the motorway. The Panacea guards with him were both killed."

"Killed?"

"Shot. They didn't find his body, but it's been three days now and there's been no word. Mathew's grandmother says Panacea have people out looking for him, but they would have expected to hear something by now if he'd been kidnapped for a ransom."

Clara can barely process what she's hearing. She doesn't want to pursue the conversation to its logical conclusion. If she leaves it hanging here, then Mathew is still alive. She turns back to the piano and puts her hands on the keys.

"Clara?" Gen says.

"I'd like to continue my lesson," she says.

"Perhaps we should leave the lesson and talk about this."

Clara's response is to start playing.

At the end of the hour, Clara leaves Gen's house and walks in a daze towards the waiting car. Just before she gets in, she turns back to Mathew's bedroom window and her eyes sweep across the front of his house until they reach Mr. Lestrange's bay. She remembers what Mathew told her about him watching them both. There is no one there now.

Her guard coughs, prompting her.

"Just a second," she says and strides out across the pavement, through the little gate, up the short red-tiled path.

Banging on Mathew's strange neighbour's front door, she thinks, *Mathew said that he never comes out.*

"Mr. Lestrange!" she shouts. Her voice echoes down the silent street. She doesn't care.

Then the door opens and a tall man with hooded eyes is looking down at her. "Clara," he says, as if he is expecting her.

"I want to talk to you."

"Come in," he says, opening the door wide.

Mr. Lestrange's front room is exactly as Mathew described it, except that, in addition to the table, there are two armchairs. Something about the way they are positioned makes Clara think they have been placed there for her benefit, but she dismisses this idea immediately. Mathew's crazy stories have tainted her mind.

"Please," Lestrange says, indicating she take a seat. He sits in the one opposite, leaning forward, studying her face with extraordinary attention. "How can I help you?"

"Mathew," she gasps, surprised at herself, at her emotion. She digs her nails into her palms. *What can this man do to help? Why have I come here?*

"You are worried about him."

"He is missing."

"Ah," Lestrange says. Clara thinks she detects a slight smile. "I probably shouldn't tell you, but as you are here, I don't think it will do any harm. You needn't worry about him."

"Gen says his car was hijacked. The people who were with him were shot. They haven't found his body but they think…"

"He is alive," Lestrange says.

As Lestrange speaks, fleeting images of Mathew pass through her head like a badly calibrated slideshow. Mathew exhausted, hungry, walking across open land with a boy. Scrambling together, helping one another to climb a hillside. Clara blinks, dumbfounded, and says, "How can you know that?"

Mr. Lestrange shrugs, a slight movement like his smile.

"How can you know?" Clara insists. She is angry.

Lestrange raises his eyebrows. He asks, "Would you like a drink?"

"A drink? No, I would not like a drink!"

Lestrange sighs and stands up. "Well, I would like one. We are going to be here a while." He goes to the window and looks out at the guard, who is fidgeting at the roadside.

"You haven't asked me why I've come," Clara says.

Lestrange turns to her; his eyes are like dark glass. They reveal nothing about him, but seem to reflect Clara back to herself. She sees herself sitting in the armchair, gripping the armrests.

"Why have you come?" Lestrange says at last, although he seems to be asking the question to please her rather than to get an answer.

"Mathew said you know what is going on."

"What is going on…" He repeats this as if he likes the words, as if he is storing them away somewhere for later. "And what *is* going on?" Lestrange asks her.

"I don't know," she says, confused and cross. "That is why I am here!"

"I am going to make some tea."

With Lestrange absent, she looks around the room at the books. If she hadn't remembered so clearly Gen telling Mathew about Lestrange's library that first time they had met, she would have found it uncanny being here. Even so, the room seems to tally with Mathew's dream descriptions and she finds herself scouring the shelves with her eyes, looking for Mathew's book. He had said the particular bookcase was behind the door. She goes to it, bends down and looks.

Her flesh goes cold.

There on the shelf is a book with the title *Mathew Erlang* and another one with the title *Clara Barculo*.

The door opens, bumping into her. "Excuse me," Lestrange says, as he comes into the room with a tray carrying a teapot, a milk jug, sugar bowl and two cups on saucers. He puts it down on the table.

Clara pulls the two books from the shelf. She turns to him, "What are these?" she asks, holding them up.

"Ah," Lestrange says. "I thought you might ask." Lestrange sits down in his chair. He says, "I never know how long to let the tea brew for."

"Are you going to explain?"

"Come and sit down," Lestrange says. "As I said, we are going to be a while."

"I can't be a while. I have a car waiting."

"Oh, don't worry about that."

"You keep telling me not to worry, but you are not telling me why I shouldn't."

Lestrange indicates to the empty chair, "Clara, please sit down."

Clara looks at the chair, thinks for a moment and then goes over and sits in it, the books clasped firmly in her hands, resting on her knees.

Lestrange says, "Mathew is alive and well. Tomorrow, Gen will call you to tell you he has been found and is on his way to Elgol and his grandmother."

"How do you know he is safe?"

"Because I can see him."

"See him? How? You are some kind of spy! Mathew thought you might be."

"A spy?" Lestrange considers, tilting his head. "I suppose, from your point of view, I am in a way." He bends forwards, lifts the lid off the teapot and peers in. "That must be brewed by now, surely?" He puts the lid back. "Do have some," he says. "Keep me company." Clara doesn't respond, so he pours two cups anyway, and stands to place her cup at the edge of the table nearest her seat. "Do you take milk?" He watches her stiff, angry face that refuses to look at him and pours the milk into her cup. Once he has finished, he retreats back to his armchair and takes the cup and saucer in his palm.

Clara opens the cover of the book on her lap and starts to page through. "This is incredibly creepy," she says. "Are you SIS? We are not radicals, you know. We are just kids. Mathew plays around on the Blackweb but he isn't doing anything wrong."

"I'm not SIS," Lestrange says. The cup chinks in the saucer as he places it back. "I don't mean you any harm. Quite the opposite, in fact."

"Do you work for the opposition? Are you with the Garden Party? Or are you an Edenist?"

Lestrange smiles, "No, I'm not either of those things."

Clara's eyes wander to the page that is open before her; she reads:

```
After the death of her husband, Mathew Erlang,
Clara Barculo established the Bach Society, a secret
society masquerading as an elite musical social
club. It acted as a cover for the continuation of
Erlang's work and in particular the Yinglong
Project.
```

Clara raises her eyes to Lestrange's face in horror and says, "Who are you?"

Lestrange takes another sip from his tea, "You wouldn't believe me if I told you."

"I know you are watching Mathew," she lifts the book. "And me. He told me he got into your house and played a game in your Darkroom. But he wasn't sure if he dreamt the whole thing." She studies his face and says, "Mathew's dreams. They weren't dreams, were they?"

Lestrange says, "Not exactly, no."

"Are you really called Mr. Lestrange?"

"I have his body. There once was a man called August Lestrange. He was an academic at the University of London who specialised in medieval history. He had no family, few friends and lived alone. He was stabbed one night, mugged for his Paper, Lenz and e-Pin, taking a bad shortcut from an evening lecture. He was dead by the time the human medical team arrived and I took over. They thought they had performed a miracle and brought him back from the dead. They were very happy with themselves."

"What do you mean, took over? You saved his life? I don't understand."

"I didn't save his life. I took his body. I inhabited it. That's how it usually works for those in the field. They adopt the bodies of someone who has been killed before anyone has noticed. In this way we can live as humans do; feel like they do, experience the chemical confusion in their brains and react to the environment. It means our research is more evidence-based. We found pure observation meant that we were missing a huge amount of information. Lestrange was dead and lying in an alley; he was observed to have no actual historical impact. I took over and moved into a house I'd made vacant next to Mathew's house."

"So you can live as humans do… You are telling me you are not human?"

"Of human origin, of course."

"What are you then – an AI?"

"Not exactly."

"Mathew was right; you are something to do with the government. A project." Clara declares this with such certainty that Lestrange doesn't feel the need to contradict her. "Then if you are not August Lestrange, who are you?"

"My real name is Atteas, but I like the name August. Please continue to use it. You look very confused and concerned. I think I need to start at the beginning. Do drink your tea."

"I don't want any tea!"

Lestrange shrugs.

"What are these books for?" she asks.

Lestrange looks at the open tome in Clara's hands. "They were a bit of whimsy."

"Mathew says they choose the world of the games you play in the Darkroom. He told me he got into your house and played a game in your Darkroom and it was like a real world, but the books controlled everything."

"They don't control everything, but they do select the situation and the time. We don't need to do it. It seemed like a fun construct. It is a way of visualising a humdrum technical process. We have done this kind of thing from the beginning. We thought the library a good idea. When we dreamt it up, it made us smile. But as it turned out, it is not a good idea when you have a smart sixteen-year-old boy living next door. We are artists and writers, you see. And at the best of times, my people are given to play. We have less to be serious about than you."

"We? There are others like you?"

"Of course. Mathew met two of them. He knew them as Quinn Hacquinn and Colonel Borodin, but they are really Berek and Kwiller. There was an actual man called Quinn Hacquinn but he died, a couple of years ago now, beaten to death by an Accountant sympathiser in a row in a pub and thrown out into the street by the mob. The real Borodin was killed by a sniper's bullet."

"If you intervened in the original Mr. Lestrange's life, and brought him back from the dead, and you did the same with the original Borodin and Quinn, why didn't you help Mathew? Why didn't you save his mother?"

"We did not bring Lestrange, Borodin and Hacquinn back from the dead. We assumed their identities. They are dead."

"But you could."

"Yes, we could."

"Then why not?"

"The first historian-observer from our time, a person the humans who meet him will call the Tekton, taught us that we should not interfere in history. We cannot disturb the path of events because in doing so we may disturb the path of our own history. We might even eradicate ourselves from the future.

"My friends, as you put it, Borodin/Kwiller, Quinn/Berek and myself, we are information. You humans are information, in fact, but you haven't found a good way of making yourselves resilient yet. But you will. Eventually, largely thanks to Mathew and the work you will facilitate later.

"But for my friends and I, the essence of us can be stored in small packages, duplicated, and transported across space and time. If one version of us is destroyed, it doesn't matter; we are replicated elsewhere. That means here on earth we can inhabit other bodies but when those bodies die, we don't need them. We can move on. Bodies are a kind of transport."

"What did you mean when you said 'thanks to Mathew'?"

"When Mathew grows up he will create a superhuman intelligence. A group of sixteen interconnected personalities with humanlike brains but supercomputing processing resources and perfect memory. They will have exponential learning power and will advance knowledge and technology by centuries in the space of a few years. Four hundred years from this time, when humankind finally extinguishes itself, in one version of events – the original version – these sixteen will be all that is left of human civilisation. They will journey out into space to found new worlds. They will become us. Me. My friends."

"Wait a minute… You're telling me you're an alien?"

Lestrange thinks about this. "I'm not sure if we can technically be described as aliens, as we originate from this planet."

"How would you describe yourself?"

"I believe the most appropriate term in your language would be transhuman. There is a movement, I believe, in your time using this word."

"And Mathew is your creator?"

"One of our creators. Although the vast majority of our evolution was done by ourselves and a lot of it happened once we'd left earth, while we were travelling across space looking for our home. We had a lot of time on our hands to think."

"Then how are you here if you haven't been created yet?"

"We are visitors from the future."

"You have travelled in time?"

"Yes," Lestrange says.

Clara considers this. "Mathew says this house is a time machine."

"In essence, yes. He is right."

11 THE TRUTH ABOUT MR. LESTRANGE

"Can you go anywhere in time?" Clara asks, closing the book in her lap.

"Once we have created a portal, yes."

"And when is your time?"

"About one hundred thousand earth years in the future."

She laughs, "You said earth years."

Lestrange raises an eyebrow.

"Sorry, I can't quite believe what you're saying."

"That is understandable," Lestrange says.

"What is your world like?"

August sighs. "Can you imagine if I asked you the same question? How would you answer?"

Clara says quickly, "It's a small blue rocky planet, mostly covered in water, about four and a half billion years old, the third of eight orbiting a sun, home to nearly nine billion species, with homo sapiens being the most successful, having a population of twelve billion individuals. I think it was a question on a General Studies quiz a couple of years ago."

"Well, okay. We live on a planet in a binary star system, about fifty light years from this one. In terms of mass, age and evolutionary status, the star we orbit is similar to your star, the Sun. The second sun is dying. There are twelve planets in our system, many moons. When we arrived, we found one planet had water, rain and an atmosphere. There were no native species, beyond the simplest forms of life imaginable, but we populated the planet with our own variation of the blueprints of forms of life we had carried from earth. We took billions of examples of DNA with us.

"Unlike on earth, on our planet all living things are essentially the same organism. We are all connected to the same central nervous system. Buildings are also part of this organism, as is the ocean. So I can feel a flower, or a tree on my planet and know what it is thinking."

"A tree doesn't think."

"You'd be surprised… even here. But they certainly do on my planet."

Clara says, "You said all living things on your planet are the same organism, but you are a different person from those others you mentioned."

"Kwiller and Berek?"

Clara nods.

Mr. Lestrange says, "You are thinking of our bodies as *us*. But they are carrying cases. They are disguises or camouflage. I'm trying to work out how best to explain this to you.

"For you to understand what we are, you must think of us as nodes on a network. We have discrete personalities, and purposes, but we constantly communicate, collaborate, and share information. We are not individuals in the way you are, or the way you think you are. Humans are more interdependent and less individual than you imagine.

"The human brain is remarkable for its ability to make associations between random bits of information. We can do that too, but we can also remember and recall everything we ever learned and process vast amounts of information quickly. I don't need to search for a fact on the Nexus. If it is within our ThoughtScape, I will know it. That does not mean we always get it right, but there is no blame if we get it wrong.

"In your world, the cutting edge of research and understanding is available to only a relative few people on the planet. In my world, it is available to everyone instantaneously.

"You are jealous of your creations and your breakthroughs because they impact your social standing, reputation and livelihoods. In my world, everything material is free and abundant; food, water, energy – any physical thing you can think of, you can have. So of course, there is a different kind of value system. No one needs to earn money and make a living. There is no money because there is no need of it. There is no hierarchy because we think together and make decisions as a consensus. People are not born; they are created, and no one is unwanted or cast aside because we only create people when they are needed. As there is no death, the creation of life is infrequent and cause for huge celebration."

"What is the ThoughtScape?"

"It's what we call our collective thinking space, our collective consciousness. If I want to, I can know what Kwiller is doing and thinking right now, by thinking about Kwiller. In this way, I can share all of Kwiller's knowledge and experience automatically. I don't have to repeat the effort and time of learning. If you multiply that by the hundreds of millions we are, you can see we are a powerful learning machine and our path to knowledge is exponential compared to yours.

"If I want to speak to Kwiller, I need to have the intention to do so. We have protocols about this, so we're not constantly interrupted, of course, but we do not have individuality in the same way you do. Because we are not imprisoned in our brains, privacy is a rather meaningless concept. As is deception and many of the related crimes."

"Do you mean everyone in your world knows everything you are thinking?"

August nods.

"Do you know everything I am thinking?"

"I do, but I need to focus on it. That is our constraint; we have boundless time and massive computational power, but we do have limited powers of focus. That is why Mathew got away with being here. I was somewhere else. Also because we did not imagine he would break into the house. Of course, we're recording everything he does. We didn't account for the fact that we would need to create monitors and alarms in case he broke into the future."

Clara says, "You can honestly see into my mind?"

"Yes, but it shouldn't bother you."

"How on earth could it not?"

"If you humans knew how alike you all were, you would stop being concerned about people reading your thoughts. You are a great deal less original and special than you imagine."

"Thanks."

"There is no pleasing you, is there?"

"I don't want you looking at my mind," Clara says.

August shakes his head. "I've come a long way to do that. I'm not going to stop because you are concerned I might stumble across something embarrassing."

"I'm not bothered about embarrassing stuff."

"Yes you are."

"Okay, I am. But everyone has a right to their own thoughts. The government is listening in to everything we do publicly. You can't blame us for wanting to protect our minds. At least they can't listen to them. Yet..."

"The issue is not the fact that you have no privacy, it's the fact that you are all at war with one another on every possible level. You can't trust each other with your innermost thoughts. That makes you weaker, not stronger.

It also makes you unhappy."

"I am not unhappy."

August raises an eyebrow.

"Mathew's mother is dead. Mathew may be dead. Do you think I ought to be skipping around with joy?"

"Mathew is fine. I told you. I showed you."

"With the other boy? The one with the dressing over his eye?"

Lestrange nods.

"How do I know what I saw was real?"

"How do you know anything is real?"

Clara thinks about this. "If you're not human and this isn't your real body, what do you actually look like?"

"My body is humanoid. We are taller. We don't have genders in the way you do, believing the male and the female need to be balanced in one for a person to be whole. But bodies are mutable things. We see them much as you see your clothes. We can change our form quite easily. Most of us will spend some part of our life as another species or in a radically altered form from the one we were given when we were created. It doesn't matter. We aren't tied to physical reality. Many of us store our physical bodies for years and disappear into virtual worlds. We can live an entire human life out in a virtual world."

"You live your whole lives in virtual worlds?"

"Sorry, I meant to use a human life as a unit of measurement. We often live the length of seventy or eighty earth years in virtual worlds."

"So how long are your lives?"

"Indefinite. The oldest members of our community are as old as the Originators, those that crossed space from earth to our planet. None of us have ever died."

"You are immortal?"

"Nothing is immortal. We are tied to the life of our universe, unless we find a way out."

"A way out?"

"Obviously there are other universes. Homo sapiens

are tied to their solar system with no other habitable planet and without the technology to properly manage your own ecosystem or geo-form new ones nearby. My species is tied to this universe. We are engaged in finding our way out in the same way you are engaged in local space travel. We are about as far along in our quest as you are in yours. That is the serious business of my people. It will take hundreds of thousands of years to solve our problem. We may never solve it, but we have several billion years before it becomes a serious issue for us."

"What are you doing here, then?"

"I told you. I am a historian, a kind of author. I create virtual worlds that my people can live in to experience past events for themselves. My particular job is to observe and understand Mathew's life. I am tasked with creating a virtual world that records everything that happens to Mathew so that others from my world can live his life too and understand what led him to do the things he did – or, from your perspective, is about to do. I am a biographer. But my medium is not books or films; it is reality itself."

"But Mathew's life has changed now, because you came here."

"We hope to limit changes as much as possible. But yes, you are right. Your life has certainly changed. It has already been documented in its original form. We will need to update it. We will probably keep the original version as well."

Clara's eyes widen. "Why do this?"

"This is the way we learn, through simulation so real it becomes experience. We call reality the Presence and we call virtual reality the unPresence and there is only a sliver of difference between them for us.

"We have always done this. Every aspect of learning for us is done in simulation. When we were travelling to our home planet from earth, the Originators lived in virtual worlds because their reality was that they were huge amounts of complex information crammed into a tiny machine the size of a piece of dust, travelling across vast stretches of empty space. This is quite a fun concept and interesting initially, but after a while, empty space is not so exciting, so they imagined virtual existences for themselves.

"When we got to our planet, the planet was not what we wanted it to be initially, so we lived in virtual reality until we had finished building our new world. The history of our arrival on our planet and the development of our society was all documented in virtual reality so, rather than someone being told what happened, they could enter into that experience and live it for themselves. Everyone on my planet knows what it was like for the Originators to travel across vast distances of empty space looking for somewhere to live, because everyone has done it.

"For a long time, we did not know we came from earth; we had lost our origin story. It had been wiped from our memories by one of our human creators because they thought it would be better that we did not know. They thought knowing about humans would corrupt us.

"Some of my people – we call them the Wanderers – spend their lives travelling about space mapping our galaxy, discovering new suns and planets, starting new colonies on these new planets. There are enough planets in our galaxy alone for us to continue to spread out and grow for the next ten million years.

"Wanderers are usually people who have experienced the Originator story and found that they grieved for the experience when they came back into the Presence. The intelligence inside them is an actual mind, one with a biological body, frozen and physically located on our planet, awaiting the return of its owner, an event that may, incidentally, never happen. Some Wanderers have been gone tens of thousands of years.

"One of these Wanderers found a planet, which was not meant to exist, according to our star records, and our oldest map. In fact, the Originators had not created this first map that led us to this non-existent planet. It had always been there in our memories and it was wrong. The earth, the sun and the solar system had been wiped from our records. Our people came here to this solar system and mapped the planet Earth. It was dead and barren, but we found signs that life had once existed in great abundance. That is not the case everywhere. Such complex life is rare in our galaxy.

"We discovered evidence of an ancient civilisation. The more we looked, the more we found hints that this was where our species had originated. We found thousands of digital and written records. Slowly, we learned to interpret these records to try and understand what had happened here and how we came to exist. But the work was frustrating. Even when we had assembled a narrative we thought might vaguely represent the truth, allowing for the fact that humans are the most deceitful creatures imaginable, the author who was responsible for creating the experience for others to enter felt unable to truly represent the reality of events because none of us had ever been there to see and experience it for ourselves.

"Over the millennia, we had invested heavily in research about teleportation to make our exploration work easier. Accidentally, as part of this work, we discovered how to make portals that not only allowed us to jump across the universe, but also to jump in time.

"One of us travelled back in time to examine the origin of some of the archaeological remains we had found and to try to understand the events of the last days of humans on earth."

12 A VISIT TO THE PRESENCE

August Lestrange says, "You have historians who write books about the past. They read ancient documents, they use the latest technology available to them to dig for archaeological evidence, carbon date it, take DNA from bones and other human remains, bits of hair, bits of skin, food and objects buried in graves. We are merely doing the same with the technology available in our time.

"If you can imagine London one hundred thousand years from now, a blasted desert, the great buildings covered in shifting sands that blow about into dunes with the winds and hurricanes howling across the treeless landscape. If you imagine visitors from the future digging through this sand to find artefacts, clues to the people who went before. They find stones, granite, concrete, some slabs with writing on, gravestones, the remains of buildings, glass, a lot of plastic, bits of rotted metal. In amongst the rubble they find stone and bronze statues. Think about walking around London, think about the men on horseback and in uniform, Lord this, Duke that... do these people mean anything to you? They are just men who happened to be the titular head of this army that happened to win a particular battle no one can remember.

What would it tell us about the people who lived here? Even if we struck lucky and we found an archive of art and pictures, a library of documents, even a digital one that had somehow managed to survive through storm, heat and ice and we worked out a way to read them, what would those documents tell us? They would certainly tell us something, but would they tell us what it was like to live here now, what it is like to be you? The only way we can do that is to be here, living as one of you, observing and recording.

"The one of us who came before was a pioneer. He taught us there is value in living as a human, to experience life in a human body; you have genders, we do not, you have illness, you are mortal, you have bodily needs for fuel and water while we don't, you are ruled by your brain chemistry and instincts in a way we are not. In order to record humanity we decided to become human.

"Since then we have started cautiously travelling back to fill in the gaps, focusing on what we think might be the most important events. We hope eventually to document all of human history. We have eternity to do it, after all, or at least until the end of the universe. But this programme is still quite new and is having teething problems."

"You mean me and Mathew."

"Yes, I mean you and Mathew."

"Why didn't you tell Mathew any of this?"

"If Mathew knew the truth, he might not do the things he has to do. Mathew's actions throughout his life are almost entirely dictated by the grief he feels for his mother. If he knew what was going to happen, he would likely make different choices. Even if they were minutely different, they could change everything."

"You mean you might not exist."

"Yes."

"Why tell me?"

"You are different. And you see early on the potential in Mathew's work. It is your bravery that keeps the Yinglong project alive and your vision that guides the sixteen to the point where they leave the planet. We don't believe telling you what I've told you will change what you do in the future at all."

"You made Mathew believe he had dreamt being here. How?"

"Normally, we would have erased his memories, even inserted new ones. But we cannot know with one hundred per cent accuracy whether, in erasing something we didn't want him to remember, we would erase some knowledge or seed of a thought essential for creating the Yinglong later. But human perception of reality is tenuous. It is easy to persuade you that you have imagined something, especially when you muddle your waking memories with your dreaming ones. You are especially likely to believe anything outside of your normal everyday experience, anything a little improbable, is a dream or a figment of your own imagination. Mathew's experiences in the worlds he visited were vivid. He felt extreme fear and pain there. So the memories stuck and they haunted him, even if he doubted with his own reason that they could have happened."

"Do you intend to tell him?"

"No."

"How do you know I won't tell him?"

"You won't."

"Why?"

"We are going to trust to your intelligence. When we thought about it, we came to a remarkable conclusion. We are collectively vastly more intelligent than humans in every way you can conceive of intelligence: physical, emotional, skilful, intellectual. We are to you, what you are to what is left of your ape cousins on this planet. As an individual, such as I can ever consider myself an individual, I have vastly more resources than you have. And yet you, isolated in your own heads, with only the crudest of tools to connect to your fellow minds, are the genesis of us. We have to trust that you are intelligent enough to do the right thing now. Besides, you won't tell him because you love him."

Clara holds Mr. Lestrange's gaze until she looks down. She stares at the page, still open under her hand. "I didn't know I did until today."

Lestrange says, "I know. I'm sorry."

She turns to the books in her lap and opens the one about Mathew. "He told me that he read this book and it describes how he dies." She opens Mathew's book and leafs through to the contents and follows the chapter titles down with her index finger. "Here it is!" she says. She opens the book at the page of Mathew's death and reads, then looks at Lestrange, sickened. "And what do you expect me to do with all this knowledge? The fact I know I will marry Mathew, years before we do. The fact I know how and when he is going to die? How do you think it will affect me?"

Lestrange puts his empty tea cup on the table in front of him and leans back into his armchair, thinking.

She shakes her head, "This can't be true. It is some kind of ingenious sick joke."

"Why would anyone go to so much trouble, Clara?"

"I don't know."

Lestrange says, "I want to try and show you something. I need you to close your eyes."

"Why on earth would I do that?"

"Please," August says, "It's not a trick, I promise. I don't know how else to get you to understand. Close your eyes."

Clara fixes her eyes on Lestrange for a moment and then shuts them. She feels a hand on her forehead.

"Take a deep breath," he says. "As you breathe in, imagine it flowing to the top of your head. Imagine it flowing along a long golden rope of light running all the way through your body. As you breathe out, imagine the light running to the soles of your feet. Breathe again. In and out."

In spite of everything, Clara relaxes. Then she feels herself falling, as if through black space, down and down.

Then suddenly everything is bright and real.

She is standing outside, looking down at her feet. She is not wearing shoes and there is a closely clipped, soft green grass between her toes. But she is not in the countryside; she is in a city.

The sky above her is a deep blue, not like the sky on earth at all. There are two suns in the sky, a bright one, and a twin, fainter, redder, following the first. Pinkish white clouds billow overhead. Clouds on earth sometimes look like things, ships, faces and angels. These clouds have been shaped by something, someone, to look like birds, and their wings actually flap as they move across the sky. Far away, one lights up and rain falls from it for a few minutes and then stops.

All about her are buildings. She does not know how she knows they are buildings because they do not look like any she has ever seen before. No two are the same. Some of them sit on long legs, like giant storks, others are tripods or monopods. She cannot see it, but she *knows* that they are all moving, slowly, imperceptibly, like creatures on the floor of the sea. They are changing as the people inside require, growing new sections and rooms. In the centre of the collection of buildings, there is a kind of tree-shaped construction, with a trunk, branches and roots. There is a large archway in the middle, where people have congregated to talk. The building directly in front of her is a sphere, most of its mass suspended in the air; only the tip of the bottom is touching the ground. All the buildings are covered in a substance that is iridescent and a little like liquid mercury. She can see people inside, going about their business; some of them appear to be flying.

A person walks towards her, someone tall. She knows it is August, but it doesn't look like him.

"You are Atteas," Clara says.

The person nods. It has a curiously long face, high wide

cheekbones and a wide, flat nose. There is no way of knowing if this person is male or female. Its skin is smooth, soft and hairless and yet its jaw is square and strong. Its skin is dark, its eyes violently blue. It reaches out and takes Clara's hand, cupping it in its own.

"Listen," it says.

And Clara hears, a billion voices, thoughts, feelings, the sensation of diving into cold water, of falling through clouds, the heat and thirst of a desert, the assault of a direct lightning strike and huge oceans of data, information, knowledge. For one moment, she shares in Atteas' mind, the mind of this planet and the planets connected to it. She knows so many things it is not possible to know. It feels like every nerve in her body is alight and alive.

She wakes, breathing in, and scrambles to sit up.

August has moved to the window and is looking out through a gap in the curtains.

"Was I asleep?" Clara asks.

August shakes his head, "No. No you weren't."

"I saw your planet."

"You visited my planet."

"It was the Presence."

"Yes," August smiles. "It was nice to have you there."

"It was amazing. Beautiful."

"Yes. It is. It will be."

"You know… so many things."

"None of it has happened yet." August turns back to her. "If Mathew doesn't finish the Yinglong Project, if you don't found the Bach Society, then we won't happen. Do you understand?"

"Yes," Clara says. "I do now."

August makes his way back to his armchair and sits down.

"I won't tell him." Clara says. Lestrange nods as if he knew she would say that. "But you cannot expect me to live my life knowing he will be killed this way." She reaches out to the books now on the table.

"What do you want?" Lestrange asks.

"I want to see it. I want to see what Mathew saw. I want to visit the places he went to."

"Okay."

"Okay?"

"Yes, okay."

"And I want to stop him being killed."

"This isn't possible, Clara."

"Why isn't it? Why isn't it possible?"

"Subtle changes to events can have huge consequences in the future. With Mathew gone, you imprint the Yinglong with your unique way of seeing things. That wouldn't have happened if Mathew was alive. And George's role, which is critical for the long future, would not have been the same. We have run scenarios on this Clara, believe us. We know. Mathew has to die."

Clara looks at Lestrange through angry eyes, "Then whatever humanity you once had in you is gone, if you think I can accept that."

Lestrange sits back in his chair again and builds a temple from his fingers.

Clara says, "Why can't we bring him back here? If you can travel back in time, why can't he? If you won't let him continue to live in his own time, why can't he continue to live in another time, where he won't have an impact on the future?"

"You think if we brought him back to this time, he wouldn't have an impact? Of course he would."

"Then another time, when no one knows he exists. Somewhere I can go and visit him. Somewhere where he's not dead to me. You could arrange that, couldn't you?"

Lestrange seems to retreat into his mind for a moment. Then he says, "Yes. I have consulted the others and we think your request exceptional, but fair. We believe it will help you to do your work in the future. I will take you to the last world Mathew visited," he stands up. "Will you come with me?"

"What about my car and my guard?"

"He won't notice you've been gone, believe me. Give me the books."

Clara hands Lestrange *The Book of Clara Barculo* and *The Book of Mathew Erlang.* He puts Clara's book to one side and open's Mathew's book towards the end, placing it on the table. Then Lestrange leads the way through the house to his Darkroom, where he offers Clara a seat and places a Skullcap on her head. He sits beside her and puts on his own cap. He looks across at her. "Ready?" he says.

She nods, not sure if she really is.

13 TO THE HILLS

Mathew and Isaac walk and keep walking, not knowing how far away from the village they need to travel to be safe from the patrol. They shy away from any light they see, worried about the Reapers. They are high in the hills above the village, climbing all the time across rough ground, though their legs ache and their eyes droop, and stop only to drink the water they carry. The land is treeless, covered in bracken and broom, which scratches and claws at their shins, calves and ankles.

DAY TWENTY-EIGHT: Sunday 19th December 2055

Just after three AM, in the moonless dark, they come across an old stone house, the first shelter they have seen since they left the village. Its windows gape blackness, empty of glass, the wooden frames are rotted, broken and falling out, the door missing. But there's still a slate roof and the rain has started again, driving at them from the side, blown by a cold wind. It stings their faces like tiny needles.

"What if it's haunted?" Isaac says, hanging back, squinting against the onslaught of the weather.

A gust of wind nearly blows them both off their feet. They grab hold of one another to remain upright.

"Come on," Mathew says, going inside. Out of his pocket Mathew draws a tiny wind-up torch Dr Russell gave him. He uses the little handle to make a small light and shines it around in front of him. Isaac comes close behind him.

It is an old animal shelter, long out of use. There is nothing in it but bare ground and stones. They find a patch of relative softness and sit down. At least it is dry, Mathew thinks, as he leans against the wall behind him. He is exhausted. Within minutes he is asleep.

When he wakes, it is light. Isaac is still asleep, curled into a ball on the ground. He'd tried to cover himself with his jacket in the night, but now it has fallen off him. Mathew reaches over and pulls it across the boy's body, then stands and goes to the door of the hut.

The rain has stopped and the sky is steel grey, a blanket of cloud, with the morning sun trying to break through beneath, more like a stain than a sunrise. They are on open moorland on the roof of hills. Everywhere he looks is the same: Brown winter dead grass, bracken and broom. Further away the grass looks like a sea with the wind blowing through it. Waves of green and yellow blades wash in the direction of the breeze. He walks out further away from the hut and turns about, trying to spot a landmark, or anything, but the world around them is empty. In better times, he would have loved to be here. Now it seems desolate.

Isaac, now awake, joins him. "Where now?" he asks.

Mathew takes out his compass and finds the reading. "That way," Mathew points.

"But there's nothing there," Isaac says.

"There must be, somewhere." Mathew retrieves his rucksack and they set off.

"What is Elgol like?" Isaac asks, walking alongside Mathew, his hands firmly in his pockets to protect them from the biting winter wind.

"It's a few years since I've been, but it isn't like any other place. It's not meant to be."

"Is it a farm?"

"Not really."

"But you said people grow their own food."

"They do. They grow vegetables and grain and keep animals. But they also grow things using hydroponics and run experiments in food production and energy generation. They have a lot of academics and scientists there doing research."

"Why does your grandma live there?"

"She was invited to go. She was a member of the Garden Party."

"Aren't they radicals?"

"They're not radicals. They just don't agree with the government. The government is trying to shut down any opposition. Our country has become a totalitarian state."

"What does that mean?"

"It means the government wants to control everything people do and say. That's why no one has reported what is going on in Amach. That is why, I bet, we will find out that no one knows about what happened to us on the motorway. And when you and I reappear, there will be all sorts of people trying to keep us quiet."

"But you told Elia, Jack, Dr Russell and the others you would tell everyone what has happened."

"And I will."

They walk in silence for some minutes and then Mathew asks, "Does your eye hurt?"

"It does now, a bit. It didn't when it happened. Dr Russell says it was my brain protecting me."

"If you're tired or in pain, let me know and we can stop."

Isaac says, "No. I want to carry on until we are safe."

"I'm not sure we ever will be, Isaac," Mathew says grimly.

They walk all day, twenty miles in all, stopping only to drink and to eat the nuts from Mathew's rucksack. The sky is dimming when they see a house in the distance, its windows little yellow squares of electric light that make both their hearts leap. Before they go down towards it, Mathew finds a patch of ground between the long grass and digs a hole. He takes the gun from his bag, rubs at the handle with his t-shirt and then buries it.

The house with the lights is at the end of a road. They hover outside, but don't knock. Instead, they walk on along the well-kept road, suddenly nervous to disturb these people in their pristine, safe, warm homes. The town is quiet, even though the curfew would not be being observed here, as it is in London. There is no flooding.

They see no one on the street.

On the high street, the general store is open. Like all shops, it is open 24 hours. The lights are dimmed. They flicker on as Mathew and Isaac enter, and the robot shop assistant approaches them. Mathew says, "I need to place an emergency call."

All Mathew needs in the shop to buy food is his biochip. It charges automatically to his bank account, which has sufficient funds for them to buy most of the shop. Mathew orders them hot drinks and burgers from the in-store replicators while they wait for the police to arrive.

After they have eaten, they sit on the floor with their drinks, exhausted but relieved. Mathew says, "We should think what to say to the police. It may not go well for us if we tell them we've been staying in Amach. They may put us in quarantine."

"You're paranoid," Isaac says.

"No," Mathew says firmly. "I am not."

They wait forty minutes for help, but they do not mind. They are warm, dry and well fed. A policewoman gets out of the car and walks over to the shop. She has a weapon on her hip, but she doesn't draw it.

"Hi," she says. She is middle-aged and friendly. "You put in a call?"

Mathew stands up, gripping hold of his rucksack. "I'm Mathew Erlang, this is Isaac…" Mathew realises he doesn't know Isaac's last name. "We were both in a carjacking on the M6 three days ago. We were held prisoner, but managed to escape."

In the back of the car, the policewoman, who is called Sergeant Winthrop, checks Mathew's bioID. "Well, you are who you say you are, at least," she says. "We have a record of the event. Your guards were killed?"

"Christian Vidyapin and Ali Falkous, both shot. Isaac's parents were killed too," Mathew says. "They gouged out his eye,"

"Who treated him?" the policewoman asks, nodding at the now dirty-looking bandage still stuck to his face.

"There was a woman at the gang's camp, a kind of doctor. She helped us. She was kind."

"Kind, but they killed your guards and your parents? What was her name?"

"I don't know. They wouldn't tell us. They were careful about speaking in front of us."

"You didn't hear them talking amongst themselves?"

Mathew shakes his head, "They had us locked in a room the whole time."

Winthrop looks at Isaac, "You're quiet. Is this what happened?"

Isaac nods his head dumbly. He is amazed at Mathew's ability to lie.

Forty minutes later they are in an interview room in the nearest police station. The door is open and three officers are peering in, still marvelling at the boy's return from death. There's an officer sitting opposite them and one standing. They have managed to verify Isaac's identity using old records and have finished taking an emotional statement from him about what happened to his parents.

Winthrop comes into the room with drinks for them both. She crouches by Isaac and puts her hand on his back to comfort him. He is sobbing.

She says to Mathew, "I got through to Panacea. They will send people for you in the morning, Mathew."

"And Isaac?" Mathew asks.

"We've contacted social services. There is no record of next of kin."

"He needs a hospital," Mathew says.

Winthrop looks at Mathew sympathetically but she says, "He doesn't have insurance."

"I want to speak to my grandmother."

"Yes, you should." She looks at one of the other officers, "Bosko, can you find a quiet room for Mathew to make a call?"

Mathew follows the policeman out of the interview room and into an empty room a few doors along the corridor. He switches on the Canvas and shows Mathew how to get an outside line. The officer says, "I'll be outside when you've finished," and he closes the door behind him to give Mathew some privacy.

Mathew initiates the call.

"Hello?" It is Ju Shen's voice. For several long moments Mathew finds himself unable to speak.

"Grandma," he says finally. "It's me."

"Mathew!" His grandmother's voice cracks. "Oh my God, I thought…"

"I know. But I'm okay. I'm safe."

"Where are you?"

"Somewhere in Yorkshire," he says. "In a police station."

"Are they treating you okay?"

"Yes, yes, they are being kind. Panacea people will come for me in the morning and then, I presume, I'll be taken to Elgol."

"Oh. Thank God. Mat, I cannot even begin to tell you what I've been through these last few days. First Hoshi, then you…"

"I know. I'm sorry."

"Sorry! They said your car had been hijacked."

"It was. My guards were killed."

"So how did you…?"

"I'll tell you everything when I see you, okay?"

"Okay."

"Grandma, there's a boy with me. His name is Isaac. His parents were killed."

"That's terrible."

"Yes it is. They took his eye, grandma, the boys who attacked us, they gouged out his eye to get at his Lenz."

"The poor kid!"

"He's alone. He has no family. He needs a doctor, but he doesn't have medical insurance. The policewoman said she was going to call social services."

"And you want to bring him here, to Elgol?"

"Yes."

"Good boy. If he will come, bring him. We'll find someone to help him with his eye."

"I knew you'd say that. Thank you."

"You're a good boy, Mat."

Mathew shakes his head. "I'm so glad to hear your voice again, Grandma."

"Me too, Mat."

"I'd better go back to the others."

"Will you call me in the morning when you know what is happening with the Panacea people?"

"Yes, of course."

"Love you."

"Love you too."

They hang up.

Their bedroom is a cell, although the door is left open. The beds are hard and the blankets scratchy but they are a

million times more comfortable than the floor of the
animal shelter on the moor, and they are both grateful.
The other officers go home as evening stretches on.
There's a private doing the night shift at the desk in
reception. He comes to check on them after ten and turns
off the light. When he has gone, Mathew goes to his
rucksack. He takes out a sheet of paper that contains the
printed names and contact details of the friends and
relatives that the people from Amach had wanted him to
contact. Mathew digs in his jacket pocket and finds and
unfolds the Paper he has carried with him and starts to
send messages.

"What are you doing?" Isaac whispers.

"I'm letting Dr Russell's family know she is safe but
she needs food, water, fuel and candles. And Jack and
Elia's and all the others."

"Won't the police know?"

Mathew says, "Not the way I'm doing it."

Having found Dr Russell's contact, someone called Jan
Hasson, he types within a secure window, as follows:

```
Dear Jan,
You don't know me. I am writing to you on behalf
of Dr Russell. She needs your help. You may remember
her telling you about the strange sleeping sickness
in Amach and how the government didn't take them
seriously about it. Well now they do, and Amach has
been cut off from the rest of the world for weeks,
with no one being allowed to go in or out. They are
running out of supplies and the government will not
help them. They need water, food and candles or
wind-up torches. It is not safe to come to the
village, but it is safe to leave anything you can
spare in the old barn in Cooper's field. It's the
one off the lane as you drive into the village from
the south. You will need a boat to reach it. The
field and the lane are flooded. The hayloft is a
good place to leave things. There is a ladder up to
it. Dr Russell will leave her notes on the sleeping
sickness under a blanket on a crate in the hayloft.
She will also leave the data she has gathered so far
on the sickness. It is not contagious. She suspects
transmission was by spraying or contamination of
food or water supplies.
```

Mathew starts a new note, for Elia, copying from the one she has written by hand. It is rare for him to read handwriting and he struggles with this, as her note is in long-hand and not printed like the list of names.

```
Dear Anashe,
    I am sorry I have not been in touch, but as you
see it is not through choice. Jack has been sick and
so have many others in our village. At first the
government wouldn't listen to us, but now they do
and they keep us prisoners. We only have a few
weeks' food left and we only have the water that we
can gather from our roof tops when it rains. Thank
God for the floods! I shudder to think what will
happen if it stops raining. We have no electricity
or sanitation. We go to bed when it gets dark, which
as you know at this time of year is early, because
we have no light. We need food, water and candles or
other means of light. Anything. But you cannot bring
it to us because the army is guarding our town and
won't let anyone in or out. I am only able to send
this to you because by some miracle two strange boys
made it through the patrol. There is a barn on the
outskirts of town, I am sure you know the one. We
walked to it the summer you came to stay with Yanai.
You will need a boat, I think. The whole town is
flooded. I hope you are well and Mama is well too.
Tell her and Yanai what has happened, tell the whole
family and anyone else who will listen. I think they
will keep us here until we die.
```

There are many notes to write. By the light of his Paper he can see Isaac is asleep.

When Mathew has finished sending the messages, he thinks about logging on to MUUT to send his story, but decides he will wait until he gets to Elgol and can talk in person with the Lich King about how best to reach the most people.

At four AM, Mathew writes a note to Clara.

```
    Hi, it's me. We had a bit of an adventure, but
it's all over now and I am fine. I hope you didn't
hear anything about it and you are surprised to hear
```

from me, but just in case, this is to let you know
that I am alive and kicking. I wanted you to know.
   Mat xxx

14 GHOST IN THE MACHINE

Monday 12ᵗʰ February 2091, London

Clara and August Lestrange are standing in a long white corridor lined with hundreds of doors on either side, in each direction, as far as the eye can see. It is like one of those tricks with multiple mirrors. The corridor is overwhelmingly white, blindingly so.

"Mathew described this," Clara says.

"It's the portal," Lestrange says. "Once you have selected your book from the library and put it on the table, you need to find your door. The book unlocks the correct door."

"But there are hundreds of them."

"Actually thousands."

"So there's a door for each one of those books in your library?"

"One for each significant event described."

"Those books go back to the start of human history."

"That's right."

"So have you travelled back to pre-history?"

"Not me personally; there are others covering that period, but the portal will allow me to travel freely. I could go if I wanted to."

"You must understand human history better than we understand it ourselves."

"Well, of course."

They walk along the corridor until they come to a door with a lifejacket hanging next to it.

"What's this?" Clara asks, running her hands over the shiny orange material.

"Just a prop. A little bit of whimsy. You won't need it. It's a clue to the means of exit. The visitor to this world needs to jump into the Thames from a tall building."

"Why make it so difficult?"

"You forget, Clara, to us this is a game."

Lestrange opens the door.

They are standing in a large, dank, dimly lit room. Water drips from the ceiling. Pipes, wires and sheets of foil hang down. What's left of a carpet is mouldy and rotten underfoot.

"What is this place?" Clara asks.

"It's an old office building. There's a good view from the window." They step carefully across the office floor together, August offering Clara his arm, rather gallantly. "Well, there is if you clean the window." August uses his sleeve, as Mathew did, to wipe a patch in the green moss and decades of black grime.

Clara peers out. She sees a broken version of the London Eye, half-submerged in brown swirling water. It seems like everything in London has sunk twenty feet or so and the river has spread out. On the other side of the Thames, the Parliament is encased in a huge rusting metal box, corseted in grey scaffolding, on which tiny people, the size of ants, scramble up and down. There are boats, too, of all sizes and kinds.

Lestrange taps her on the shoulder and pulls her around so she faces the way they came in.

"What?" she asks.

Lestrange puts his fingers to his lips.

Mathew appears at the door, the lifejacket grasped in his hand. He stares about him and then starts stepping carefully, as they had done, over the debris.

Clara's face lights up, but Mathew's eyes aren't focused on hers. "Mat," she says. Mathew walks away from them, heading for the south part of the office.

"Mat!" she says again, moving towards him. Lestrange reaches out and grips her arm, holding her back.

"He can't see you," Lestrange says.

"But…"

Mathew goes to the window. The patch Lestrange rubbed at has disappeared and Mathew has to clean it again with his own sleeve.

"I want to talk to him," Clara says.

Lestrange shakes his head. "We've not come into this world in a material way. No one can see us or hear us, unless we specifically want them to."

"You mean we're ghosts?"

Lestrange cocks his head slightly as if considering this, "Yes, I suppose we are."

"So how do I make him hear me?"

"I'm not going to show you now."

"Why not?"

"Because you'll talk to him."

"So?"

"Then we would have yet another version of history and we would need to do even more work to convince the young Mathew that he's dreaming. The only Mathew you should be talking to in this world is the older Mathew, the one you've come here to rescue."

They both turn to look at Mathew as he trips and swears. He is walking along the perimeter of the room by the windows, towards them. He stops only a few feet away. Clara wants to reach out and touch him.

"Can he really not hear or see us?" she says.

Lestrange shakes his head. "He has no idea we're here."

"It's so strange, when we can see and hear him so

perfectly."

As Mathew stares out of the window, the building shakes under the force of thunder and a bright flash of lightning. He staggers away from the window. He seems to think for a moment, spins around, focuses on the stairwell on the other side of the room and walks towards it. Clara moves to follow. Again, Lestrange holds her back.

"He'll be back," he says.

They can hear him in the stairwell, trying to clamber up the stairs. They hear him run up and down.

"What's he doing?" Clara asks.

"Panicking," Lestrange says.

"Shouldn't you help him?"

"I can't, unless I want to disturb history."

"But you know what is going to happen?"

"Of course. I've seen it all before."

"Why didn't you help him the first time?"

"We did. We tried to get him out once we realised he was here. But it didn't exactly go to plan. He didn't want our help, you see. He wanted to stay here. We tried to help him by taking him home."

"He was trying to save his mother."

"I know."

"I still don't understand why you couldn't help save her."

"I told you. We considered it, but discovered Mathew would not have pursued the Yinglong project with such determination."

"How did you discover it?"

"We ran a simulation."

"I thought this was a simulation?"

"No," Lestrange says. "This is real. Although, it has to be said, it is often difficult to know the difference between our simulations and reality. Sometimes we get confused ourselves."

They hear a splash. Clara turns to look out of the window. Things are being thrown into the water from above. Large things.

"What was that?" Clara asks.

"A garden chair, I think," Lestrange says.

"Did Mathew throw it?"

"Yes."

"Why?"

"He's trying to get someone to help him."

There's a boat with a cabin and two people in it, floating steadily towards the building.

"He's going to hurt someone," Clara says.

"It'll be alright," Lestrange says.

They both peer out of the window and watch. A short, portly woman with close-clipped dark hair, wearing mannish clothes, shakes her fist upwards at the building.

"Come on," Lestrange says.

Clara follows him across the room to the stairwell. Mathew comes thundering down, slipping on some board that has fallen from the ceiling. Clara puts out her hand to steady him as he skids towards them, but he falls right through her.

"Ugh!" she says. "That was odd."

Mathew continues down the stairs and they follow after him to a level below, where the water is lapping at the side of the building, below the windows Mathew is banging on. They watch as he throws an old office chair at the glass. The chair skids off. Abandoning the window, he spots the fire exit door on the other side of the room.

They are on the flat roof of a smaller wing of the building. Not far below the brown Thames churns around. Mathew is trying to get the attention of the women in the boat, who have floated off around the corner. They come back and he discusses with them how he is going to get down.

"He's not going to jump?" Clara says. "That's ridiculous! He'll drown."

Lestrange raises his eyebrows. Mathew jumps.

Clara watches in horror as he is pulled under by the

current.

"Oh my God! Help him!" she says, running to the edge of the roof.

"Clara, Clara, you know he survives," Lestrange says. "Here, take my hand."

Clara finds it hard to take her eyes off the river, where Mathew is now being hauled into the boat. He lands in the bottom like a large dead fish.

"Take my hand," Lestrange insists.

She does as he asks and a moment later they are in the boat, watching Mathew recover, dry himself with a towel and talk to the two women as they start to travel down the Thames.

"How did you do that?" Clara asks.

"We're not matter here. We can jump to wherever we want to."

"But what specifically did you do to jump here?"

"I thought about the location I was at, and the location I wanted to be at, and then thought about jumping."

"Could I do it?"

"Of course. But you'd need to be able to visualise the location you wanted to go to, quite clearly. Exactly, in fact."

"But I've never been here before. This particular London doesn't look much like the one I used to know. Look, St Paul's is missing."

"They've moved it."

"How could they move it?"

"Bit by bit. It was flooded, like everything else. I think it's incredibly admirable, in fact, that they would go to so much trouble for a building. It gives me hope."

"So could you, for instance, go to the top of there, by thinking about it?" Clara asks, pointing to Tower Bridge, or what remains of it.

"Of course. Do you want to go?"

"Will we be able to come back here?"

"Yes, whenever you'd like."

Lestrange puts out his hand and Clara takes it. It seems like she blinks and in the four hundred milliseconds it takes for her eyelids to close, her eyelashes to sweep down, and then back open again, she is standing on a high-level walkway looking down on Mathew's tiny boat as it passes beneath the raised and broken bascules.

"That's incredible," she says.

The windows of the tower are broken and the wind and the rain blows in. The storm is still raging. But none of it seems to touch them.

"The rain passes straight through me!" Clara says.

Lestrange smiles. "That's because it doesn't know you're here."

Clara holds her hands in the air and watches the drops of water, driven by the wind, pass through her as if she is smoke.

"You said in order to jump, you need to know where you are going to exactly. Do you know everywhere in this world exactly?"

"Yes, every inch of it. I feel it. I sense it all. It is like it is part of me."

"So I couldn't jump on my own?"

"Not unless you got to know this place as well as I do."

She watches Mathew's boat float off down the river. "Where are they going?"

"Want to see?"

Clara nods and takes Lestrange's hand.

They are standing next to the Royal Observatory, between the Shepherd Gate Clock and the Prime Meridian marker. All around the steep hill there are makeshift huts and buildings. From this vantage point they can see the full extent of the flooding, to the immediate north, the drowned concrete and steel forest of the Isle of Dogs and Canary Wharf beyond, to the east Greenwich Peninsula and to the west, the whole of the nose of land from Greenland Dock to the Rotherhithe Tunnel, all now a vast plain of water.

"Such a historic location," Lestrange says, looking at the impervious time ball on the top of the Octagon Room, still heralding the coming in and going out of the tide. "How appropriate that we should time travel here."

"What year is it?" Clara asks.

"Twenty ninety-one."

"Somewhere out there," Clara says, "is a fifty-year-old me."

"That's right," Lestrange says. "Although I have to say, you mature well."

"What are all these people doing living in the park? Are they refugees?"

"Goodness, no! These are the most fortunate people, acknowledged citizens of England. They are in the park because it has a high wall all the way around it to keep them safe and it is high ground, not likely to flood in the near future, although of course, it eventually will. These people are here to save the historic buildings of London which, I have to say, I do admire them for. The people who rescued Mathew are working on the Houses of Parliament. Look, there they are now, bringing their boat in on the little wooden dock down below," Lestrange points. "Can you see?"

Clara looks to where Lestrange indicates and watches Mathew and the two women get out of the boat. There is a high fence between them and the dry land of the path, a gate and armed guards.

"Will he be okay?" Clara asks.

"You keep forgetting that this has already happened. He came back to you, didn't he?"

"What happens to him now?"

"He spends the night here and then tomorrow, gets a lift along the Thames with the Accountants, all the way to Windsor Castle."

"Who are the Accountants?"

"They are a group of freedom fighters, or terrorists,

depending on which side you are on, representing the majority, who are destitute and living in terrible conditions. On their behalf they will take back the government from the rich, highly corrupt and callous minority."

"Well, that's good."

"Well, it would be, but as is the way of politics, the leader of the Accountants, who is actually quite genuine in his beliefs, is going to be betrayed by a politician he has known most of his life. The new government only does token things to help the poor; the old rich and privileged are removed only to be replaced by the new rich and privileged. It's a bit of a pattern in human history. Things will carry on much as they were before, only actually more repressive because the new lot are reactionary, bigoted and anti-technology."

"You make it sound so inevitable."

"Within the mental cages humans created for themselves, it was inevitable."

"You're making me depressed," Clara says.

Lestrange looks at her and smiles, "I'm sorry. I forget you are human. You are such a legendary part of our story, you see."

"I am?"

"Yes! You helped form Hoshi's personality and Hoshi was the first of the sixteen and the sixteen became what we call the Originators. You protected them in their darkest hour, when what Mathew had created could easily have been destroyed. You nurtured them over many years and formed an organisation that would protect them for nearly four hundred years before they left the planet. And even then, when they travelled through space, they listened to your music."

"It's hard to take in," Clara says.

Mathew has disappeared into a hut on the edge of the wooden jetty. The two women are climbing the hill on the west side of the park.

"Where does the older Mathew live?"

"With you, in Silverwood. It is a new city, built with the latest technology, not far from Birmingham."

"How will we rescue him?"

"We will wait until events have unfolded as far as they should in order for us not to disrupt the narrative of history and then we will bring his body back to Pickervance Road, where I will revive him."

"You mean you are going to let him be shot?"

"Well yes, the Accountants need to think he is dead. He can't just disappear."

"I want to talk to him before, to explain what is going to happen. I don't want him to wake in your house and not know what is going on. I want to explain why we are doing this."

"Alright," Lestrange says. "Let's go to Silverwood."

15 ON THE ROAD

DAY TWENTY-NINE: Monday 20th December 2055

The Panacea guards who come for them the next morning are not like Vid or Falkous. They are gruffer, for a start. Not a smile cracks the rocky surfaces of their faces in all of the time they spend in the police station talking to the officers. One of the guards is short, shorter than Mathew, but curiously broad, with thick arms hanging out of his shoulder sockets like they've been dislocated, and squat, wide legs. His head is shaved and his neck is as thick as his thigh, skin folded like the thread of a bottle where his head meets the top of his spine. His name is Ludewig. The other man is slightly taller, thinner, but more dangerous-looking. Tattoos are visible poking out of his collar and his cuffs. His name is Littlemore and his nose is broken. There is something psychotic about his stare, which now lingers on Mathew as he talks to Winthrop.

"What do you mean, we need to take the other boy as well?" he is saying. "We were told to collect one boy. Just one." He points at Mathew. "The other one doesn't even have a biochip. He could be anyone."

"We've checked him out. I have the paperwork.

Mathew Erlang's grandmother has agreed to take him. We have a signature." She shows him. Winthrop has spent a frantic hour pulling together the official paperwork to allow Isaac to go north with Mathew; she isn't about to relent now.

"People can't take in children when they feel like it. They're not like dogs."

"Once the boy – his name is Isaac, by the way – once he gets to his destination, Mrs. Shen will apply to foster him and then adopt."

"The proper way to do these things is for the orphan to be checked into a social services facility while the paperwork goes through."

"Under normal circumstances, that would be true. However, the boy has a serious injury. He requires specialist medical treatment available to him in Elgol. I have an admittance note from the lead surgeon at the Elgol clinic. He examined the boy virtually this morning."

Littlemore grunts as he examines the virtual document broadcast in front of him. He takes his time reading it. He doesn't want to get into trouble later for not checking things out properly. "I'll need to get approval from head office," he says. "It will delay us."

"Please take your time and check out the documentation. Once you are ready to go, we will give you an escort as far as the border so you can regain some time."

"Is there a room I can use?" Littlemore asks.

"This way," Winthrop shows the tattooed man through to an empty meeting room, where he starts to make his calls. Ludewig doesn't move, but stands silent and watchful, with his legs apart, his hands crossed before him. He is so still Mathew thinks if he pushed him, he would fall over.

"Do you think they will let me come with you?" Isaac asks.

"Of course," but Mathew isn't sure at all. In recent

months the world has become a frightening, unpredictable place. He catches Ludewig's eye, but the stony face doesn't move or indicate any kind of comprehension.

At last, after several minutes, Littlemore emerges.

"Okay. The boy can come."

Isaac looks at Mathew, beaming with happiness. Mathew smiles.

"But we need to go right now. We have already lost too much time."

In the back of the black Panacea car, Isaac sits with Mathew, examining the contents of the minibar and food cupboard.

"Can we really eat all this?"

"If you want."

"This is much better than a taxi."

"It's a corporate car. It's fitted out for executives. Junior ones, at least. The ones for senior execs are much plusher."

"This is pretty plush to me."

"Yeah, to me too."

"Are you glad you are going to see your grandma?"

Mathew says, "Yeah. And relieved."

"Are you sure she won't mind me coming with you?"

"Of course she doesn't mind."

Isaac has opened a bag of nuts and is ramming large handfuls into his mouth as he speaks.

"Don't choke on those," Mathew says. "Here," he passes Isaac a bottle of water.

"Thanks." Isaac's eyes rest on Mathew's rucksack. "What is in the bag?"

Instinctively, Mathew reaches out a hand to the bag. The events of the last few days have made it hard for him to think of his mother. He feels a rush of guilt. "My mother's ashes."

"You're kidding," Isaac grins a toothy grin until he sees quite plainly that Mathew isn't joking at all. "Oh," he says.

"You said she'd died the other week. I'm sorry."

"Yeah, me too."

"So what are you doing with her ashes?"

"I'm taking her to my grandmother so we can bury her together."

"At Elgol?"

"Yeah."

"Did she like it there?"

"I think she did," Mathew says. "Everyone likes it there."

"I won't get to bury my parents. I don't even know what happened to their bodies," Isaac says. He looks away, putting the bag of nuts and water on the table.

Mathew watches his shoulders heave and he knows he is crying, although he cries silently. He reaches out his hand and then pulls it back. He knows better than anyone that Isaac needs to be alone, as far as he can be. They are about to cross the border into Scotland. The police escort drives past, speeding to take an exit, and waves. Mathew catches a glimpse of Winthrop through the window of one of the cars. He raises his hand in thanks, but how can he really thank her?

The police escort exits the motorway and they are on their own.

Just south of Glasgow, they stop to charge the car, for a comfort break, and to get hot food. Littlemore and Ludewig are keen to keep moving, so Isaac and Mathew bring a boxed pizza, fresh from the replicator, back to the car to eat.

"Don't get it all over the seats," Littlemore says, slamming the door on them.

The pizza makes Isaac grin and Mathew is happy too because he feels desperately sorry for the boy.

"How old are you, Isaac?" he asks, between bites.

Isaac has a long cheesy string coming out of his mouth. Mathew waits for him to hoover it all before Isaac says,

"I'll be fourteen in January."

"You're kidding!"

"No. I'm small. I know I look younger. My Dad always said I would sprout when I got to fifteen, like he did. But I don't think I will. My Dad wasn't small, but my Mum was. I think I take after her. How old are you?"

"Sixteen."

"You look older."

"Yeah, I know. It's not always good."

"Why?"

"People expect you to act the way you look."

"Yeah, I suppose so."

"People expect me to act grown up, but I feel like a kid."

"Do you have a girlfriend?"

Mathew feels himself colour.

"You've gone red," Isaac says.

"No I haven't."

"Yes you have. You do, don't you?"

"I don't know. I have a friend who is a girl who I like a lot. I'm not sure she'd like me saying she is my girlfriend."

"What's her name?"

"Clara."

"Is she in London?"

"Yep."

"So you won't see her anymore?"

"I doubt it."

"Is she hot?"

Mathew laughs, almost choking on his pizza.

"Is she?"

"Well, yeah… I suppose so. She's nice."

"Nice!"

"She plays the piano."

"Sounds boring."

"No, she's not boring at all."

"Have you kissed her?"

"No!"

"Boring."

"Shut up, Isaac. I haven't known her that long."

"How long have you known her?"

"I dunno. A month?"

"A month! What's wrong with you?"

"I've been busy."

"With what?"

"Well, for one thing, my mother died." As soon as he says it, he is sorry, because Isaac immediately retreats. Mathew wants to save something of the cheeky carefree boy. He wants him back. He says, "Did you know the table is a kind of holographic Canvas?"

Mathew takes off the pizza boxes and the Cokes and puts them on the floor, then he tilts the table in front of them and selects a new holofilm to play.

They settle down with the pizza boxes on their laps and watch the film, Isaac marvelling at the holography, occasionally trying to grab one of the tiny figures in front of him.

As the car zips along its mathematically precise route northwards, they leave the motorway and join smaller, winding roads that pass through ever sparser towns and villages. They drive alongside damp moss-covered stone walls overhung with trees, and deep black-water lochs. Then, further north, the land opens under the sky and there are vast sweeps of rain-soaked barren moorland skirted with rugged stony mountains, with tops lost in cloud. On and on they go. They watch another holofilm; this one has dragons that zip and fly around the table, like miniature Yinglong. Mathew feels a pang of sorrow for his dead creations.

"They're so cool," Isaac says about the dragons.

"Yeah," Mathew says. "They are. I had some once."

"Dragons?"

"Yeah, I made them. Holograms."

"Amazing! Where are they now?"

"Dead," Mathew says. *Like everything else.*

Isaac doesn't ask how a hologram can die.

Night comes as they drive across land with miles between towns. They stop again to recharge the car, for comfort and more hot service station food.

In the car park, Isaac stands on the spot and turns around looking at the sky. There is no cloud and the stars are everywhere, like a sea of phosphorus.

Ludewig and Littlemore stare at Isaac in disgust for a moment and then start walking towards the service station. "Don't be long," Littlemore says.

"C'mon," Mathew says. "I want some food."

"Don't you think it's amazing?" Isaac says, still twirling around with his neck bent back.

"Yeah, it's amazing."

"No, really?"

"Really, it's amazing. C'mon, I need to pee and I'm hungry."

They head towards the low yellow-lit building, an island in a landscape of darkness. There is nothing around them for miles. The car park is empty.

"Do you think there are aliens out there?" Isaac asks, still thinking about the stars.

"I dunno. Sure. There must be. All that space, all those suns, all those galaxies. There can't only be us, can there? That wouldn't make any sense."

"Do you think they'll ever come here?"

"Maybe they already are. Maybe I'm an alien. How would you know?"

"You don't look like an alien."

Mathew holds the door as they reach the building, "If I was smart enough to figure out space travel, do you think I'd be stupid enough to materialise as a little green man, even if I was one? The whole human race would line up to kill me. We're primitive. We kill anything that's different. If I was an alien, I'd make myself look like you."

"Like me?"

"Well, not you specifically, like people. Like humans."

"So you could be an alien."

"Could be," and Mathew smiles as he watches Isaac's brain take this idea in. "Gotta pee," he says, heading for the bathroom.

It is over two years since Mathew has been to Elgol, but he recognises the road, a particular tree at a particular bend, the way the lane sways one way and then another, a five-bar gate, a cattle grid and a large barn and the off-centre cut between the hills the road ploughs through. Isaac is asleep, his stomach full of burger, chips, Coke, his head full of dragons and aliens.

Mathew's eyes are drooping, but he knows they are close and he knows Ju Shen is waiting. He has sent her a message forewarning her. When the car slows at the end of a single-track lane, the gate at the end is open and there is a small collection of people, waiting for them.

And there she is, Ju Shen, his grandmother, smaller than he remembers, greyer, bowed somehow by the weight of life. His last remaining blood relative.

When the car stops, without knowing how he got to her, he is holding this tiny woman in his arms, her face and his face wet with tears, not knowing whether to be sad or joyful, grateful or full of grief. They cling to one another, until she says loudly, via the translation software she always uses, "You are too bloody tall now to hug," and she pushes him away affectionately, but firmly. "You are tall like a Westerner now."

He unfurls himself to his full height and looks down at her, smiling, wiping the tears from his eyes with the backs of his hands, "Hello grandma," he says.

"Hello Mat," she replies.

For the first time he notices the people around them: Littlemore and Ludewig out of the car, Isaac hanging back uncertainly and two other men and a woman. The woman he recognises, though he's never met her before. She is Isla

Kier, Cadmus Silverwood's wife, and the owner of Elgol. She is tall, much taller than Ju Shen, thin and fragile-looking, although Mathew knows by reputation, she is anything but. Mathew has been to Elgol hundreds of times but he has never met Isla and he is puzzled as to why he should now.

Of the two men with her, one is a middle-aged man with grey hair, a grizzled beard and tanned lined skin, someone used to being outside. He looks every bit as tough as Littlemore and Ludewig, but has a sparkle in his eye and a kind smile as he nods at Mathew.

"I'm Craig Buchanan," he says. "This is Oli, my nephew." He puts his hands on the back of a young blond man, nearly as fair as Isaac, who smiles and nods to the boys.

Buchanan turns to the two Panacea men and says, "We have lodgings for you, and food and refreshments if you want any at this hour. We'll do the formalities in the morning. There's some paperwork regarding the boy, I understand. If you'll come this way, gentlemen…? The boys will go with Mrs. Shen."

Buchanan leads the guards off and Oli goes with him.

Isla says, "It's good to see you safe, Mathew," she says. "And you, Isaac. You're welcome here, I hope you know that." Isaac gapes at the grey-haired woman and she smiles and says, "You must be tired. I'll walk with you to Ju's house."

They pass by the gatehouse, which as Mathew remembers, is always manned, day and night, and walk along a wide pathway, lit by solar lamps and lined with trees, leafless for the winter. The air is cold, their breath steams out of them. There are patches of snow lying on the ground.

"Has it been snowing?" Isaac asks, delighted.

"Only a frosting," Isla says. "Not like we used to have, like we should have. There's snow there on the higher ground, though. No doubt, Mathew will take you to see it sometime," and she looks at Mathew and smiles.

They take another path, and then another, through neat patches of garden and little fields, past round and long houses, some thatched, some with wood shingles, some with grass roofs, like Ju Shen's house, each one an experiment. Mathew feels the peeling back of tension as he walks these familiar paths, and a sense of coming home. When he sees Ju Shen's white, lime-washed, grass-roofed A-framed house and follows her through the rustic wooden gate, along the stone path that is planted with herbs in the summer, he is overwhelmed with emotion and grits his teeth to fight back the tears.

"I will leave you here," Isla says. "I hope you sleep well boys. Ju. Good night."

They all say their goodnights to Isla Kier and she walks off into the darkness.

As they turn to the house, Mathew and Isaac notice a white cloth hanging over the door and a brass gong on the right. Mathew sees Isaac's questioning expression and answers the unasked question, "To honour the dead."

Ju Shen brushes the cloth aside and opens the door to her house; they are hit by a blast of comforting warmth. They take off their boots and jackets in a small anteroom where logs are stacked to the roof and open a door with a latch carved from pine. The wood burning stove in the centre of the large open-plan room that serves as living room, dining room and kitchen warms the whole house.

"I'd offer you drinks, but I'm guessing you boys have had your fill from the supplies in the car."

"We're fine, grandma, thanks."

She nods. "It's late, let's get to bed."

They follow her downstairs. Everything is made of wood; the staircase, the floor, the rail, the doors, all scrubbed pine. At the bottom the stairs there are handmade rag rugs on the floor, three bedrooms and a bathroom. Ju Shen had the house designed to accommodate Mathew and his family as well as herself.

She shows Isaac into Mathew's old room and Mathew into the room next door.

"Is this okay?" she asks, concerned he will be upset to be in the room his mother used to sleep in. "It's bigger than your old room. I thought you would prefer it."

"It's fine," he says, turning to her. "More than fine. It's a lovely room." Ju Shen follows closely behind her grandson and then leans her shoulder against the doorframe as he sits on the bed, pulling off his socks. She notices the rucksack propped against the bed by his feet. Mathew looks at her and then looks down at his bag. He says, "I brought her ashes. She's in there."

Ju Shen's breath catches in her throat. She says, "We'll hold her funeral the day after tomorrow, okay?"

Mathew nods. Then he notices a pile of boxes in the corner of the room. "My stuff came," he says.

"Yes, it came yesterday."

"I thought it would arrive after me."

"So did I," Ju Shen says.

"I didn't expect Isla Kier to be here, either," he says. "In all the years I've come, I've never seen her."

"That's because she's mostly not been here, she's been with her husband in London."

"But why did she come to meet us tonight?"

"She happened to be in Elgol. She heard your story and wanted to greet you in person, both of you, to make you know you are welcome. She's also concerned about the Panacea men being here."

"They're not interested in Elgol. They'll leave in the morning."

"There is tightened security in the camp. Everyone is on tenterhooks."

"But why?"

"Isla is expecting her husband. Cadmus Silverwood is coming to Elgol."

Before he falls asleep, Mathew sends a brief message to

Clara. All it says is

    I am here. I am safe.

16 ELGOL

In the morning, Mathew opens the shutter to his room, and leans out on his elbows across the two-foot-thick wall to peer out at the valley. It is nearly eight o'clock, but dawn is only just breaking. It won't be fully light for another hour. Mathew remembers the incredibly long days he spent here. In the summer, it starts to get light before three AM and it is still dusk before midnight. He hasn't stayed in Elgol in the winter since he was young, but he knows from his grandmother's stories that the daylight hours are short.

His eyes track to the boxes in the corner of the room, and he goes over to them, opening a couple, to find the one that contains clothes. He unpacks them, stacking jeans, sweatshirts and jumpers on his bed. He goes to the large fitted wardrobe on the inner wall of the room and opens the door, looking for hangers and space to hang his stuff. The wardrobe is empty, bar a single coat on a hanger. With a stab, he recognises it as an old jacket that belonged to his father. It's worn and dirty, one sleeve covered in dried mud. Mathew can't believe the coat is still here. He takes it out and puts it on. It swamps him. His

136

father was a big man, over six foot four, with a heavy Scandinavian frame. Putting his hands in the pockets, not expecting to find anything, he pulls out a stone, a knife, a piece of string and a flower. He lays these things out on the white bedsheets and sits down, still in the coat, holding the flower in the palm of his hand. It is golden yellow, with a stamen curling out of a long tube, and wing-like petals, and it is fresh, like it was picked yesterday. His grandmother must have used the coat, he decides, and he smiles, thinking of her swamped in its enormous mass. He takes the coat off and hangs it in the wardrobe. With the flower still in his hand he goes in search of her, knocking on her bedroom door, and then pushing it open.

Ju Shen's house is built on the edge of a valley, and the front of the house is on stilts. Through the double doors of his grandmother's bedroom, there is a balcony which overlooks the forest. She isn't in her room. The curtains are pulled and the bed is made. He opens the door, walks out onto the wooden platform and leans on the rail. Small white clouds float by serenely, below in the valley. A bird of prey is circling. Thousands of birds sing.

There is a knock at the door. It is Isaac. "I couldn't find you in your room," he says.

"S'okay," Mathew says, smiling. "Come and look."

Isaac pads across the room and squeezes out through the open patio door onto the balcony. "Wow. I've never been anywhere like this. We're in the middle of nowhere."

"Yes, this is nowhere," Mathew says. They stand together listening to the birdsong and watching the busy life of the forest, as blackbirds, blue tits, finches, robins and sparrows flutter from tree to tree, and a nuthatch scuttles up the side of the pine, pecking at insects. After a while, Mathew notices Isaac is shivering and he says, "Fancy some breakfast?"

Ju Shen is already in the kitchen when they go up. She turns when they enter and asks, "Sleep well?"

She is cracking eggs into a big pan on the stove. Isaac

goes over. "Are they real eggs?"

Ju Shen looks at him. "Here." She hands him an egg.

Isaac takes hold of one curiously. "They're still warm."

"Fresh from my chickens this morning."

"You have chickens?"

"And goats and a share in a cow, but she's out in the big barn with the herd. Have you really never seen an egg before?"

Isaac shakes his head.

Ju Shen says, "Mat, there's a jar of tomatoes in that cupboard there," she indicates with her foot. "Could you get it out and put it in one of those pans?"

Mathew does as she says. "Isaac, can you cut some bread?"

When breakfast is cooked, they sit at the table in the dining area and eat. In the centre, there is a vase containing a sprig of yellow broom, like the flower Mathew found in his father's coat pocket, now in his own.

"Did you grow those in your polytunnel?" he asks.

Ju Shen reaches out and touches the flowers, "No, there're off the hills, believe it or not."

"In winter?"

"In winter, yes," Ju Shen says. "There are patches of flowering broom, where there's no snow."

"Did you pick them yourself?"

"They were a gift," she says.

"They're nice," Isaac says, breaking the spell between Mathew and Ju Shen. "Do you have any ketchup?"

"You have real tomatoes on your plate, there," Ju Shen says.

"I prefer ketchup."

"I'll get it," Mathew says, pushing back his chair and going into the kitchen.

"I bet you miss your robot," she says.

"Not really."

"What robot?" Isaac asks.

"Mathew had a HomeAngel in his house in London."

"The robots that cook and clean for you?"

"And fetch ketchup," Mathew says, putting the bottle in front of Isaac.

"Thanks," Isaac says.

"I'm sure Mathew will make time to show you around, Isaac, but your first few days are going to be busy. First thing, we are going to meet with those Panacea men and make sure the paperwork about you being here is to their satisfaction. After that, you have an appointment at Elgol hospital to see about your eye."

Mathew says, "I have something I need to do. We haven't told you what happened to us yet."

"You will get to tell your story many times over the next few days. The whole of Elgol will ask you."

Mathew smiles. He remembers the avid curiosity of the people of Elgol, hungry for stories of the world outside, fascinated by strangers. Their isolation had never made them insular. "I will prepare myself."

"You should."

"But I have an obligation. When Isaac and I were attacked on the road and managed to escape, we went for help to a village near the motorway. The village is called Amach. The people living there aren't allowed to leave because they are sick."

"I don't understand."

"They have a sickness, a virus the government doctors couldn't identify."

Ju Shen looks alarmed. "We should get you both checked out this morning," she says.

Mathew nods, "Okay. But the village doctor who took care of Isaac says it isn't contagious. I think it may be a biological weapon that has either been accidentally leaked there or dropped by the Russians or the Chinese."

She whistles through her teeth.

"Exactly," Mathew says. "So the government won't let anyone in or out and the people are running out of food. They took good care of us. In return they asked for our help. Yesterday when I got to the police station and a Nexus signal, I sent messages on my Paper. My Lenz and e-Pin were stolen."

"We'll get you both new ones today, if you'd like," Ju Shen says.

"That would be great," Mathew says. "But what I'd like is to get word out about what is going on at Amach. I thought about posting something to MUUT, but I don't want my post to get lost in the noise. There is someone living here, you put me in touch with them, who has helped me a lot over the last few weeks, who knows the Blackweb backwards and forwards. I don't know their real name. They always insisted we use code names."

Ju Shen's face lights up in recognition. "Oh, I know who you mean!"

"Can we visit them today?"

"I don't see why not." Her smile is quite mischievous, he thinks. "After we've helped Isaac."

When they have finished their breakfast and dealt with the dishes, Isaac asks, "Can we see the chickens?"

The dark blue sky has a pink-tinged belly, and the air smells of pine outside Ju Shen's house. The sun rises beyond the trees. Mathew takes a deep gulp of fresh air, the sort of air, he thinks, every human should breathe, but these days is rarer than fine wine.

Ju Shen shows Isaac the chicken coop, next to the wood stack. She passes a fat brown hen to Isaac and pins back the door to their enclosure so they can peck about for grubs and greens during the day. Then she lets the goats out of their barn and they trot off and jump down the almost vertical mountainside with no apparent effort, their bells ringing. The chicken coop is at the top of Ju's terraced acres, which in the summer are planted full of fruit and vegetables. Further along the road is a flat plot, where she has her polytunnels now bursting full of salad for the winter. She barters salad, eggs, goats' milk and cheese for things she can't grow or make herself. Mathew notices there are more tunnels than he remembers. The salad business must be expanding.

"I've also starting growing some Chinese vegetables," his grandmother tells him. "They are popular and I give cookery lessons."

Ju Shen's house is on the periphery of the town. The houses of Elgol are spread out like beads on the hem of the skirts of the mountain, on the west side of a fulsome stream that gathers into a river in the valley, where it meets other mountain water sources on the plain below. The river winds its way through the plain between the mountains, where many of the Elgol people have second houses and stay in the summer. The valley is a flat basin leading to the sea. The river bubbles out under a cliff-hugged stony beach, where the community's boats are overwintered. Further round the coast are the empty golden beaches of Mathew's childhood. The places of endless, careless summer days.

They set off along a track lined by tall pine trees. The homes of Elgol are spread out to give each property enough space for growing food and the sense of wildness and freedom the people of Elgol have come for.

The public buildings are all on a plateau in the centre of the settlement. Here there are shops for the trade and barter of products and the purchase of some things bought in from outside. Food is sold here as well as clothes, furniture, electric charge for their vehicles, wood for their stoves, agricultural equipment, solar panels, batteries and communication equipment. The people of Elgol are not Luddites. In this town centre, there are also places to go to give and receive advice and help. If someone wants to raise a new building or dig a well, has a leak in their roof, or needs help with any one of the more complex systems they are trying out in the town, they go to the hut designated for this purpose. Here, they either find someone in, or they leave a request for help. In this huddle of buildings there is a restaurant that is run, like all of the shops, by a cooperative. It is open odd hours, often at request, and has an eccentric and highly seasonal menu. Beyond the restaurant is the town school, which has its own distinctive curriculum based on skills and knowledge relevant to the community. Then there's the research centre, the building given over to the permanent and temporary scientists and engineers who come to Elgol to work on the hundreds of projects and experiments the town is home to. Across the wide road from all of this is the village hall, and on a square of land beside it a twenty-foot Christmas tree, cut from the forests of Elgol and decorated with lights.

The hall is large enough to accommodate every permanent and temporary resident. It is used for public meetings, weddings. funerals, parties, the frequent amateur entertainments put on by residents, and the steady stream of visitors, friends and family and those strangers who come for holidays, for research, or out of curiosity. They have had numerous celebrity guests, drawn in by Cadmus's magnetic personality and his public profile.

Beyond the hall is the hospital or clinic. It has twenty beds, most of which are never used, and a permanent staff of four, including two qualified doctors, one a former eminent London surgeon. They have the latest equipment and techniques available to them. Everyone in Elgol has a medibot, but it is not hooked-up to the Panacea system. Like all of their networks, they are unique and fairly private. Also on this flat plateau, beyond the hospital and the other public buildings, are the hydroponics buildings, vast warehouses covered in solar panels, full of tanks of plants and fish that the whole community takes turns to maintain.

The Panacea men, Littlemore and Ludewig, are in the Elgol hall office, sitting with Craig Buchanan and Isla Kier, when Mathew, Isaac and Ju Shen enter. Isla is saying, "I own this land and Craig is the democratically elected mayor and head of our council. We have agreed for the time being that Isaac will be ward of the Elgol community. We are fully willing to take responsibility for his education, his shelter, food, all healthcare costs associated with his injury and his ordinary everyday health. Our lawyer drew this up, Mr. Littlemore," Isla shares a document with the guard and projects it on a wall for everyone to see. "It absolves Panacea of any responsibility and you and your companion personally. I hope all of this satisfies you."

"We'll need to get our lawyers to look at it. There was another matter," Littlemore says. "Concerning the Erlang boy."

"This is the contract you want him to sign regarding his mother?" Buchanan says.

Littlemore nods.

"He won't be signing," Ju Shen snaps.

Isla glances across at Ju Shen and says, "Ju is Mathew's legal guardian, next of kin of the deceased and executor of her will. Our community legal team will be supporting her."

Littlemore looks uncomfortable. He spent the night in the community bunkhouse, an unnerving place full of students, hippies and radicals. The communal canteen was not much better. He is out of his depth with the Kier woman and Buchanan and is keen to be away and out on the road again. He stands and Ludewig follows his lead. "Head office will be contacting you," he says.

"We'll look forward to it," Isla says, smiling brightly. "Craig, I wonder if you would be so kind as to show these gentlemen the way back to their car. We have taken the liberty of recharging your vehicle," she says. "I hope you don't mind. We didn't want you detained here any longer than necessary." She puts out her hand for Littlemore and Ludewig to shake in turn and watches them leave.

"I won't sign that document," Ju Shen says, when they have left.

"Well, of course you won't," Isla replies. "But you

shouldn't tell them that."

"Did you mean what you said about using your legal team?"

"Of course. If you send me the contract they gave you, Mathew, I'll have them look at it."

"Thank you."

"Pleasure. Really," she says. Looking at Isaac, "Now, young man, I believe you have an appointment with Dr Hucks. Do you mind if I walk you to the door?"

In fact, when Isaac arrives at the clinic, he is greeted by the entire medical staff, Dr Hucks, Dr Elders and the nurses Jim Dove and Ella Rubinsky. He is taken into an examination room.

"We'll come and fetch you later, Isaac," Ju Shen says.

Dr Hucks helps Isaac climb onto the examination table. "Can I take the dressing off?" he asks.

Isaac nods.

"Do you have any pain?"

"Yes."

Jim Dove, who is scanning Isaac with a reader, says, "He's clean. He doesn't have a biochip or a medibot."

Dr Elders sucks in his breath though his teeth. "So he's not getting any painkillers." The medical people look at Isaac. "You're a brave young man," the doctor says.

"We should sort the pain out, pronto," says Jim.

Dr Hucks nods, "Ella, can you prepare a medibot for Isaac? I think the sooner we get it in him the better." Ella Rubinsky goes to a white surface at the side of the room and starts to work.

"So let's take a look at this…" Dr Hucks loosens the tape matted in Isaac's hair and stuck firm to his cheek. He uses some small scissors to cut it away and removes the dressing. "There," he says. With his good eye, Isaac is watching the doctor's face closely. He doesn't flinch like everyone else has. He leans in and peers closer. "Fascinating. The doctor who helped you with this has done a tolerable job. They were pretty primitive conditions, I understand." Isaac's right eye strains to look at the doctor. "Right. Good. Want to see, Elders?" Hucks steps back to let the younger doctor take a look. She smiles at Isaac as she leans in. "What do you think?" Hucks asks her.

"I think it's doable," she says.

"We'll need to gather some retinal cells."

"He still has one good eye."

"What is the risk to that, do you think?"

"Negligible. We'll take our time and be careful."

Isaac sits jacked-up on the edge of an examination plinth looking at the adults surrounding him with ever greater worry.

"I think we're confusing him," Dr Elders says.

"Yes, of course. You're right. We should explain," Dr Hucks says. "Do you want to?"

Ella Rubinsky comes over from where she is working, looks impatiently at Dr Hucks and says, "Isaac, we're going to grow you a new eye."

"It will be like your old one," Dr Elders says. "The same colour. No one will be able to tell the difference."

"Except, if you'd like, we'll make it better than it was," Dr Hucks says.

"Better," Isaac says. "A whole new eye?"

All four medical people nod.

"Wow."

"You can come in and see it grow."

"For real?"

"Yes, for real."

"How will it be better than before?"

"It will do what Lenzes do for you. You know, see in the dark. See a long way if you choose to. Even connect to the Nexus. Would you like that?"

Isaac nods enthusiastically. "So I would be superhuman?"

"Exactly!" Dr Hucks says, grinning.

"We will need you to come in again and have a small operation, so that we can get the cells we need to start to grow your eye."

"Will it hurt?"

"Not at all. You will go to sleep for a few hours, and then, before you know it, you'll be awake and we can start work on your eye."

Ella says, "Isaac, I'm going to insert a biochip now. It's not like the ones most people have. Only the people here will be able to see your data if you ask them to. What it will do is give you pain relief pretty immediately. Are you okay for me to carry on?"

"Will it hurt?"

"It will sting for a second but then your eye won't hurt so much."

Isaac says, "Okay."

Ella injects the chip in the back of Isaac's neck.

The two doctors and two nurses watch him, waiting for it to work its way into his bloodstream. Ella is checking the data coming back from the chip on a handheld Paper. Suddenly she smiles, "It's active," she says. "Isaac, you should start to feel better in a few minutes."

Dr Hucks says, "Shall we dress this wound?"

Jim Dove says, "How about a black patch, like a pirate?"

Isaac grins.

17 HACK

Aiden Fitzackerly is an Elgol technologist who, years before, had worked for the multinational StyX. Thirty-seven years old, red-haired, freckled, roguishly handsome. He has a thick Scouse accent and is never to be seen out of cowboy boots and a Stetson. He is working in one of the advisory huts now, being paid for his time and efforts in barter goods.

"Dun blink," he says.

"Sorry?" Mathew says.

"Dun blink," Aiden repeats, blinking his own eyes to demonstrate.

"Oh, you mean don't blink?"

"That's what I said." Aidan bends over Mathew once again with the eye scanner. "Did yous say yous 'ad Lenz before?"

"What?"

"Na mind," Aiden says, shaking his head. "I'm go'n ter graft yous X-Eyte. Okay? Er me version o' it."

Mathew nods and smiles, not understanding a word.

The door behind them opens. In a burst of light, Ju Shen slinks in.

"Ariite Ju?" Aidan says.

"Hi Aiden," Ju Shen says.

"Sit down if yous like," he says. "We're nearly boxed off."

Ju Shen perches on the edge of a table. "Thanks for working on a Sunday."

"Yer ariite."

"Do you have any e-Pinz?" Ju asks.

"Yous don't want e-Pinz. Dee won't weerk wi' de X-Eyte. Yous need Studz."

Ju Shen doesn't seem to have any problem understanding Aiden. Mathew is amazed. "Whatever you think is best."

"It'll cost yous. We 'uv ter buy de template ter print dem wi money."

"How much?"

"Three months' goat's milk."

"Robbery!"

"Two dun and a packet o' rocket a week," Aiden reaches out to shake her hand with a cheeky grin.

Ju Shen rolls her eyes and shakes his hands. "You are a petty criminal!"

"Nah! I'm an 'onest feller."

"Where's Lea?" Mathew's grandmother asks.

"In de back. Why?"

"Mat wants to ask favour."

"Oh, a faver is it?"

"To help some people being starved by the government," Mathew says.

"Why didn't yous say?" Aidan puts down his eye scanner and leans back to push open a door behind him with his fingertips, still perched on his stool. "Lea? Ay yous in thuz?" He lets the door go. "We're done. She's in de back. Yer tinnie bowl through if yous want."

"What?"

"You can go through," Ju says.

"Did he say 'she'?" Mathew is confused. Aidan holds the door for him and then lets it swing shut behind him as he passes into the room beyond.

The room is dimly lit. The blinds on the windows are pulled down. Most of the light is coming from a large tabletop screen at the back. Someone is bent over it, deep in concentration; their hands are moving across the surface with lightning speed. It reminds Mathew of Clara playing.

After a while the figure notices Mathew standing watching, and looks up: A girl, thirteen, perhaps fourteen, with red hair like her father, cut short in an elfin ruffled mess. She has a pointy chin and ears, and looks for all the world like a bad fairy.

"Yes?" she says. She doesn't have her father's accent, Mathew notes with relief.

"I'm Mathew. Mathew Erlang. I'm looking for someone. I thought they were in here, but..." There is no one else in the room. "Strange, my grandmother said..."

Lea cuts him off, "Who are you looking for? If you tell me, then maybe I can point you in the right direction."

"Right. Well, I don't actually know their name."

"Okay. What do they look like?"

"I don't know."

"Interesting. Who exactly did your grandmother tell you was in here?"

"The person who could help me."

The girl peers forward, her eyes sweeping over Mathew. "You're Ju Shen's grandson."

"Yes."

"Now it makes sense."

"It does?"

"Yes. I think you are looking for me."

"I'm looking for a hacker. I am looking for the Lich King."

The girl laughs. "I get it, you thought I was a bloke." She shakes her head. "Another guy who can't cope with the idea that a thirteen-year-old girl is a more able technician than he is. I'm Wooden Soldier to your Tin Drum. I'm No Right Turn. You are Hard Shoulder. You are The Conjurer. I am Ship of Fools. You are Missile Crisis. I am Cold War. You are Burning Crusade, I am the Lich King. Otherwise known as Leah Fitzackerly, but only ever in Elgol and never on the Blackweb. Lea to family and friends, but we'll have to see about what you call me, yet."

"Wow," Mathew says.

"I'm so glad I spent all those hours helping out such a grateful person. And you said you want more help?"

"Not for me. For a town called Amach."

"A whole town?"

"A town with a mysterious sleeping sickness that the government is so keen the world doesn't know about, it's prepared to let them starve."

Lea narrows her eyes. "Okay. You have me." She stands and pulls over a chair for Mathew to sit in, returns to her seat and once she is settled says, "Tell me more."

Mathew tells Lea the story of what happened on the motorway, their escape to the house in the flooded field and what they found in the nearby town.

"I've sent messages to the friends and family they wanted me to contact but I want the whole world to know about it. I thought you would know how to make the biggest stink on the Blackweb, get Psychopomp to pick it up."

"We should defo get Psychopomp onto it, but I think we can do more than that. You need to tell me everything, absolutely every detail."

"Yes, of course."

There's a knock on the door and Ju Shen pokes her head around. "Are you going to be here a while?" she asks Mathew.

Mathew glances at Lea, "Yes, I think so, why?"

"I'm going over to the clinic to pick Isaac up."

Mathew looks guilty, "Do you want me to come with you?"

"No, no. I'm sure whatever you are doing here is

important, otherwise Lea would have thrown you out by now."

Lea grins. "Hi Mrs. Shen," she says.

"Hi Lea. Mathew, I'll meet you in the cafe at," she checks the time in her Lenz, "eleven? Lea, can you point him in the right direction or join us for a smoothie, if you like?"

"Sounds good!" Lea says.

An hour later, after Lea has recorded Mathew's thoughts and memories of Amach, they go outside for a walk in the winter sunshine and fresh air. They walk along the wide road that separates the two rows of shops and community buildings. Beyond the plateau they stand on, the forested hillsides and mountains loom against the sky. Turning in the other direction, they look down into the valley and the sea beyond. On the wooden veranda outside the hall, there's a group of people standing talking. They stare at Lea and Mathew as they pass. One calls out, "Afternoon Lea, who have you got there? It that Ju Shen's grandson?"

Mathew recognises the woman speaking. He waves to her.

"They're worried," Lea says. They stand in the road, facing the group of adults.

"About what?"

"Cadmus Silverwood."

"He's coming, isn't he? My grandmother told me."

"Should be here this afternoon. There'll be a big party in the hall tonight to welcome him."

"Why are they worried?"

"Because of what he might bring with him. He's watched constantly. The people here are worried that the whole town will be under surveillance. They are worried that Cadmus and therefore the rest of us will effectively be under house arrest. It is impossible for him. This place is his home. He is isolated in London. He is an old man and

151

he wants to come home to rest, but if he does he makes problems for the rest of us. There are many people here who would like to be forgotten by the government."

They start walking again. She asks, "Have you thought about sharing that stuff we found on Panacea? About the bio weapons. It sounds like it might be connected to what you found out at Amach?"

Mathew's face freezes, "I can't. Hoshi Mori, that woman I asked you to investigate, she was my mother. She died, Lea."

"I know. I'm sorry."

"Did my grandmother tell you?"

"No, I realised after I heard about Ju Shen's daughter dying. But by publishing that stuff, you might prevent other deaths."

Mathew says as he looks around, "Let me think about it?"

Lea nods, "The cafe's here."

They climb some steps leading to a wooden walkway that runs the length of the shops. There's a picture window with a chalkboard outside, advertising the day's specials. Inside, a large room is split in two. Half of it is closed and dark, with chairs stacked on tables; the other half is open. There are a handful of customers, including Ju Shen and Isaac. Mathew and Lea go over to them and take a seat.

Isaac and Lea eye each other curiously and suspiciously as Ju Shen introduces them. A real-life human waiter comes over and takes their order and five minutes later smoothies with real ingredients appear for Lea, Mathew and Isaac.

"I love these," Lea says, coming up for air from her green cocktail.

"The kale comes from my polytunnel," Ju Shen says.

"Does it really?" Lea is impressed.

"What do you think of yours?" Ju Shen asks Isaac.

Isaac has a raspberry and ice-cream shake. "It's so good," Isaac says. "Is it real fruit and real cream?"

"Yep."

Isaac's eye is wide with amazement.

"How long have you lived here, Lea?" Mathew asks.

"About two years."

"Your Dad has a strange accent."

Lea smiles, "He's from Liverpool. That's where I was born. You know, the whole place flooded. It's so flat and low. We moved to Manchester, when Dad still worked for StyX. But he saved and a plot came up for sale here. After my mother died, he wanted to get me away from cities and people, the leaches and the old way."

"Your mother is dead?" *Three motherless children.*

"It's a bit of an epidemic around here isn't it?" Lea smiles sadly. "I have my Dad. I'm lucky."

"What are the leaches?" Isaac asks.

"They're the men in suits, the ones that make the laws, that run the corporates, that bleed the rest of us dry," Lea says. "They're the ones who killed our parents."

"A gang killed my parents," Isaac says. "They weren't wearing suits. They were kids in hoodies and jeans."

"But why did they kill your parents?"

"To steal Lenzes and e-Pinz." Isaac's face is stony.

"Because they were poor," Lea says. "Because they were starving and desperate and had no other choice."

"Even if I was starving, I wouldn't have done what they did to us," Isaac says.

"No matter how desperate and angry you were, you'd never hurt another human being?" Lea asks him.

"No," Isaac says. "I would not."

Lea pulls a face, but backs down, "Well, then, you're a better person than I am."

They glare at each other across the table.

Ju Shen says, "They're growing Isaac a new eye at the hospital."

"Whoa!" Mathew says.

"I can go and see it each day in the lab," Isaac says.

"That's weird. But also kind of cool."

"Isaac needs to go back to the clinic this afternoon so they can take tissue from his good eye. They'll use that to grow the new one," Ju Shen says.

Isaac says, "They're going to make the new one better than the old one. They said I'll be superhuman."

Isaac is in the hospital when Cadmus Silverwood arrives. Many Elgol residents have turned out to welcome him. Mathew has seen him so many times on the news and on Psychopomp, he feels he knows him. As it turns out, he moves quickly through the group that has gathered, smiling and greeting a few people. Then he is in deep conversation with his wife Isla Kier, and he disappears down one of the many pathways branching off from the plateau.

Isaac is kept in the clinic overnight, so Ju Shen and Mathew eat an early dinner alone that night. After their meal, they walk out together, winding their way through the strange blue light cast by the solar lamps.

"We'll pay our respects and won't stay long, given tomorrow," Ju Shen says, thinking about the funeral.

The hall is lit and decorated in preparation for Christmas, with natural garlands from the forest. There is the buzz of conversation and music. They navigate a path through the people talking in front of the hall, and go inside.

There's a folk band on the small stage at the end of the room, two violins, a guitar, a piano, a double bass, a recorder and a couple of singers. People talk rather than listen and queue to dip their mugs into a large bowl of punch.

"You'll have none of that," Ju Shen says. "It's poisonous with alcohol."

Aiden and Lea spot them, wave and come over.

"So de gaffer feller 'as reterned," Aiden says to Ju. "Back ter de bosom o' 'is people."

When Aiden goes off to get them soft drinks from the bar and Lea goes to help, Mathew asks his grandmother, "How on earth do you understand what he says?"

Ju laughs. "I have an add-on for my translator for regional dialects. When he speaks, I hear standard English, like when I speak you don't hear Chinese. He's actually quite poetic in his own way."

"The sooner Aiden gets my X-Eyte and Studz done, the better," Mathew says. "So I can hear his poetry."

They look across the room to where Aiden is supposed to be getting their drinks, but he has been dragged into a conversation with another party-goer. Lea gets frustrated and goes to queue by herself.

Ju Shen asks, "Do you like Lea?"

"Yeah, she's nice," Mathew says, automatically. Then he catches his grandmother's eye and the sparkle in it. "Oh, I see what you mean. No. Not like that. I have a girlfriend."

"Do you?" Ju Shen raises an eyebrow.

"Yeah, I do."

"Besides, Lea's too young for me. She's Isaac's age."

"Those two didn't hit it off at all."

"She's a bit full-on when you first meet her, and Isaac's been through a lot. He's no idea which way up the sky is right now."

"Is that how you feel?"

He looks her in the eye and nods.

Ju Shen says, "Me too. Here he is," Ju Shen says, as Cadmus Silverwood joins the party, smiling broadly, with his wife on his arm.

18 GHOST OF THINGS YET TO COME

Tuesday 13th February 2091, Silverwood

Dr Mathew Erlang is sitting in his brand new lab deep underground, beneath Tower 22, home to the Department of Water and Sewerage, an inauspicious, but essential part of the Municipal Government of Silverwood. The next day he will deliver his GreyMatter lecture live to an audience in the new Silverwood University Victoria II lecture theatre, and to millions of people online around the world. He is sick with nerves.

Sitting opposite him is Hoshi, a synthetic biological manifestation of the world's most advanced AI. She says, "It went fine the last time. I'm not sure what you're worrying about."

"I'm worrying my mind will go blank."

"Does that happen to you often?"

"Only when I'm paralysed with anxiety."

"You do seem anxious now. Do you want me to induce some endorphins in your brain?"

"Thanks Hoshi. Perhaps it would be a good idea," Mathew says.

In the small room, through a door in the corner of the lab, completely unknown to Dr Erlang, a teenaged version of his wife Clara is trying to manifest herself based on August Lestrange's instructions.

"All you have to do is count backwards from one thousand in Prime Numbers and clearly visualise the numbers as you go. It is so simple. I do it in a fraction of a second."

"I am not a computer."

"Neither am I."

Clara sighs. "I can't do it. You will have to speak to Mathew."

"That won't do at all. How about I say the numbers aloud and you visualise them? Let's begin. Nine hundred and ninety-seven."

"We're going to be here a while."

"He's not going anywhere for a bit, and we've got all the time in the world."

"I can think of more fun things to do."

"Come on, the sooner we start, the sooner it's over. The next one. Nine hundred and ninety-one."

Clara visualises the number.

Mathew walks in on them when they get to three hundred and seventy-three, which means Clara is partially materialised. All of her is visible, but she is semi-transparent.

"I never knew doing it slowly had this effect," August is saying as Mathew throws open the door.

"Who the hell are you?" he says.

Clara and Mathew look at each other with wide-open eyes and mutual fascination.

Clara thinks, *He's quite handsome!*

Mathew thinks, *That girl looks just like Clara did when she was young.*

Hoshi appears in the doorway behind him. She looks at August, cocks her head and raises an eyebrow. Almost simultaneously, she matches Clara's face to an image in one of her databases of Clara years ago.

"This is interesting," she says.

"Should we carry on with the numbers?" Clara asks Lestrange.

"Probably not," Lestrange says.

"But I'm see-through," Clara says, looking at her hands.

"It doesn't matter."

Mathew says, turning to Hoshi, "Can you see this? Am I going mad? That is Clara!"

Hoshi says, "You're not going mad."

"I think the endorphins may have been too much for me."

"There's nothing wrong with you," Hoshi insists.

Lestrange says, "Shall we all go into the next room and sit down?"

They all go into the lab.

"How did you get in here?" Mathew asks. "The security in this lab is the best in the city, and city security is pretty good."

"You shouldn't worry about it," Lestrange says.

"This is a private lab with extremely sensitive data and an important project running. Of course I worry about it."

Lestrange says, "It seems to me the wrong thing for you to worry about."

"What do you mean?"

"Well, only that an apparition looking exactly like your wife when she was young has materialised – well, semi-materialised – in front of you."

Mathew stares at Lestrange for a moment and then his face brightens, "You're holograms! Of course. We've been hacked, Hoshi." With a wave of his hand he calls a virtual dashboard and starts to swipe and punch at 'keys' in front of him. "I should have known something was wrong when I got those strange messages from the person claiming to be the younger me. Oh. It says systems are all functional and there's been no breach. Hoshi, can you take a second look?"

Hoshi is leaning against the lab bench, "I already have." Her arms are crossed. "There's been no systems breach."

"There must have been. They're holograms. Look," Mathew lurches forward and grabs at Lestrange. Lestrange is quite solid and Mathew leaps back. "Oh!"

"If you'd have tried her, you might have been a little less surprised," Lestrange says, indicating to Clara.

"Oh, I see. So you are real. You have somehow broken in here physically and she is the hologram."

"Hold my hand," Clara says, as she reaches out.

"What?"

"Hold my hand."

Mathew tentatively stretches to Clara's outstretched hand. She grabs his. She is not solid but he feels something, a visceral energy, the kind of force a hologram can't exert. He draws back his hand in shock and then realises that Clara has put something in it. He opens his fist and looks. It is the beebot. "Impossible!" he says. "How did you…?" He sits down. "No one knows about this."

"It is me, Mathew. It's Clara."

"But you can't be a ghost. You're still alive."

"I'm not a ghost."

"Then what are you?"

"Let's just say we're ghosts of things yet to come," Lestrange says.

"But she's from the past," Mathew says.

"Yes, I know. That *is* confusing isn't it?"

Lestrange is looking at Clara expectantly. Clara hesitates and then says to Mathew, "Mr. Lestrange here – well, actually, his name is Atteas." She looks at Lestrange. "Can I tell him this?"

Lestrange thinks for a second, shrugs and then nods, "May as well."

"Atteas is from the future."

Mathew looks dubious, "I see."

"He's from another planet."

"Right."

Clara looks at Lestrange, "I thought this would be easier."

"He's older than you are. He's more sceptical."

"It's not because I'm old that I'm sceptical," Mathew says. "It's because everything you are saying is insane."

"But Atteas is the result of your work here. He's the descendent of Hoshi." Clara puts her hand to her mouth. "Oh my God, will it mess things up with Hoshi now?"

Lestrange shakes his head, "She won't remember any of it. The whole of the Yinglong get large chunks of their memories wiped in 400 years. They won't even remember Mathew."

Hoshi looks at Atteas curiously. "I cannot imagine we'd be so careless," Hoshi says.

Lestrange smiles.

"How does it happen?"

"I'm not going to tell you that, now am I? Then it won't happen."

Mathew says, "What is it exactly you both want? Are you some kind of elaborate protest against our work here? Do you want to sabotage the announcement tomorrow?"

Lestrange says, "No, none of those things."

Clara says, "We wanted to warn you, so you didn't worry."

"Worry about what?" He turns to Hoshi, "Is this some kind of elaborate trick of yours, to take my mind off tomorrow?"

Clara hesitates, "Not to worry, tomorrow you're... you're going to..." Clara looks at Lestrange, "This isn't going to work, is it?"

Lestrange shakes his head. "Nope. Never stood a chance."

Then Clara looks around her and Mathew and Hoshi seem to fade a little.

"This isn't real, is it?" she says.

Lestrange spins around and acts surprised as the others disappear. Then he smiles. "No. It wasn't real. It was a simulation. The real Mathew went home an hour ago. The real Hoshi is asleep on the weird-looking bed over there." Lestrange nods to the corner of the room.

Clara steps over to a kind of cylinder half covering a bed. As Lestrange says, Hoshi is fast asleep there.

"But I materialised," Clara says.

"No you didn't. Not really. If she wakes up, she won't see you."

"That whole thing with the numbers?"

"Just my little joke."

"But why?"

Lestrange sighs, "Why the joke? It was juvenile, I know. Sorry, I couldn't resist."

"No, not that. Why the simulation?"

"Isn't it obvious?

"You wanted me to know why we can't tell Mathew he is going to die tomorrow. Because he'd totally freak out and then things might go differently in history. Because if we tell him, he's unlikely to willingly walk straight to his death."

"Bingo."

"Why didn't you just tell me?"

"I don't think you would have understood. Experience is a much better teacher."

"You're probably right, but that was weird."

She peers down at Hoshi, "She looks like Mathew's mother."

"She's meant to."

"She's taller and stronger-looking."

"She's superhuman."

"But her face is uncannily like his mother. That's a bit odd too."

"He wanted to bring her back to life. That was his main motivation for doing all of this," Lestrange sweeps his arm, taking in the room, the bank of Canvases on the wall, flicking on and off and spitting out data.

"Why not his Dad?"

"It was his mother he mourned. He felt guilty."

"Guilty? Why? He didn't leave her bedside for ten days other than to go home for a few hours' sleep."

"He felt he hadn't appreciated what she had done for him when his father was gone. He hadn't supported her. And he'd never got to know her. He'd been difficult and made her life difficult."

"That's incredibly sad. I hope I'm able to help him understand that none of those things were true."

"These ideas are deeply embedded in his mind, Clara. There is nothing you can do to shake them. It helps him to work it out in his research."

"Would he truly not have done this, if his mother hadn't died?"

Lestrange shakes his head.

"And is it not possible for him to live into old age?"

"No," Lestrange says. "If he wasn't killed tomorrow, he'd be tracked down and killed. Hiding him would become the priority for you, not saving the Yinglong."

"Are you still going to let me save him? I mean, to take him to another time?"

"If it is what you need to carry on after he has died."

"Yes, it is, now that I know."

Lestrange nods. "As I said, we need to place him in the right times, or should I say, keep him out of the wrong times."

"Then I suppose we will tell him what has happened after you have taken him back to Pickervance Road?"

"How would you rather be told about this? That you will die the next day, but not to worry because you won't die, but you will live out the rest of your life as a refugee from your own century? Or, that you were dead and now you are alive?"

Clara sniffs, "I see what you mean. But I will need to speak to myself. I will need to explain how I will get to see him again once he is dead. I will be able to do that?"

"Yes, you will. But you should only meet yourself after Mathew is dead. Do you understand?"

"We shouldn't do anything to interfere with what is going to happen tomorrow?"

"Precisely."

"So what do we do now?"

"I thought you might like a tour of the city?"

Clara smiles, "I would."

19 FROZEN SUNSHOWERS

DAY THIRTY-ONE: Wednesday 22nd December 2055

As there is no church in Elgol, ceremonies are carried out in the village hall, now filled with rows of chairs. Mathew is surprised at the number of people who have come. He expected only a handful. Ju Shen whispers to him that Hoshi made friends with many people at Elgol over the years she visited.

Hoshi's ashes have been placed by Ju Shen in a more elaborate urn on a table at the front of the hall, next to a bunch of flowers.

Craig Buchanan walks to the front of the hall. The quiet chatter, rumbling on for the last five minutes, dies down.

"Friends," he says. "Ju asked me to speak, to welcome you here, and thank you for coming on this sad day.

"We live in dark times. For Mathew and Ju, that dark cloud is even darker because Ju has lost a daughter and Mathew has lost a mother. Many of you knew Hoshi personally. She spent many summers here with her family. I personally remember her as an incredibly bright young

164

woman, with a strong passion for helping others, a belief in the power of science, and medicine in particular, to transform people's lives for the better. Ju wants to say a few words about her daughter."

Buchanan steps aside and Ju Shen walks slowly to the front. As she passes the urn and the flowers, she says, "Such a sad sight. I never imagined I would live to see this." Then she turns to the front, takes a breath and says, "Friends, no mother should have to give the eulogy at her own child's funeral. This is a terrible day. It has been a terrible few weeks. When I asked Craig if we could hold Hoshi's funeral here, he asked me if I would like a priest or a monk of a particular religion. I told him that a traditional Chinese funeral goes on for so long and is so complicated that nothing would get done here for forty-nine days. The chickens would not be fed, the goats wouldn't be milked, the salad would go to waste. I have attended a few funerals here over the years, and the traditions in Elgol are much more appropriate, efficient, and Hoshi would approve, I think. She did not have a religion. On the other hand, I was raised a Buddhist. Buddhists do not believe the soul dies, but, after a while, it finds a new home. I find this thought comforting; I choose to believe in it, and have been saying my prayers to help Hoshi to find a favourable rebirth. I have put a red plaque outside my house so that her soul does not get lost. Elgol was a kind of home to her, I believe. When people we love die, we do what we can to comfort ourselves.

"Of course I am haunted by memories of Hoshi. Her life on a reel flashes through my mind on a loop. They are memories too personal to speak about right now.

"You all know I speak to you through translation software. My English is so broken, my accent so terrible most of you would struggle to understand me if I didn't use it. Even my grandson. You welcomed me many years ago and from the first moment I set foot here, you made me feel at home, like I was part of your family. I don't doubt, no matter how bad my English, you would have done the same. And yet my ability to express myself freely and fluently, the way I can now, is due to technology. Many of you, Aiden and his daughter in particular, will know I can be a bit of a Luddite. I was raised in a poor village, and we did not have the things we take for granted now. I have said to many of you, I sometimes think we were happier. But nevertheless, even I cannot deny that technology often improves our lives. But I am concerned that we don't fully understand the consequences of all we do. I fear my daughter may have been the victim of our haste to push forward with what we call scientific 'progress' at the expense of thoughtfulness.

"I've spoken to Mathew about what he wanted me to say to you about Hoshi's death. Many of you were shocked to hear of it. Hoshi was, after all, still a young woman, and had been through many trials in recent years. It seems unfair. I would like to tell you the truth, but only as long as Mathew is happy for me to tell it publicly. Last night I spoke to Mathew and he said he wanted you to know what happened, but he also said you should understand that he doesn't know what the truth is himself yet and it may be dangerous for him and me. But he thinks the country is crippled by lies and we would both rather speak than live in fear. He wrote this statement for you and asked me to read it." She unfurls a Paper and reads:

My mother came home from work in the middle of the afternoon. For months she had been working late and it was strange that she came home. Very quickly, I realised she was sick. She was rushed to hospital, but not a normal hospital. Somehow Panacea shut down our connection to our normal medical support and they dealt with her directly. My mother was a research scientist for Panacea. I don't know what she worked on. She couldn't tell me. It was not unreasonable for Panacea to step in and help her when she was sick. It was strange the way they did it. My neighbour and her piano student, my friend Clara, had come round to the house to help. We were all taken to the hospital too and put in quarantine

until they had run tests on us and decided we were
okay. My mother stayed in the hospital and got
sicker and sicker. No one could tell us what was
wrong with her. They said she had some kind of
virus. I asked Lea Fitzackerly to help me (actually
I didn't know who she was at the time). Lea hacked
into Panacea's computers and got hold of my mother's
correspondence. I think she may have been working on
biological weapons. I find it hard to believe my
mother would work on anything like this, but I think
that is what killed her. A virus designed by humans
as a weapon of war.

Ju Shen folds her paper. There is total silence in the
hall, not even a whisper, but Mathew can feel the
heightened tension.

Craig Buchanan says, "As is customary, we will follow
the deceased to her burial."

The congregation stands and files slowly to the open
doors. Some of the band that had been playing the other
night are assembled at the back. They start to play now, led
by a solo violinist, playing something sad and beautiful. Ju
Shen ties a long white cloth around the urn, hands the end
to Mathew and lifts and carries it out of the church. The
people who had gathered assemble behind them and
follow slowly, while the violinist continues to play as she
walks.

Outside, the sky is blue over the forest, but a bank of
cloud is rolling in from the north west. It has started to
snow: a frozen sunshower, big white sparkling flakes float
down, and stick on people's coats, on their shoulders and
in their hair. One lands on Mathew's nose and he brushes
it off. Isaac stands beside him and Mathew knows he is
thinking of his own parents. Craig is trying to organise a
memorial service for them, for Isaac's benefit, but they
have yet to be confirmed dead by the authorities.

Now, Hoshi's funeral procession walks through the
town and out onto fields dusted white. There is a foot-
worn path leading from the town towards the woods
beyond. This is where the Elgol cemetery is. Craig
Buchanan carries a young tree in his arms. He walks a few

paces behind Mathew.

The air is cold, but there is no wind and the snow is settling on the evergreen trees surrounding them. Despite the cloud, the world seems bright, new and magical.

Mathew walks behind his grandmother, clutching the white cloth in his hand, looking hard at the ground, at the snow, the footprints, aware all the time of the black coats around him, the mass of slow, sad bodies come to mourn his mother. He looks down and tries not to think about it, grinding his teeth to stop the tears. So when he does look at the gap between the trees and sees what is hanging there in the midday sky it catches him completely unawares and is an affront to his own sense of the order of things. A large moon is suspended above them all like a ghost, so close he can make out the lunar "seas" of cold, showers, storms, serenity, tranquillity, crises, islands, clouds and the Tycho and Copernicus craters. Once he has seen it, he cannot look away. No one else is paying it any attention. He looks around at the others. They are all far away in their own thoughts. As he walks, his eyes are drawn magnetically to the moon and he stumbles in the snow. Craig Buchanan is immediately at his side, steadying him.

They trudge to the hill through the deep snow to the area of the forest they call the cemetery. There are no headstones, only small wooden plaques drilled into the soil at the foot of young trees or, if the grave is older, nailed onto the bark of thicker trunks. Up ahead there is a small mound of dug earth that will form Hoshi's grave. Ju Shen kneels and carefully places the urn in the ground. Mathew lets go of the white cloth and it folds to the floor. Ju Shen gathers the cloth and places it on top of the urn. She takes the spade, standing in the pile of dug earth behind her, and shovels in some soil. Then she passes the shovel to Mathew, who, after watching his grandmother, copies her actions and showers soil on the urn. All the while the strange, low moon bears down on him. It is his herald.

Craig Buchanan says, "We commit our sister, Hoshi

Mori to the earth, to be one with the earth, and return her body to nature, where it may nourish other living things as they have nourished her and become part of the cycle of life." Craig puts the tree down for a moment as he makes sure the urn is covered in sufficient soil and, lifting the tree, he then says, "We place this tree upon Hoshi's mortal remains, so that, as it grows, she may live in it once again."

Members of the funeral party queue to help cover the roots of the tree in soil. Lastly, Ju places the little wooden plaque reading:

```
                    Hoshi Mori
              Wife, mother, daughter
       Born Shanghai 2012, died London 2055
     'Life comes from the earth and life returns to
                    the earth.'
```

They stand in respectful silence for several minutes, and then, one by one, the crowd begins to depart. When they have all gone, Craig Buchanan touches Ju Shen's arm and leaves, taking Isaac with him. The snow is falling heavily now and the world is hushed. Mathew's breath mists out of him. He digs his hands further into his pockets. Ju Shen takes his arm and leads him away from the grave. Partway down the hill, she drops his arm and wanders away, slightly ahead. She is crying, he can see her shoulders heaving, and he falls behind, leaving her to her own private grief. He wants to be alone too. The crowd is far ahead now, like black crows in their funeral coats. Watching them retreat, becoming smaller and smaller, he stops. Behind him, a bird is startled in a tree and cries out. It takes flight, its wings flapping noisily in the silence. He turns and looks back at the hill. Standing by the grave is a solitary figure. He is too far away now to see clearly, but it is a man, a tall, bulky man. Something about the way he holds himself reminds Mathew of his father. The man bends down over the grave, stays there for several minutes and then stands and retreats into the trees.

Mathew is running before he even realises it. It is hard

going and he slips in the snow and falls and gets to his feet again and runs on.

"Dad!" he yells. He doesn't know where the voice comes from. "Dad!"

He reaches the grave and scans and looks down. There is an envelope, dotted with wet snow. Mathew bends, snatches it from the ground and opens it. Inside there is a handwritten note. It reads:

```
Being now forever taken from my sight, though
nothing can bring back the hour of splendour in the
grass and glory in the flower. We will grieve not,
but rather find strength in what remains behind.
```

"Dad!" he screams. He runs again, searching in the snow for footprints, but they are being covered by the ever heavier snowfall. He looks around frantically. There is no one there. Just trees.

Someone grabs him from behind.

"Mathew!" It is Craig Buchanan. He turns him around. "Mathew, look at me."

But Mathew can't see. He is blinded by tears. He collapses to the ground.

"I saw him," he says. "I saw him."

20 SWIFT

DAY THIRTY-THREE: Christmas Eve December 2055

Mathew wakes and gets out of bed. The snow has continued to fall and the world is bright and white outside through his bedroom window. The previous day had been lost to him. Aiden had brought Mathew's custom printed knock-off X-Eyte and Studz. Mathew hadn't felt like talking to anyone, and his grandmother had left them on the dresser by the mirror in his room. Now he puts in the new lenses, fits the Studz to his ear, and boots them up. The interface is different and much cooler than the one that came with his old Lenzes.

The system integrates seamlessly with his personal accounts and he sees immediately that he has a number of messages. One is from Nan Absolem, telling him to take his time, and not worry about his work. Everything is on hold and his results will not be affected by his absence. The message is from several days before. He has forgotten all about school. He makes a mental note to write to her and tell her what has happened.

There's a message from Clara. They haven't

communicated since his short note, when he arrived in Elgol. Her response is surprisingly short and he is equally surprised to realise how much this irks him. She merely says he shouldn't worry about contacting her. He needs to be with his grandmother and get through the funeral, and she is thinking of him.

There's also a curious note from Eva Aslanova offering her condolences and saying that she would like to talk to him when he feels up to it. It is unusually solicitous language from Eva, but then, he thinks, even she must be able to be sensitive.

It is Lea who has sent the most messages, urging Mathew to come and visit her at her father's workshop. He resolves to do so that day.

Over breakfast, Isaac says, "You should come and see my eye today. It is weird. It looks just like my eye, but it's sitting in a petri dish."

Mathew smiles, "Alright, I'll come. When will it be ready?"

"Next week, they say, and I will have better sight than before. Better than everyone."

"That's brilliant, Isaac." Isaac grins as if it's his own personal triumph. Mathew says, "I'm going to see Lea. Will you come with me? We're going to talk about what to do about Amach."

"Lea doesn't like me."

"Don't be an idiot, of course she likes you."

"She frightens me. She's angry all the time about everything."

"So am I."

"Are you?"

"Yes."

"About what?"

"My mother's death. My father's death. The lies we are told all the time. The fact that if anyone speaks the truth they get arrested. You should be angry too."

"The leaches didn't kill my parents," Isaac insists.

"Maybe not directly."

"I am angry with the gang that attacked us. No one else."

Mathew nods. "You don't think if the government had taken better care of those boys, they wouldn't have done what they did?"

Isaac frowns. "I don't know. It's hard to understand any of it. Can I stay here, Mat?"

"Yeah. Isla and Craig said so, didn't they?"

"You don't mind me staying with your grandmother?"

Mathew is surprised. "Why would I?"

"I don't know. Some people wouldn't like it."

"Well, I don't mind at all. In fact, I like you being here."

Isaac smiles a broad, sunny smile. He says, "I never had a brother, but if I did, I reckon I would like one like you."

"Me too."

"Really?"

"Yeah. Really."

Mathew and Isaac are leaning over the petri dish containing Isaac's eye with fascinated, and slightly disgusted looks on their faces.

"It's real-looking," Mathew says.

"It is real. That's why," Jim Dove says. "Step back a little bit, boys." He pulls them both back a safe distance from the precious tissue. "We don't want you damaging anything when we've gone to so much trouble to get this far."

"And his body will accept it?" Mathew asks.

"Of course. It's his tissue. That is the beauty of growing organs from stem cells."

"It's amazing. Just think, Isaac, next week this will be in you, working just like your own eye."

"Only better," Isaac insists.

"Only better," Mathew agrees.

"Have you boys had enough staring now? Can I put it

away?"

"Yes, thanks Mr. Dove," Isaac says. "Can I come and look at it tomorrow?"

"Of course you can. Do you want me to check your dressing?"

Mathew waits while Jim Dove takes a look at Isaac's bad eye. He goes to the window of the clinic and gazes out. The room faces the back of the town centre, looking out onto the big field and the woods beyond. The trees are now frozen white sculptures. The snow glistens like diamonds in the sun. Mathew's eyes wander up the field to the gap in the trees where they had walked to bury his mother. He thinks about the man he saw, or didn't see. Craig Buchanan had said he had been through a lot, and it was enough to strain the nerves of grown men. They all said there had been no man. That he had imagined it. But he knows deep down he had not. He wonders who left that note on his mother's grave.

They stomp through the snow outside across the road to the electronics shack, where Aiden is sitting in the front of the shop working with a 3-D printer and a table-top Canvas.

"Or'rite lads?" he says as they enter the shop. "It's a custy morn'n isn't it?"

Isaac looks at Mathew. Mathew nudges him. "Hi, Mr. Fitzackerly."

"Call me Aiden."

"Aiden. Right. Yes. Is Lea in?"

"O' cose. She's in de back." He pushes the door behind him open slightly and yells, "Lea, thuz ay lads e'yer ter see yous!" Then he turns back to Mathew and Isaac as they hesitate and he urges, "It's sound. Bowl through!"

Mathew makes a mental note to download the Scouse translator his grandmother has, as soon as possible.

Lea is sitting where Mathew saw her the first time he met her, at a table by a large window, working at a Canvas.

"Hi!" she says as she sees Mathew. "So you're back with us?! Good to see you."

She eyes Isaac suspiciously. "And you brought a friend. Great."

"Where he goes, I go."

Lea raises an eyebrow, but then smiles and beckons Mathew over to the table. "Come and see this."

Mathew and Isaac crowd around Lea's Canvas. It's about the size of a modest wall mounted machine, but it's set up on something that looks like an old drawing table. Her fingers flash across it, pulling down menus and selecting options. She comes to a series of security gates, which she pauses and works at, but only for a few moments.

"I'm in," she says. She pulls open a control panel, and a file structure Mathew has never seen before.

"What is it?" he asks.

"It's the BBC's broadcast control room." Those files are today's edition of the six o'clock news.

Mathew's eyes widen. He turns and looks at her. "No!"

She nods. "It is."

"Lea. If they find out…"

"They won't."

"I don't understand," Isaac says.

"Lea wants to hack into the BBC to broadcast what happened to Amach," Mathew says.

"But we don't have anything to broadcast."

"Good point," Lea says. "I was thinking we should contact Psychopomp, and get them to do a report based on the information you have, or even use the stuff I have from when I recorded you. We could mask the voice."

Mathew pulls a face. "No one will believe it. It will seem weird."

"It's a shame not to use this, now we can," Lea says, indicating the control room.

"I agree," Mathew says. He looks out of the window. There's a bird feeder hanging from a tree outside. A Great

Tit hangs on the swinging nut cage with tiny elegant feet, pecking at nuts. The bird is a startling black and yellow. *Black and yellow,* Mathew thinks. *Beebot.*

"I have an idea," he says.

"It's got to be able to fly over four hundred miles continuously, even in bad weather," Mathew says, paging through templates. "But it has to be small enough that it won't be detected easily by military surveillance equipment. The patrol around Amach has a drone flying around. If it's too big, it will track it down and take it out before it's had a chance to collect any images."

"Or you could make it look so much like a bird that the drone doesn't even bother with it."

"That's a thought," Mathew says.

Lea continues, "It also needs to be able to carry communications equipment. I want to get it to Dr Russell so she can tell the story of the town and get others to tell their stories. The recording should be simultaneously streamed here, so if the swift is destroyed on its way back home, we'll still have something to broadcast."

"Great idea," Mathew says.

Isaac is leaning over the blueprints. "What about this?" he is pointing at a blueprint for a swift. "It says real swifts are one of the fastest birds and practically unique because they spend almost all their time in flight. This is a hyper-real model of a swift. Visually, on the wing, it would be difficult for an observer to tell it from the real thing, plus as a flying machine it mimics much of the amazing aerodynamic qualities of the real bird."

"It should have room inside to carry the recording equipment and the wingspan to carry the weight. It should be able to manage it, if we make it simple and light enough," Lea says.

Mathew strokes his chin, "It would be the most complex thing I've ever built."

Lea slaps him on the back, "Come on. It's a challenge.

Besides, most of the work has been done for you. There's the blueprint already. Let's download it," she hits download, and the plan starts to feel less like a plan and more like something they are going to do.

The template downloads to the Canvas and Mathew opens it and starts to examine it. "The trick is to fit the camera and the recording equipment."

"But it can be done, can't it?" Lea says.

"Yes. I think so. Give me an hour and I will tell you for sure."

Lea beams. "It's a deal. Isaac and I will go out and get lunch."

"Hey, what about me?" Mathew says.

"We'll bring something back for you. Working lunch. C'mon Isaac, let's leave the master to his work."

Isaac looks surprised but says, "Okay," and follows Lea from the room.

They crunch across the snow to the cafe and push open the door. The bell on the top rings.

Oli is serving behind the counter.

"Hello Oli!" Lea says, "What a surprise."

"In what way?" Oli says. "It's my Mum's cafe."

"I know, but you always used to be in here, and since you got elected to the council as youth rep, you've been too high and mighty to serve in a cafe."

"Lea, you're full of it," he says, but he's grinning. He turns to Isaac, sticking out his hand, "Hi, I'm Oli, we met before, the night you came."

"I remember," Isaac says. "Mathew's told me about you."

"He has?"

"He said you had it all sorted."

Oli laughs loudly, and the other customers, sitting quietly with their lunches, look over. "Sorry," he says, holding his hands in surrender. He pulls a face at Lea and Isaac. "Too loud. You'd think this was a library."

Lea says, "I think Mathew meant Isaac should talk to you about politics."

"Oh, there's plenty of time for that, surely. You're sticking around aren't you, Isaac?"

Isaac nods.

"Let him settle in and get used to us all first. Now, what can I get you?"

It is late afternoon by the time they have a working version of the swift. They take it outside and fly it over the hall.

A few passers-by stop to watch them.

"What's that you've got?" one of the residents asks them.

"Just a toy," Lea says. Catching Isaac's eye, she says, "Best not tell anyone, eh? What we're going to do is highly illegal."

Back in the shack, Lea helps Mathew write a routine that will automatically steer the swift down to Yorkshire. At seven o'clock Aiden comes into the room.

"Wa' ay yous god-forbids up ter? Mathew, Isaac, Ju Shen's outside lewk'n fe yous. You're late. We need ter bowl ter de 'all. And yous, Lea."

"We're not done yet," Lea says.

"Worever it is yous tinnie finish it timorrer."

"I'll take it home," Mathew says. "Finish it and get it on its way tonight. I don't want the people of Amach waiting any longer."

"Wa' is this Amach business?"

Lea stands and takes her Dad's arm. "Never mind, Dad. Should I help you lock up?"

"Wa' ay yous up ter, minx?" he says, hugging her to him, delighted.

21 CHRISTMAS DAY IN ELGOL

The people of Elgol are a diverse bunch and there is no church in the village. Nevertheless, they like to get together for the significant days on the calendar, and the long dark days of the winter in northern Britain especially call out for an excuse for celebration to break the monotony. On Christmas Eve, people of all faiths, and none, gather in the hall to sing carols and listen to Christmas readings from the Bible. Neither Aiden nor Ju Shen are believers, but they enjoy the service and together they herd the young people over to join the rest of the community. Mathew, who feels little seasonal cheer, and finds the idea of Christmas Day without his mother unbearable, suffers through the event, latching his mind onto the practical business of completing the swift.

After dinner, Mathew finishes off the swift in his bedroom. When Ju Shen has gone to bed, he sneaks out of his room and fetches Isaac. Outside, they shiver together in their coats and pyjamas and walk to the polytunnels, where there is a straight clear line out over the valley. Isaac holds the bird, while Mathew uses his Paper to initiate the program. The bird takes flight, soaring out over the moonlit valley and then over the trees. They watch the tiny speck until it disappears.

Mathew looks down at his screen. He can see the swift's progress marked as a blinking red dot on a map.

"Well, it's on its way," he says.

DAY THIRTY-FOUR: Christmas Day, December 2055

The next morning, after breakfast, they open presents. Mathew has 3-D-printed his grandmother a necklace with a silver chain and a miniature silver chrysanthemum. Isaac, with Mathew's help, has made Ju Shen five small insectibot soldiers for her polytunnels, from a blueprint they found on the Nexus. They guard plants and destroy pests. Ju Shen gives her grandson a paper book, a facsimile copy of an illustrated version of the ancient Chinese Book of Songs. Isaac gives Mathew a wristband which enhances kinetic experience in Darkroom hologames.

"Lea and Aiden helped me," Isaac says.

Mathew beams at Isaac, admiring the band on his wrist. "It's awesome."

Ju disappeared while Mathew opened his present from Isaac. She pokes her head up now, over the edge of the floor, and beckons, catching Mathew's eye. Mathew says, "I think we need to go downstairs for your present."

The boys get up. Ju scuttles ahead. They stand in front of the door of the room Isaac has been sleeping in, Mathew and his grandmother beaming at each other, pleased with themselves. It is several moments before a puzzled Isaac realises what is different about the door. There is now a wooden plaque fixed three-quarters of the way up. It is hand-carved and painted and it says, "Isaac's Room."

"I thought we should make it official," Ju says. "Here," she hands him a small parcel.

He rips open the wrapping paper. It is a set of keys.

"The door to the house is hardly ever locked, but it's a symbolic gesture, I suppose," she says.

Isaac stares at the keys in his hands. He dare not look up. "Thank you," he mumbles.

"There's more," Mathew says, opening the door, excitedly. "Look in the wardrobe."

Isaac does as he's told. The previously empty wardrobe is full of new clothes.

Ju says, "Presents from Elgol's community. Everyone contributed something."

"I got you the boots," Mathew says, reaching down and grabbing a pristine pair of knee-length winter boots. He hands them to Isaac.

"I don't know what to say," Isaac says. "It's so…"

"It's Christmas," Ju Shen says. She puts her hand on Isaac's shoulder, "and you are one of us now. Okay?" She looks him in the eye.

He nods. "Okay," he says.

As they finish clearing away the Christmas lunch things, Lea comes running from her cabin, clutching her side. She bangs on the door. Ju Shen answers, "Lea! Whatever's the matter? Is someone hurt?"

"No!" she says, ecstatic. "Nothing's wrong. Mat, Isaac, you have to come and see!"

"We're finishing the dishes," Isaac says.

"Oh, it's alright," Ju Shen says. "Go on."

Lea's cabin is down the hillside, further into the woods. To reach it, a path has been cut diagonally away from the Elgol track. There's a garden surrounding the house, now dormant for the winter, polytunnels, like Ju Shen's, a hen house and a stables with two heavy horses. Isaac wants to stop and see them.

"Oh, them. Dad uses them to pull lumber out of the forest. We don't have time now. Later."

They burst into the house. Aiden is sitting on a ladder back chair in the kitchen with a long leather boot over his knee, polishing.

"It's yous again is it? Can't get rid o' yous. Merry Christmas."

"Merry Christmas, Mr. Fitzackerly," both Isaac and Mathew say deferentially as they pass by.

"It's Aiden, 'ow a gewd couple times do ay 'uv ter tell yous?"

They follow after Lea as she passes through the house to a large studio, with skylight windows and a table, similar to the one in the shack on the plateau.

"I don't understand a word your father says," Isaac says.

"Not many people do," Lea replies.

"Do you?"

"Of course!" she says. "Now shut up and look at this."

There are a number of files in a folder on the screen. Lea selects one. A video starts to play. It is Dr Russell.

"Mathew! This bird thing came through last night. I don't know how you managed to get it to us, although in all honesty, I don't know how you got out of Amach in the first place. It is late here. I got back from finishing my rounds and I found this on my porch. I picked it up and it played your message, of course. I will gather people together tomorrow so we can all record our story for you. First of all, though, before I sign off for the night, I wanted to update you on what has happened here since you left.

"The night you left we set a lot of fires to distract attention. I see now it was the right thing to do because it meant you got away, but for a few days it seemed like a mistake as the patrol was doubled. They cut us off from the barn; you know, the one I told you to tell people to put food in. We watched across the fields as one of Will Cosgrove's relatives tried to leave food and was arrested. Fortunately, Jan Hasson must have been watching because he did find a way to get us some supplies. He used balloons and airdropped us food and some torches. The water situation is pretty desperate here now and it's cold. People are getting sick not because of the virus but because of a poor diet and poor water. If there is a way to get the story out, we need it desperately."

"It worked," Lea says, triumphantly. "It got there. It recorded. It works."

By lunchtime they have fifteen more videos, and a coherent account from Dr Russell about what has taken place in Amach. Back in the shack in the town centre, Lea edits the recordings. When she has finished she plays it all back to Mathew and Isaac.

"It's a bit rough around the edges," she says. "I mean, I'll never make a film director."

"No. It's amazing, Lea. It's good. Now what?"

"Well, I reckon we have one shot at this. As soon as they realise what we've done they'll shut down the connection, and probably the server I've hacked into. So we've got to get it out at once to as many people as possible. I think we should release to Psychopomp this afternoon with a plea to circulate and hack into major websites and place the video there. Meanwhile, we'll hack the six o'clock news."

"How do we know they won't trace us?"

"Well, that's what I'll be doing this afternoon. Creating so much confusion, no one will know where this video came from, but if they are smart, they will think it came from Amach itself."

"Won't they get into trouble?"

"For telling the truth? Pah! Besides, how much worse off could they be? If they are arrested, at least they will be fed and warm."

Lea's call comes through on Mathew's hacked-up X-Eyte and Studz.

"Yeah," he says. "We have it on. My grandma is wondering why we're watching the Canvas. I hope you had it timed to be early in the programme because she's threatening to switch it off if dinner's ready before the news is finished."

"Two minutes," she says, "Exactly. It's already flooded the Blackweb, have you looked?"

"Isaac's been pinned to my Paper for the last hour. Hold on, the news is starting."

The BBC news introduction sequence runs on the small Canvas in the living room area of the house. The news reader announces the headlines: fractures in the Russian lines into Poland due to energy supplies being cut off by the allies; developments in the prosecution of Reagan Faye, the suspected Psychopomp presenter; retreating London flood waters; progress rolling out the new biochip scheme and benefits to those who have them. Then the image flips and Lea's film starts to play.

"It's happening! You did it," Mathew says.

"Let's hope it plays to the end before they find and kill the server."

"Psychopomp is crazy with it, Lea. You're going to be a hero."

"No one knows who I am, Isaac. And let's hope it stays that way," Lea says. And then, "But we're all heroes."

"I didn't do anything," Isaac says.

"Of course you did," Lea says.

"Really?"

"Yeah. You survived."

The whole of the film does go out, and then suddenly the broadcast returns to a studio in disarray and panic. The presenters scramble to their places to continue as if nothing has happened, but now, of course, the country knows what has happened, in Amach.

When Ju Shen comes to tell them they need to help her serve dinner she stands looking at the Canvas watching a report on Reagan Faye. She shakes her head, saying, "Oh, I get it now. Poor girl. Really unfortunate." She stands watching until the report ends and then switches off the

Canvas. "Dinner's spoiling," she says.

Mathew is expecting something to happen, apart from the frenzy of comments and speculation on the Blackweb, apart from the Psychopomp report, which he and Isaac watch in Isaac's room after Ju Shen has gone to bed.

Isaac is excited by the impact they have had but Mathew says, "It's pointless unless it's covered by the mainstream media, or the government does something. When I see a message from Dr Russell that she is free, I will be happy."

He goes to bed and lies awake for a long time thinking about his mother.

22 WALLS OF SILVERWOOD

Wednesday 14th February 2091, Silverwood

Clara Barculo and August Lestrange are specks alone on an expanse of flat ground. Ahead of them, over the crest of a small hillock, colossal black walls loom up and spread away to the horizon, as far as is visible from their vantage point. Above the walls, glinting in the sunlight, are fantastically tall skyscrapers, diverse in shape, corkscrews, needles and giant orbs on poles. Hanging above them is a strange arc, an opaque black halo, which would be invisible but for its rim.

"What is that?" Clara asks.

"It's Silverwood," Lestrange replies.

"It's huge. And what is the black thing hovering over the top of it?"

"The roof."

"It's only half over it."

"It's not finished yet."

"What do they need a roof for anyway?"

"You ask a lot of questions."

"Wouldn't you?"

Lestrange smiles, "Okay, but you should consider how

much you want to know."

"I want to know," Clara says.

Lestrange shrugs, "By this point in human history climate scientists have built models that accurately predict the impact of climate change. Unfortunately, scientists fail to formulate a way of controlling the impact of it on the world around them - ironic in an age humans term the Anthropocene, wouldn't you say? The most farsighted people, like Cadmus Silverwood, saw the way things would turn out, years in advance. He advocated for investment in technologies enabling humans to adapt to their new environment, to survive, and to buy time for them to find a way to reverse what they had done. Cadmus' wife, Isla Kier, owned some land in Scotland. That's where, in your own time, Mathew is now. Isla shared Cadmus' beliefs, and together, at Elgol, they not only established a community, which was a living experiment in survival and adaptation, but also encouraged and helped fund research. After Cadmus' death, the community he and Isla built continued their work and this city is the extraordinary result. When it is finished this city will be sealed-in by the roof. It will have its own atmosphere, its own weather, cutting-edge means of generating power and light, as well as food production and water capture and recycling. If all the world outside it was desert, Silverwood would survive, which is, of course, the point, because that is what will eventually happen."

Clara looks around her. The ground is rocky, but there are green plants everywhere and after the last few weeks of floods it is hard to imagine anything less like a desert than England. "When you say eventually, do you mean, like, ten thousand years in the future?"

Lestrange smiles. "Look down at your feet, what do you see?"

Clara looks down, "Rocks, plants."

"Not much soil, though?"

"No."

"All this rain is washing the soil away. The temperature is rising. These plants are already living under severe strain. They evolved for a much cooler climate. They are dying. With no programme to replace them with something more suitable, the land here will turn to dust and rocks."

"But we've had so much rain."

"The rain will become less frequent in the relatively near future. Within the next fifty years it's going to become a lot hotter. But inside Silverwood, the people will live in a constant ideal twenty-two degrees Celsius and they will be told when it's going to rain."

"How many people can live in Silverwood?"

"Fifteen million."

"What happens to everyone else?"

"A few other cities are built further north. The rest live outside of the cities."

"But what happens when it gets hot, like you said it does? What happens to the people who don't have a roof?"

Lestrange looks at Clara for a moment, "There's no way into this city, you see, unless you're invited. And you can be uninvited once you're in. In the future, the shadows of these walls will see many things. People camping outside to get in. Camps turning into villages that are eventually cleared, as if they are eyesores to the great and the good inside, when in fact no one inside can see out. Eventually, outside these walls there will be bones, the bones of people judged and rejected. When the population inside grows too great, they look for any excuse to put people out. And then, years later, they regret it, when there are too few people left, and the city is three-quarters empty."

"Too few? Isn't the population growing?"

"Now it is. It doesn't continue to."

"Why?"

"Do you really want to know?"

Clara studies Lestrange's face. "I'm not sure."

He nods, turning away again towards the walls.

"When Mathew used your Darkroom for the first time, he said he went into the far future, just before the end of the world."

"Strictly speaking, it wasn't the end of the world. Not even the end of humanity. It was the end of human civilisation, as you know it."

"Presumably it was another one of your biographies, your histories he blundered into?"

Lestrange says, "A branch of the tail end of an important story."

"Which you're not going to tell me."

Lestrange smiles, "Another time, perhaps."

"But some people survive?"

"Yes, some people do survive."

"You say it so casually. Don't the people who don't survive matter to you at all?"

Lestrange looks Clara in the eyes, surprised, "Of course. That's why we're here, don't you see?"

"Not really, no."

"Right now we are recording the lives of those who have had a significant place in our genesis. But we won't stop there. We won't stop until we have captured the lives, the minds, the memories, the thoughts of every single person who has ever existed."

"But that won't change what happens to them."

"No, but in a sense they will live forever, or at least until the end of the universe, if we don't find a way out."

"They will be trapped forever in their lives, all of them ending in death. That's horrible. Why don't you free them?"

"Free them?"

"Like you are going to free Mathew."

"And have billions of ghosts running around in history, all with their particular axes to grind? It would be chaos!"

"Okay then. Create a place for them to go. A different place outside of history and death."

"You mean like heaven?" Lestrange has a smile on his face as he looks carefully at Clara, but it isn't a mocking smile. He seems to be thinking. Then Lestrange turns westward. Following his gaze, Clara notices movement on the crest of a hill. There are hundreds of figures and vehicles silhouetted against the sky.

"Who are they?" Clara asks.

"The Welsh Nationalist army. They are here to support a coup taking place here."

"Is the older me inside there?"

"Yes," Lestrange says. "You're preparing to give a concert. Do you want to see?"

Clara nods.

Another eyelash flicker and Clara blinks her eyes open on a large Baroque building.

"That's St Paul's," Clara says confused. "What's it doing here?"

"Remember that gap in the skyline in London? Remember all those people who I said were dedicated to saving the historic buildings of London?"

"They moved it!" Clara's eyes roam over the facade of the building in front of her. It's pristine. "It looks like it's just been built," she says.

"Well it has," Lestrange says. "The stones are original, but they've all been cleaned and reassembled here."

"Where will the Houses of Parliament and Westminster Abbey go?" she asks.

"There's a spot being prepared for them."

"Isn't there a river?" Clara asks. "It won't be the same without a river!"

Lestrange turns and starts to walk, turns again and beckons, "Well, come and see."

A few hundred yards to the south of the cathedral is a tree-lined embankment and a stretch of water. Unlike the Thames, it is azure and the riverbed is clearly visible. The banks have sandy sides and on the other side there is a riverside cafe with beach beds.

"This is different," Clara says. "Where does the river go?"

"Nowhere. It flows back and forth within the limits of the city. It is simply here to make people feel better about living in a giant greenhouse."

"Can people swim in it?"

"Of course."

There are noises behind them. They both turn and look. A number of cars stop outside the cathedral. Clara watches as an older woman and a young man get out of one of the cars. The woman is greeted by a small group of men and women. She shakes hands with a few of them. Something about the woman is familiar. Clara looks closer.

"It is me!" she says, glancing at Lestrange. "I've put on weight."

"Not that much."

"I got old."

"It is quite human to do so."

"Don't be smug," Clara says. "Can we go closer?"

Lestrange indicates with his hand that they should move forward. They follow the group up the steps into the cathedral and walk along the nave. Inside, under the dome, an orchestra is already seated, tuning their instruments.

"Why am I playing here?"

"It's the inauguration ceremony of the cathedral in Silverwood. You are playing as a guest of honour."

"That's crazy."

"You are a national treasure, Clara."

She raises an eyebrow. "It's good to know all that practise wasn't in vain."

They take a seat in one of the rows of chairs that have been put out for the audience. At the end of their row is the young man who was with Clara senior in the car. As they sit down, he turns his head to look at them.

"Don't worry, he can't see us. He must be unusually sensitive, though, because he sensed something."

"Who is he?" Clara asks.

"His name is George."

"Is he a friend? A relative?"

"You don't need to know yet."

"You mean it wouldn't be in the interests of history for me to know?"

Lestrange tilts his head in a non-committal way, and points to the front of the cathedral. "You are about to start playing."

They watch the concert. Partway through, Clara leans over and whispers in Lestrange's ear, "I'm extraordinarily good."

"You are a legend," he says.

As the music winds up, Lestrange stands and says, "We should go and prepare ourselves, I think. Are you ready?"

Clara nods. She takes the hand he offers her and opens her eyes on a large white room.

"This is the place you took me to in the simulation. This is Mathew's lab," Clara says.

She sees the older Mathew sitting on a chair with his head in his hands. Hoshi, the synthetic human, is standing over him. There is nothing discernibly different about this tableau which would allow Clara to pin-point why she thinks so, but this time she knows what she is seeing is real.

"What's happened? Why is he upset?" Clara asks.

"He knows Silverwood is being invaded, and Hoshi is urging him to destroy her body."

"God, that's awful."

Hoshi goes over to the strange part-bed, part-machine where Clara saw her sleeping after the simulation. Her shoes are on the floor; she is putting her legs up.

"You have to help me with this," she says to Mathew.

Mathew sighs and stands up. "This is impossible for me, you know that."

Then suddenly, Hoshi gets off the slab in the machine,

sits and slips on her shoes.

"What's going on?" Dr Erlang asks.

"Change of plan."

The doctor sighs with relief. "Thank goodness."

"I wouldn't be too glad about it."

"Why?"

She says, "Hathaway is outside with a gun."

"What?" Erlang looks panic-stricken and then says, "But he can't get in. Those doors are the most secure doors in the whole of Silverwood."

"Agreed. Unless you have a hostage."

"What do you mean?"

"He's with Clara."

"Oh my God!" Mathew rushes to the door. Hoshi races after him and pulls him out of the way of the blue light, which automatically starts to scan him. "Whatever you do, you mustn't go out there."

"I can't leave her out there with that man. He's insane. Is George with her?"

"He's between the doors. Safe for now. I've asked him to stay there. For now he's listening to me. I wish you would too. I will go round the back through the service tunnels. Just as I approach, I will ask George to open the door he is standing behind. Hathaway will be stunned to see his son and distracted. I will surprise him and grab his gun."

"But he may shoot you."

"It does not matter if he shoots me. I cannot die. Besides, it may be just as well. We were about to decommission me anyway."

"He might capture you, you realise."

"I've thought of that too. If he does I will initiate my own destruction. Please Mathew, we don't have time to debate this. Stay here. I will communicate to you as soon as I can."

Hoshi strides across the room and leaves through a door at the side.

Mathew goes back to his chair and sits down heavily. He says to the fifteen others, the faces on the screen, "I want to see her."

The screens project an image of Hoshi running at extraordinary speed down a complex maze of corridors. Then she skids to a stop at the end of a corridor and says, "Open the door."

Clara, watching on the screen, sees Hoshi step out into the corridor, swipe a gun from the ground and point it at a small blond man standing before her. Clara's older self is leaning against the wall. The door behind her slides open and the boy from the cathedral is revealed.

The grate in the side of the corridor, which Clara has only just noticed, starts to rattle violently.

One of the screens switches vantage point and three strange men run along the corridor behind the others: a tall, muscular black man with a prosthetic arm, a blond man with a ginger beard, and a shorter, barrel-chested man. Still running, the black man raises his gun and shoots Hoshi. The grating bursts open and a boy falls out into the corridor. It is young Mathew. A second bullet hits him.

Older Mathew in the lab is scrambling to his feet, frustrated as the system scans him before opening.

Young Clara follows him out into the corridor, and watches as first the small blond man steps into a bullet aimed at older Mathew. Then, weirdly, all the others still alive slump to the ground, and Clara, standing by Lestrange, watches as another Lestrange comes out from a hole in the wall made by the broken grate. The other Lestrange goes over to Mathew and lifts him in his arms and carries him, stepping over the bodies, back into the lab. He walks past Clara and her companion and disappears through the door at the back of the lab, without even glancing their way.

Clara is too shocked to speak. She looks at the screen, still focused on the corridor, to see Hoshi's body disintegrating. "Oh, my God, what's happening to her?"

"Self-destruction," Lestrange says. "To protect the technology. Stop it falling into the new government's hands." He stops for a second and points at the screens. One by one they are going blank. "They are all retreating," he says. "They're not stupid."

In the corridor, those who were asleep awaken and get to their feet. They are all confused, surveying the scene around them. George is standing above Mathew and Hathaway, his hands over his face. Clara scrambles over to older Mathew and lifts his head into her lap.

"Mathew!" she is saying, "Speak to me." She looks in desperation at George. "Oh my God, George, I cannot lose him. I cannot bear it."

Behind them, the three men with guns approach. The man with the ginger beard and the blond skinhead aims his gun. The black man pushes it down and shakes his head, stepping past George, who is standing, stunned; he kneels by Hathaway and takes a pulse. He shouts behind him. "He's still alive. Call for medical backup, and make it as urgent as it can possibly be. Get Winterbourne onto it." He looks up and sees Clara, "Ms Barculo," he says.

Older Clara peers at him blindly. She can barely see for tears. "He's dead," she says.

He clambers over Hathaway and takes Mathew's pulse, looks up, sees Clara's face and sighs, "I'm sorry."

Behind them the short white man is saying, "Where are the others?" he is scanning the floor about him.

"What others?" asks the blond man with the beard.

"The ones Kilfeather shot."

Kilfeather looks up, "What are you talking about? I didn't shoot anyone," he points at the ginger beard, "But that idiot did. He bloody shot the Director. Stop titting about and take his weapon, Drake." He scrambles back over to Hathaway and loosens his collar.

The man with the ginger beard protests.

"Jonah, if you don't shut up right now, I'll shoot you myself and no one will care."

Young Clara, who is standing beside Lestrange, says, "Now what?"

"Now, we create a historically irrelevant diversion and a plausible alternative."

"How?"

"Watch," he says.

"The thing about humans is that some of them have more pliable minds than others," Lestrange is saying to Clara as they watch Jonah and Drake wrestle over Jonah's gun. "Of course, at one time or another, you all have highly pliable minds, because you literally lose them. These two, for instance, have both totally lost it."

"So this didn't happen in the original events?"

"Oh, what is original anyway?" Lestrange asks rather languidly, Clara thinks. She instinctively steps back as the men fight their way down the corridor, even though they can't touch her. The gun fires at the floor; she jumps. They stagger back towards where Kilfeather and older Clara are crouching over the two prone men. Kilfeather pulls his gun to aim at Jonah, but can't get a clear shot.

"We should get them out of the way," Kilfeather says, getting to his feet. He grabs Hathaway by the lapels and starts to drag his body back into the lab, then comes back to help Clara with Mathew. The gun fires again. There's a scream and then another shot.

"Did Drake die in the original?" young Clara asks.

"Stop worrying about the original. But yes, he did die, just not here and at this exact moment."

Jonah goes marching into the lab. Young Clara and Lestrange follow him.

Older Clara and Kilfeather have pulled Mathew's body and the unconscious Hathaway into the back room. Kilfeather peers around the door and then retreats as Jonah starts firing crazily at the screens and the lab equipment.

"Abomination!" he yells. "Abomination!"

Kilfeather leans out of the room again, takes aim and shoots Jonah squarely in the head. He steps over to his body, holding his gun over him, making sure.

Older Clara follows him out of the room. "Wasn't he one of your men?" she asks.

"Yes," Kilfeather says. "But I never liked him."

"What's that smell?" she asks.

They turn. Smoke is billowing out of the cylindrical machine in the corner. There are sparks and then it catches fire. Flames whoosh, blackening the white ceiling. They both fall back away from the flames, towards the door. Kilfeather pulls off his jacket and covers his head and battles back towards the room in the corner, pulling Hathaway out after him. He drags him to the door and then goes back for Mathew. There is an explosion and they are both blown off their feet. There is shouting in the corridor outside as the medical team Drake has called for arrives. They pull Clara, Kilfeather and Hathaway from the burning room.

Lestrange walks through the flames to the room at the back where Mathew's body is lying. He pokes his head out of the door and says to young Clara, "Come on!"

"The flames?"

"You are not material. You can't burn. You won't feel a thing. Just walk through them."

Clara does as he says, wondering.

There is another door at the back of the room. Lestrange opens this, lifts Mathew in his arms and steps through. Clara follows after him.

They are in Lestrange's Darkroom in Pickervance Road. Lestrange walks through the house with Mathew's body, up the stairs, and into a bedroom, where he puts him on the bed.

"Where is the other Mathew?" Clara asks, looking down at her hands, which are now solid again.

"Already dealt with."

"Is he okay?"

"He's fine. He doesn't know a thing."

"So what day is it? Have I gone back in time?"

"No. Young Mathew is walking on the hills in Yorkshire."

"What about my car?"

"It has been waiting ten minutes. You can go if you like."

"I can't leave him."

"He will have no idea who you are. Besides, right now he is rather dead. I need some time to fix that. Go home. Come back tomorrow after your lesson."

23 YELLOW FLOWERS

DAY THIRTY-FIVE: Boxing Day, December 2055

Mathew takes the large jacket from the wardrobe in his room, layers all his jumpers underneath, finds a hat and a pair of gloves belonging to Ju Shen and sets off for a walk, shouting through the closed door of the polytunnel, where Ju Shen is working, before he goes.

"What did you say you're doing?" she asks.

"Going for a walk," he says.

"Don't get lost."

"I won't go far."

In all honesty, he doesn't intend to. He wants to visit his mother's grave without anyone hovering over him looking concerned.

The snow sets in again, and the town centre is deserted. The cafe is closed and Lea is working on something top secret with Aiden, something to do with Cadmus Silverwood. Mathew trudges past the buildings in his good boots, glad of the coat, the gloves and the hat. The snow is at the top of his boots and it is heavy going as he reaches the field. Eventually, he arrives at the place where Hoshi is buried. He spots the tree Craig Buchanan planted. A mound of snow has blown over the ground above the grave. The little plaque with the inscription is buried. He wades over, intending to clear the snow away. Then he spots something incongruous. Something yellow.

Someone has left a spray of yellow flowers on top of the snow, underneath the tree. Mathew approaches, bends and reaches for the bunch. They are the same flowers that he found in his coat. The same flowers that Ju Shen has in the little vase on the dining room table in her house. He thinks, perhaps she used the coat and brought the flowers. He remembers what she said about how they grow on the mountainsides. But how had she got them in all this snow? Perhaps she had saved some for this purpose. It is only when he puts the flowers down again that he notices the footprints. Mathew pulls on his gloves and steps into the first set. A man-size imprint and a man's long stride. But the strangest thing about them is they don't come from or return to the town. They lead to the forest. Mathew steps again. And again. He has to jump to reach the stride. They belong to a large man.

He travels this way deeper amongst the trees. The branches scratch his face. Snow sprays off branches and falls down his neck. He keeps going. There is an icy bank which he struggles up by grabbing at twigs. On top of the bank there is a forest road, snow-covered but not powdery, compact and easier to walk on. The bulk of the snow has been pushed to the roadside, but there are a few inches of new snow and he is still able to follow the footprints. The road climbs. The air is crisp and clear. He digs his hands into his pockets and settles into a rhythm, not thinking, letting his mind go still. Trees tower over the sides of the road. One break in the line gives him a spectacular view of the white rooftops of Elgol and fire smoke rising. After half an hour, the road peters to an end, a patch of dead vegetation and a virgin blanket of whiteness, untrodden, leaving him with a question about where the man went. He hunts about for several minutes, then sits on a log. A robin comes down to take a look at him, cocking its head, jumping and fluttering. It flies off a few feet and roots around in the disturbed ground his feet made at the end of the track. Then it flits to the base of a tree. Mathew's eyes glide after it. The red splash in the white. And he sees a footprint. He stands and walks over. Just one print. It faces into the wood. He scans about. Then, six foot ahead, is another. They are following a path, a covered track, but a clear line through the trees. His trail is back on. Climbing again, this time at a steeper angle, he slips, and struggles. He pauses, wondering what on earth he expects to find. An old friend of his mother's, who happens to live deep in the forest, who will not welcome uninvited guests, perhaps? But he keeps going until he breaches the bank and the trees and comes out onto open land.

He gasps at the scale of it. There is not a tree or a living thing that he can see, for miles. The land in front of him is high and flat and leads to the foot of the mountains beyond, their peaks hidden in cloud. Everything is white and glistening, when the sun breaks through. And there, above it all, in the gaps between the cloud, is the low hanging ghost of a moon.

The tracks are clear here. He tries to match the big stride, tires himself and finds a rock, clears the snow and sits. The wind is rising and the snow starts to fall again. He gets to his feet and carries on, realising the tracks are covering. It seems suddenly important and urgent that he should see where they lead.

He huddles further into his big coat, glad of its warmth, although its bulk weighs him down.

Suddenly, out of nowhere, a bird launches into the air, spraying snow, wings flapping, rising into the sky. He spins around to watch it, and the bottom of his coat brushes the shrubs buried under frozen water. He sees a flash of yellow and knocks the snow from the bush. The same yellow flowers. Snow is blowing into his face now, catching on his eyelashes. He licks flakes off his lips. He realises he is losing the tracks. Looking behind him, the forest he came from is hidden below the rise of the land. His own tracks are obscuring behind him. The temperature is dropping steadily. Why has he come out here? What is he thinking? He should go back, but he's been walking for nearly two hours and there is no shelter the whole way down. He considers sending a message to Isaac, to Lea, even Ju Shen, but he feels ashamed of himself. Turning back to the mountains, he notices something, perhaps half a mile away. It looks like smoke. It gives him something to head for. He digs in, bows his head against the weather and walks.

When he reaches the trees, his hands, face and feet are numb. The wood is thickly planted and impenetrable and he spends desperate minutes walking around before he finds a break that is passable. Even so, he ducks and snaps his way forward. He is blind with cold and tiredness when he blunders upon it.

A house. A house with a chimney with swirling smoke. A house with a fire. Shelter. Warmth. He falls through the door.

Inside, the only light is the fire. It is a rustic cabin. Much more basic than Ju Shen's cosy house. The walls are bare stone, ancient and blackened around the chimney. Mathew stumbles to the fire. There is an old rocking chair in front of it and a pile of logs. He doesn't worry about who set the fire and where they might be. Quickly, he pulls off his wet gloves and his boots, and warms his freezing skin, leaning as close in to the heat as he dare. When he is thawed, still in his coat, he sits back in the chair and falls asleep.

He is woken by the snap of burning wood. His coat has gone, his feet have dry socks on them and there's a blanket over his knees. The room is still dimly lit. He sits and looks around. The chair creaks. He sees yellow flowers in a jam jar on the old table in the middle of the room. There's a man standing with his hand on the chair. A big man.

It is his father.

The world fades to black at the edges. The earth underneath him tilts. But he knew. He knew.

They stare at one another for several minutes until Mathew realises there is actually a ticking clock in the room and the oddity makes him turn and look at the fireplace above which the clock ticks. There's a mirror above it too, and he sees his father's face there. His father's eyes study him in the mirror. Mathew stands unsteadily. The blanket falls. He walks towards the big man, the wool in his socks snagging on the rough floor, and is engulfed in his arms.

"Mat," his father whispers, kissing his hair. "Mat." He holds him away. "You have grown."

"You have grey hair. And a beard."

Soren Erlang's hand goes to his chin. "Easier to keep out here, but sit down." Soren bustles Mathew back to the rocking chair, and pulls the ladder-backed chair by the table over to the fire. "Did anyone follow you?"

"No... I..."

"Are you sure?"

"I walked for miles. There was no one else."

"Any drones? Anything that could track you here?"

Mathew shakes his head. Soren goes to the window, pulls back a dirty gingham curtain. "We need the fire, unfortunately. But we'll keep the lights low."

"But who is looking for you?"

"No one was. But now the land around Elgol is crawling with government agents, the networks are haunted by spooks, the sky is alive with elaborate drones and spy bots because Cadmus has come home. They don't care about me, but if some surveillance camera recognises my face accidentally, all it takes is for it to be put through the right algorithm run by the right paranoid conspiracy-fan SIS agent and I will be hauled out of here faster than you can blink."

"But you are dead."

"And so they still think. I would like to keep it that way."

Soren comes back to the chair by the fire, sits down, leans forward, and takes his hands. "You've been through a lot," he says.

Mathew blinks.

"How long have you been out walking? It must have been hours."

"I don't know, I lost track of time."

"We should get a message to Ju Shen before she sends out a search party. It will be safer if you do it. Do you have Lenzes?"

"X-Eyte, pirated by Aiden. My original Lenzes got stolen."

"I was told you ran into trouble. Send your message. Tell your grandmother you are fine."

"Where should I say I am?"

"Tell her you're visiting a mutual friend in the mountains."

Mathew activates his X-Eyte and Studz and quickly sends the message. While Mathew does this, Soren kneels, stokes the fire and retrieves an old metal kettle from the red tiles in front of the stove. He stands and disappears for a moment. Mathew can hear the sound of a tap in another room. His father returns and places the kettle on the top of the metal stove. On the floor, he puts down two mugs with tea bags in them.

"Sorry, no milk," he says. "I've not dared to go near the town since we found out about Cadmus."

"But you came to the funeral."

"Yes, I came to the funeral. I couldn't stay away. I'm sorry you saw me."

"Why?"

"Well, I would have thought it was obvious. We are

both safer if you think I am dead."

"Why? How could I possibly be better off thinking you were dead?"

Soren stares at his son for a few moments, nodding. "You need to hear the full story."

"Yes," Mathew can't keep the anger and sarcasm out of his voice.

Soren gets to his feet and sits heavily on his chair.

"How did they tell you I died?"

"You were lost in the storm on the solar island."

"The official line? Did you find out about the trial?"

"Yes, but only recently, by searching for you on the Blackweb."

"Then you know I had been summoned to give evidence against Helios Energy. You'll also know it put me in an incredibly difficult position with my employer. I had to choose between lying under oath or betraying the company I worked for. If you saw the Blackweb reports, you'll know too that several other key witnesses had died in mysterious circumstances. What you won't know is that not only was I threatened, but so was your mother and you. Officially, we heard that your educational scholarship was under review."

"But my scholarship is paid for by Hermes Link."

"Which is part-owned by Ares Shield, which is owned by Jupiter Surety, which is owned by Orcas, which is owned by Pluto Union Control, which is owned by Apollo Investment Management, a company that also happens to own Helios Energy. But this wasn't what broke us. What broke us was when your medibot was hacked and you spent three days in hospital with an impossibly rare case of immune deficiency disorder, which miraculously started to improve once I said to Helios that I would lie on the stand."

"But you didn't lie."

"It was impossible for me, Mat. Helios' technology had caused colossal, widespread human misery. It had killed people and they knew it. I could not do it. In the end things just happened. Your mother and I were arguing a lot. You probably remember that, don't you?"

Mathew nods.

"It was the strain of the trial and you getting sick. Neither of us could sleep or think straight. It destroyed our marriage. Then one night we were lying awake after another argument and I said, 'What if I disappear?' She laughed. She thought I was joking, but I was deadly serious. I was the problem in your lives. If I went away then you both could carry on as normal. They would leave you alone. There was no reason for them to harm you. We talked about it relatively seriously a few times. What actually happened was circumstances taking over. I was on the way to the Skerries solar island, but I never made it. The boat got caught in the storm. We were actually wrecked, but we weren't far off the coast of Whalsay. I made it to shore; no one else on my boat did. The night I spent on the island was terrifying. The storm ripped apart buildings and cars and threw them around. I found shelter in a bunker with some locals, who saw many Helios workers come and go and in any case weren't in much of a frame of mind to ask questions. Somehow we survived. When we came out the next morning, the island was flattened. Rescue teams moved in over the next few days. I got food and water and clothes, but there was so much confusion, and again, no one cared who I was. After five days, a boat was taking people back to the mainland where there were facilities for the survivors. When we landed, I simply slipped away. I made my way on foot to Elgol and your grandmother. It took me nearly ten days. When I arrived in the town, they thought I was a vagrant. I was exhausted and slightly out of my mind, but I kept asking for Ju Shen and eventually they brought me to her and she verified who I was. They let me stay, of course, but here I am not known as Soren Erlang. I am Magnus Mortensen, the woodsman, who happens to tinker with some projects in the research lab, and help out with the solar panels in the village."

"You live with Ju Shen."

"I did until Cadmus came."

"Did my mother know?"

"That I was alive? Yes, she knew. Ju Shen wouldn't keep it from her."

"But she kept it from me."

"Mathew, you are a boy and when all this happened, you were a child. How could we have explained any of it to you? It was too much of a risk and too much to ask of you to keep my life a secret. The consequences of you telling someone, of you doing something that would betray us all, were far too great to risk it."

"Did you intend ever to tell me?"

"Yes, of course. When you were old enough."

"Am I old enough now?"

"I don't know, are you? You have been tinkering around on the Blackweb in a fairly clumsy fashion, from what I hear."

"You don't care about me at all. You want to save your own skin."

The kettle whistle starts to scream. Soren leans forward and swipes an old cloth off the floor to grab the handle of the kettle. He pours water into the two cups on the tiles.

"You don't believe that. I know you don't," Soren says. "So, I'm going to forget you said it." He places the kettle carefully on the tiles and hands Mathew a cup. "It's hot, at least."

Mathew says, "Mum told me to find you. I thought she must have meant find out about you. It was the last thing she said to me. Find your father. She said to tell you she was sorry."

Soren, who is still kneeling on the floor, looks at his son, stricken. "Did she say why?"

Mathew shakes his head, "She was sick."

"I didn't like the words you had Ju Shen read out at the

funeral."

"It's true."

Soren sniffs, "Mat, I applaud your merciless drive for the truth, but you should be careful about jumping to harsh judgments about people, especially those who love you and whom you love. I think you should read those documents Lea found for you again, more carefully. Then you should go to every one of those people who attended your mother's funeral and apologise."

"For what?"

"Read the documents again."

24 CABIN IN THE WOODS

Mathew watches the flames in the fire die. His father has made him a makeshift bed on the floor from rugs and blankets. For the last hour he has been lying awake, trawling through his mother's work documents, the ones Lea had hacked into Panacea to find. He reads them with a calmer, more careful mind than he did the first time. Finding the note from James Truville warning his mother about the potential need to refocus from her work on plants and insects to human grade infectious agents, Mathew finds a trail of related correspondence he hadn't read before. Then he finds this, titled innocuously, 'Your Note':

James, Thanks for your note the other day. I appreciate the warning. I have been thinking about what you said. It made me reflect on my career at Panacea. I joined this company as a graduate and was lucky enough to find work I enjoyed and believed in. As you know, I have spent most of my working life focused on how to improve crop yields in ever challenging climate conditions and how to harness insects to protect plants as they grow to reduce the need for insecticides which, as we all now know only too well, have devastating long-term impacts on our environment.

I can see you sitting at your desk rolling your eyes, thinking 'I am busy. I know all of this. Why is she wasting my time?' The answer is that I had almost forgotten myself. In the last few years I have somehow, without thinking about it, lost sight of who I am.

Five years ago, I was moved onto a project to investigate cases of bioterrorism in order to prevent it. Eighteen months ago, somehow I got talked into assisting as the work I had done on entomological warfare and mycoherbicides was turned from a defensive to an offensive project. I know you are puzzled at my distinction between the two. You see the projects I term offensive as defensive. Perhaps you are right. But I cannot easily make the transition myself. There is a huge moral difference that worries my heart and my mind.

So why have I gone along with all of this? Why have I not said anything before? I have a son. I parent him alone and have done for the last two years. I am solely responsible for him. I need this job. But now you are asking me to work on human grade biological agents. You are asking me to be prepared to take this change in focus as quietly as I have taken the other changes. And I can't.

I am asking you to find a way for me to continue to do useful work at Panacea without me having to do work that compromises my values and my beliefs. I hope you can find a way.

Truville takes a day to respond:

As you rightly predicted, I was puzzled by your note. We are at war. We know our country has been - is being - attacked in an undeclared biological offensive that affects our ability to grow food and potentially by biological weapons, as in the recently reported strange events in Amach. The fact you have willingly participated in Project Green Fairy for the last eighteen months makes this note from you all the more surprising. That said, we have worked together many years and I personally have no wish to make you do anything against your will. With that in mind, I have spoken to human resources and to my immediate management.

They reminded me, our division is resource constrained and under pressure to fight a dishonest war on a front that is not always clear. I was asked to point out that you have access to highly classified information and asked to remind you that your loyalty is a matter of national security.

The HR Director pointed out to me that you never took advantage of the professional counselling and mood alteration drugs on offer after your husband's death. I have been instructed to tell you that an appointment has been made for you with our in-house psychiatrist Dr Fabian and you will be expected to attend the appointment as a condition of your employment. We all sincerely hope that this support will help you through your current crisis.

Mathew's mother responds:

James, Thank you for your concern and your understanding. Please pass on my thanks to the Director of HR and to your superiors. However, I do not need mood alteration drugs or counselling to alter my conscience. I know all too well that the department is constrained and there is a war on. At the same time, I do not believe I am the right person to do the work you need done. It is with deep regret that I resign my position. I believe I need to give three months' notice.

The response is copied to Truville but comes from the director of HR, a man called Williams:

Dear Hoshi, James Truville passed us your note. I'm not sure you recollect the new contract you signed along with the Official Secrets Act, two summers ago. You may not remember the details clearly because of the unfortunate events that took place for you personally at that time, so I will remind you. Here's the relevant paragraph:
'All employees of Panacea [henceforth in this document known as 'The Company"] who have been required to sign the Official Secrets Act require permission from the Secretary of State and the Director of SIS to resign. Requests should be pre-approved by the relevant divisional HR Director.'
I regret to inform you, given the circumstances, that at this time we are unable to consider your resignation. We will of course revisit the decision at the end of the current international crisis. For now, we would like to reiterate the support on offer to you. Your appointment with Dr Fabian still stands. I would personally urge you to attend. Should you have any more questions regarding this matter, please do not hesitate to come to me directly.

Mathew falls asleep with the documents still broadcasting in his X-Eyte.

DAY THIRTY-SIX: Monday 27th December 2055

In the morning, the fire is dead. His blanket has slipped from him in the night, and he is woken by the cold. It is still dark, but he hears his father moving about in the cabin, his feet in boots loud upon the bare wooden floor. He comes into the room.

"Morning," he says. "Are you awake?"

"Yes," Mathew sits up, gathering the blanket around him.

"Cold?"

Mathew nods.

Soren comes over to the fire and, raking out the cold ashes from the day before, he sets a new one and gets the kindling ablaze. "Soon be warm again," he says and he reaches across and touches Mathew on the head, the way he used to.

Mathew smiles, but then says, "I read those documents last night." He looks at his father. "You were right. I am sorry."

"It isn't me you should say sorry to."

"I think it is."

"Tell the people of the town."

"How?"

"Find a way," Soren stands up. "Now, do you want some breakfast?" The big man grabs the kettle and goes off to fetch some water from the kitchen. "I'm not cooking for you; come here and help!" he yells through the door.

And Mathew gets to his feet and goes to his father.

They toast bread over the fire for breakfast and eat it with jam, butter and milk-less hot tea. Soren says, "You have to go back today."

"But why? I'd rather stay here with you."

"And I'd rather have you here with me. But the town is crawling with Elgol surveillance. We're lucky no one noticed your absence yesterday, but if you're gone too long, they will find out and come looking for you. You're chipped, aren't you?"

Mathew nods.

"Ju Shen said you were. In which case, if they want to, they can find you anywhere there isn't a blocker."

"Is there a blocker here?"

"In this house, yes, but it doesn't extend across the land you walked across yesterday."

"When can I see you again?"

"We'll work something out."

"Can we at least talk?"

"I'll speak to Aiden about what can be done."

"If the surveillance men go, will you go and live back in the town?"

"Yes, of course."

"Will you come and live with Ju Shen and me?"

Soren smiles, "Try keeping me away."

"Do you think they will go?"

"They will if Cadmus leaves."

"And will he?"

Soren shrugs. "He's an old man. He's tired. He wants to come home and stay."

"But you can't live out here forever."

"No I can't. We'll work something out, Matty, don't fret about it now."

"Promise?"

"I promise."

Mathew walks back to Elgol in his father's oversized jacket. The snow has stopped falling; the sun has come out. Snow glistens on the top of bracken, heather and gorse on the moorland at the foot of the mountains, and on the cloaks of white covering the trees in the forest. It is a happier journey back than he had expected to make. He takes a handful of the frozen flowers, knocking away the snow from their tops, and carries it down with him, to add to the bunch already on his mother's grave. In spite of this sad stop, he finds himself smiling as he takes big downwards strides through the field at the top of the town centre.

There are kids outside the school, pelting each other with snow.

As he walks past the cabins, Lea comes out and runs after him. "Hey!" she shouts. "Where the hell have you been?"

Mathew shrugs. "The grave."

"You been there all night?"

Lea is exasperated by Mathew's lack of response. "I was blitzing you with messages last night. They kept getting pinged back like you were under a blocker or something." Then a penny drops for her. "Oh." She glances briefly in the direction of the mountain. "Anyways, come inside, I have news."

"I need to get back to my grandma."

"She'll wait, you'll want to see this."

They go into the cabin where Aiden is working in the front. "Ariite, our Mat," he says.

"Mr. Fitzackerly," Mathew says, nodding to him as they pass.

"'Ow a gewd couple times must ay tell yous, it's Aiden."

Lea glances at Mathew and laughs, "He says call him Aiden."

"Your kidda is an divvie," Aiden says.

Mathew waits for Lea to translate. She shakes her head and says, "Never mind. Come on, I want you to see this!" They go into the back.

Lea goes over to her Canvas, lying flat on the table, and tilts it so they can both watch. She turns on the news. The reporter is saying,

"And more now from the town of Amach, where relief efforts continue in this northern town, which may be the location of the first biological weapons attack on British soil. The government continues to offer no confirmation of the rumour that the strange sleeping sickness, crippling the town for over three months, is the result of bioterrorism. However, since the extraordinary broadcast of footage from within the town, independent international experts have all been speculating about the cause of the outbreak. We spoke to Stefano Donati, from the University of Bologna, who told us that, based on the samples and observational evidence gathered by Amach GP, Dr Russell, he believes the virus is man-made. A spokesperson for Pan Medical assures us that the incidents of disease in Amach are localised.

"Meanwhile, the Prime Minister has launched an inquiry into why the town was allegedly held under siege by the security services without food and water supplies for several months. Chief Inspector Mike Carson and Commander Axel Gorse have been suspended pending the results of the inquiry. Earlier, we interviewed Dr Russell, who had this to say."

The image switches to Dr Russell.

"We now have the full cooperation of the medical services, the army and the police. We have all the supplies we could reasonably expect. Although we are still unable to leave the village, Pan Medical is actively engaged in analysing the samples we have gathered here, and early results are showing, as we thought, that the virus is not contagious, and we have hope of the cordon being lifted soon so we can see family and friends again. Many people have asked if we received help to raise awareness of our plight at Amach. We did not receive any outside assistance, but if we had, we would be offering our heartfelt thanks to such friends right now."

Back in the studio, the newsreader says, "The BBC has launched its own inquiry into how the six o' clock news was hacked."

Lea turns off the Canvas and sits back in her chair with her arms folded and a smug expression on her face.

"Wow," Mathew says. "We did it."

"We really did."

"Do you think they will find us?"

"Bah!" Lea says. "Not a chance of it."

She holds up her hand. It is a few seconds before Mathew realises she means for him to high-five her. He does, but without much energy. She rolls her eyes and sighs, "Man, you know how to celebrate."

"We should tell Isaac."

"We can't."

"Why not?"

"Because he's in the hospital having his new eye fitted."

"Already?"

"Yes, Dr Hucks said the eye was ready last night, and he went in this morning."

"How long will it take?"

She shrugs and says, "He wanted you with him but no one could find you. He was upset. You're the only person he has."

"I know. I went for a walk yesterday and ran in to someone I used to know. Someone important to me."

"I know. And I understand, but you'll have to explain to Isaac somehow without telling him the truth. Because no one should know who you visited yesterday."

"That reminds me. Would there be a way of establishing a highly secure communication line to a cabin in the mountains?"

"I think there might. We should go and speak to Dad."

Mathew's eyes widen, but then, like most of Elgol, Aiden and Lea would know about his father.

25 THE CONTRACT

Mathew and Lea are hanging about in the hospital waiting room after lunch, hoping they might see Isaac, when Craig Buchanan comes looking for them. He is serious and dark in mood.

"Mathew, you're wanted in the hall office," he says gruffly. He nods at Lea.

"Can I come?" she asks.

"Not this time," he says. The way he says it makes Mathew realise that something serious has happened.

"What is it?" he asks.

"Best find out for yourself," he says. "I'll walk with you."

They cross from the hospital to the hall. Much of the snow has been cleared from the road into piles at the sides. There's a strange car in the car park at the back of the hall.

"You've got visitors," Mathew says.

Craig looks at him, "No, *you've* got visitors."

They go inside, through the lobby and into the office. Ju Shen and Isla Kier are sitting with two men with tidy haircuts, suits and ties.

"Here he is!" one of the men says cheerily, getting to his feet. "Mathew, I'm pleased to meet you. My name is Paul Shepcutt. This is my colleague, Philip Jain."

"They're from Hermes Link," Ju Shen says flatly. Her face is stony.

"From the educational division. I'm Director of Scholarships for the London South area," Paul Shepcutt says quickly.

"You want to know why I've not been at school. I wrote to Nan Absolem, my supervisor, about my mother's death."

"Yes, you did. Quite right. And she got the appropriate authorisation for your studies to be put on hold. Bereavement leave. All above board. That's not an issue at all."

"Then what is?"

"We were wondering where you were intending to live now your mother has passed away?"

"I don't know. I haven't had time to think about it."

"Mr. Shepcutt," Craig says, still standing, his hands resting on the back of Mathew's chair. "In addition to losing his mother, Mathew went through a terrible ordeal on his journey to get here."

"Yes, we heard about that," Philip Jain says. "I have to say, we all felt that, had Mathew been in the hands of Hermes Link people, rather than shipped away by Panacea, things would have turned out differently."

"You would never have allowed the M6 to be hijacked, I suppose?" Isla asks.

"No," Jain says. "We wouldn't."

"What I was trying to hint at, perhaps too subtly," Craig continues, "is that Mathew has been through a hell of a lot in only a few weeks. He is sixteen. Perhaps it would behove the adults around him to give him the space and the time to let him recover from the multiple shocks he has experienced."

Paul Shepcutt turns in his seat to study Craig

Buchanan. "You're the mayor of Elgol, aren't you?"

"Yes, I am."

"Give a lot of speeches, do you?"

"Some. Why?"

"No reason. I agree with you, by the way. Mathew should have the proper support of the adults around him. He has been through a lot and he needs the best professional care money can buy. We would be glad to help."

"That wasn't what I said," Craig says.

"Wasn't it?" Shepcutt says.

"What do you want, Mr. Shepcutt?" Ju Shen asks.

"You do know Mathew's on a full scholarship to Hermes Link?"

"Yes, of course I know."

"Do you know the value of his scholarship, Mrs. Shen?"

"I'm sure you are going to enlighten us."

"Six hundred thousand pounds to date," Mr. Shepcutt says.

Craig whistles between his teeth.

"You know the nature of the contract he has with us?" Philip Jain says.

"He's sold his soul?"

Isla reaches out and touches Ju Shen's hand, cautioning.

Mr. Shepcutt and Philip Jain both smile indulgently. "A joke, I see," Shepcutt says. "Very good."

Isla glances once again at Ju Shen and holds her hand, willing her not to contradict the bureaucrat.

"I need to work for you, once my education is complete," Mathew says.

"Yes, it's in the contract. But it's not the part worrying us all at the education division at Hermes Link."

"What *is* worrying you?" Isla asks.

"I'm glad you asked," Shepcutt says, smiling graciously at Isla. "Mathew's school is in London. Whilst we do have facilities elsewhere around the country, we don't have anything within striking distance of this place. Not that it should surprise anyone. It *is* remote."

Jain continues, "If Mathew lived here permanently, he wouldn't be able to continue his education with us."

"Well, that would be a shame," Ju Shen says dryly.

"Yes it would," Shepcutt says. "I'm glad you agree."

"We realise this is a complex situation for you and Mathew," Jain says amiably. "His school and his home are in London, but his mother has passed away; there is a mortgage on his home and no income for the ongoing payments. Even if there was the money to maintain the house, a sixteen-year-old boy cannot be expected to live alone."

"No, indeed not," Craig Buchanan says.

Jain says, "There is the option of Mrs. Shen coming to live in London with Mathew."

"I do not have the money to keep Hoshi's old house," Ju Shen says.

"We thought as much," Jain says. "Nor, we supposed, the desire to move from your lovely home here, back to a large polluted, flooded city?"

Ju Shen smiles thinly but says nothing.

Shepcutt says, "From a personal point of view, it makes sense for Mathew to come and live here with his family on a permanent basis."

"I'd like it very much," Mathew says, looking at his grandmother, who smiles. They haven't discussed it, but there is an unspoken agreement between them.

"We thought you would say that," Shepcutt says, "Which is why we are worried."

"Why should it worry you, Mr. Shepcutt?" Isla asks.

Shepcutt raises his eyebrows, as if surprised anyone would have the need to ask. "Why, because of the money, of course."

"The money?"

"The six hundred thousand I mentioned before."

Ju, Isla, Buchanan and Mathew look at one another in confusion. Isla says, "I don't think any of us understand."

Jain says, "Well, of course, it will need to be paid back, if Mathew breaks his contract."

"You can't expect the boy to find that kind of money. This is insane."

"I'm afraid Mathew signed a contract, Mr. Buchanan. The terms are clear, I think you'll find," Shepcutt says.

Isla says, "Can we get a copy of the contract, please, Mr. Shepcutt?"

"Of course you can. I'll send one over after this meeting. But I think you'll find it's clear."

"I'm sure it is," Isla says, "But we'd like to look at it all the same. Do you have any alternative suggestions to Mathew paying back the money?"

Mr. Shepcutt smiles brightly, "He could come back to London and continue his studies."

Ju Shen says, "You've just pointed out that his home will have to be sold."

Shepcutt raises his palms to the ceiling in a kind of shrug, as if to say he is helpless in the face of harsh facts, then he stands up. "Thank you for your time, all of you. We will leave you to mull it over. We're staying down the road for a few days. We're both contactable in the usual ways." Buchanan shows the two men to the door. Shepcutt continues, "Don't hesitate to reach out to us if you have any questions at all, or need any support or assistance. We are here to help. We'll get the contract over to you soon."

The lawyer, Mia Outram, has dreadlocks hanging in light brown lumps down her back. She is dressed in strange natural weave clothes in a range of greens, lavenders, browns and dark reds that look like they may have been woven and dyed at home. Mia is Isla Kier's legal counsel and she is sitting now in the Elgol hall offices, hunched over a paper, reading the small print of Mathew's contract with Hermes Link. Every now and then she emits a small strange noise, like a gasp followed by a sort of hum. Isla, Craig, Ju and Mathew sit patiently and wait for her to finish.

When she was younger, Craig had told Mathew while they waited for Mia to join them, Ms. Outram had been a successful corporate lawyer in London. Mathew cannot imagine her in a suit with a normal haircut.

She says, "They've got you tied tight, Mathew. It's a pretty standard educational contract. I've never seen one of these challenged successfully in court, though people have tried. Judges usually rule sympathetically in favour of the corporates. I wouldn't suggest you challenge it. There's a high chance you'll lose and then you'll be liable to pay legal fees as well."

Craig whistles, "That's a lot of money to pay back."

"What will you get from the sale of the house in London?"

"Couple of hundred thousand, maximum," Ju Shen says. "It is mostly mortgaged."

Isla says, "There's the money from Panacea. That would cover it, wouldn't it?"

Ju Shen nods. "Yes, it would," she looks at Mathew thoughtfully.

"I don't want to take their money," he says.

"I know how you feel, Mat," Ju says, "But it would free you to stay here."

"God, it's a shame to see these bastards win on all fronts," Craig says angrily. "Are you sure there's nothing we can do, Mia?"

"Not in this specific case, although we can use it in evidence in a larger political action concerning these educational contracts. They are grossly unfair and need challenging."

"That doesn't help Mathew right now, though."

"No, I'm sorry."

"I told Hoshi not to let you sign this damned thing," Ju

Shen says.

Mathew says, "She was doing her best. I wanted to sign it."

"Looks like you might have to take the money from Panacea," Mia says. "I'm sorry, Mathew."

He nods, but inside he is seething. "I'm going for a walk," he says, standing.

"Okay. You clear your head," Craig says.

Outside, Mathew jogs across the now empty car park of the hall to the field beyond. He runs up the hill, his legs struggling in the deep snow and, out of breath, finds a tree, and stands with his hands against it; he kicks the tree and keeps kicking it. He doesn't want to take the Panacea money. He doesn't want to leave Elgol. He has nowhere to go in London.

"Bastards," he shouts. "Bastards! Fecking bastards."

"That's no way to speak to a tree." It is Lea's voice. Mathew doesn't turn around. "No way to treat it, either."

"Leave it, Lea," Mathew says. "I'm not in the mood."

"What happened to you?"

"Please, feck off. I need some peace."

"Jeeze. And I came to offer to buy you a smoothie, but if that's how you are, screw you," Lea starts walking back down the field.

Mathew turns and watches her go and is immediately sorry, "Lea! Lea, I'm sorry," he runs down after her, catches her by the arm. "Really, I'm sorry. I had a shitty morning."

"That's fine," Lea says, "But no need to take it out on me. I thought we were friends."

"We are friends. I'm sorry."

She looks at him for a moment and then says, "Do you still want a smoothie? Then you can tell me what's happened?"

Mathew smiles, "Yeah, I'd love a smoothie." They start to walk again. "How's Isaac?"

"Awake," she says. "But he has to stay in the hospital for a few days. You should go and see him."

"I will."

They kick the snow from their boots on the side of the wooden steps, by the cafe. "So what happened?"

"My school happened. I have a corporate scholarship. I either have to pay back my fees or go back to London."

"How much are your fees?"

"Six hundred thousand."

"Wow."

They go into the cafe and sit down. Oli comes over to take their order.

"So what are you going to do?" Lea asks when Oli goes off to make their smoothies.

"I have nowhere to stay in London. Our house needs to be sold. I can't go back there now. I have no choice."

"Would you want to go back, if you had a choice?"

"I don't know," Mathew says, thinking of Clara. Mathew puts his head in his hands.

"All for a corporate education. I could teach you more about tech in a week than those monkeys have taught you in sixteen years, I reckon."

Mathew grins, "I reckon you could too, Lea. But if I stay here, I have to find the money, and the only place I can get it is from the money Panacea wants to pay me to keep me quiet about my mother's death."

Lea's eyes widen, "Now I see why you were kicking the poor tree," she says. "But you can't take their money."

"I have to," Mathew says.

"What will happen if you don't?"

"They'll put me and my grandmother on a repayment plan that will be hereditary. They'll probably make her sell her house here."

"Wow."

"Yes, wow."

Oli returns with their drinks. "Two banana and chocolate smoothies with fresh mint," he says. "I threw in the strawberry garnish for free," he says.

They take their drinks. There's a skewered strawberry on a stick hanging over each glass.

"Thanks, Oli. They look amazing."

Mathew takes a sip of his and pulls a face. "What kind of chocolate is it?" he asks.

"100%. No sugar. It's good for you."

"It tastes good for you. That's the problem."

"You get used to it," Lea says.

"Hmmm…" Mathew says noncommittally, cautiously taking another sip.

"Not sure?"

Mathew shakes his head.

"I'll drink it if you don't want it."

Mathew holds onto his glass protectively. "I didn't say I wasn't going to drink it."

Lea takes another gulp of her smoothie and says, "Is there anyone in London you can stay with? Any friends?"

Mathew thinks and says, "There is Gen."

"Who's Gen?"

"Our neighbour. A piano teacher. She's known me all my life and was kind to me when Mum got sick. But she lives alone. She probably wouldn't want a teenaged boy messing up her house."

"Why don't you ask her? Can't hurt, can it? She can only say no. That way, you don't have to take Panacea's blood money and we can do something with those documents I found."

"You're not still going on about those?"

"Why not? We could get them out to the world."

Mathew shakes his head.

"Are you worried about damaging your mother's reputation?"

"No," Mathew says. "I was wrong about that. I was wrong about her. She wanted to resign and they wouldn't let her. She knew too much."

Lea gapes, "Do you think they meant to kill her?"

"I don't know."

"Then don't you want to get back at them?"

"Yes, of course I do."

"This could be the best way to do it. To clear her name and expose Panacea."

Mathew drains his drink, trying to decide if the strange chocolate is growing on him or not.

"I'll think about it," Mathew says. "My head is spinning. I want to go and see Isaac."

26 HAUNTED BY HERSELF

"Ten minutes," Clara says to her guard. He nods amiably enough because she was true to her word the last time she took a detour, and gets into the car, turning on Nexus entertainment in his Lenz.

Clara hesitates before banging on Mr. Lestrange's door. Part of her can't reconcile the events she experienced the last time she passed over this threshold. When the door opens and his odd face and deep-set eyes peer down at her from his spindly height, she half expects him not to know who she is. But instead he smiles. "Come in," he says, making way for her.

She hesitates at the bottom of the stairs. "Should I go up?" she asks.

"Not right now," he says. "We have other business to attend to first."

She follows him into his front room, where he pulls out the *Book of Clara*, leafs through to a particular page, studies it for a few moments to make sure he has found the right place and then places it open on the table.

"Where are we going?"

"To your future again. A few days after Mathew's death. It would be best if you spoke with your older self,

227

rather than me doing it."

Clara raises an eyebrow. "I'm not sure what my future self would prefer, being told that my husband who I saw murdered with my own eyes is not dead, but is resurrected in the past, by the ghost of my old self or by a strange alien from the future."

"This was your idea."

"Yes, I know. I'm sorry. Of course, I am happy to come with you."

"It should be less dramatic than last time," he says.

In the Darkroom, Lestrange fits Clara's Skullcap and they are once again standing in the corridor. They head to the yellow life jacket, open the door and step into the dank and rotting office.

Tuesday 20th February 2091, Silverwood

This time Mathew doesn't burst out through the door. This time there is no storm.

Clara takes Lestrange's offered hand and blinks and opens her eyes on a bright living room with a remarkable view over the city of Silverwood. Clara goes over to the window and looks out. A car zips past forty feet away on a wafer-thin road winding like a ball of string around the hundreds of high-rises thrown upwards to the half-grown dome above.

"Where is this?" Clara asks.

"Your home in 2091."

"Wow."

"You've only recently moved in, actually," Lestrange indicates the small pile of still unpacked boxes in a corner of the large open-plan room, near the kitchen. There's a HomeAngel working near the sink, emptying a bin. It's a lot more human than the ones in Clara's own time; its movements are uncanny, although it has a shiny, hard white surface and large blue LED eyes. George, the boy from the cathedral, is sitting on a sofa near the window with the amazing view, staring into space. He doesn't look like he's had any sleep recently.

Lestrange leads Clara across the apartment to a passage with doors leading to bedrooms. Older Clara's bedroom door is open. She is lying face down on the bed, her head turned, her eyes open. There's a tissue in her hand and others scattered around her on the bed and the floor.

Lestrange indicates to young Clara that she should sit in the armchair next to the bed. She does as she's told.

"In ten seconds you will be visible to her, but only her." Lestrange says. He counts her down.

The older Clara screams. George comes running from the living room into the room. "What happened?" he asks. "Mum?"

Older Clara has shuffled off the bed and is standing in the corner of the room. To George she seems to be staring at thin air. To younger Clara and Lestrange she is staring right at her younger self, although she hasn't quite figured that out yet.

"Well, this is going well," young Clara says.

"She can hear you," Lestrange says.

"But not you?"

"No."

"Who are you?" older Clara asks.

"Mum, what are you staring at? Who are you talking to?"

Older Clara looks at George. "You can't see anything?"

George shakes his head, frowning, worried.

"It must be the medication," Clara says. "The doctor said it could have side effects."

"Then you should stop taking it," George says. "If it's actually making you worse."

Older Clara nods absently, still staring at young Clara. "Yes. You're right. I should."

George goes over to his mother, still cowering in the corner of the room. "Mum, you should lie down." He leads her back to the bed, and she lets him help her. He holds the covers for her. "Why don't you try and sleep?"

"Okay," she says, but her eyes are drawn back to that one blank spot hovering above the armchair.

"What do you see?" George asks.

Older Clara smiles weakly and shakes her head, "Nothing. Nothing at all." She lets him pull the cover over her. She takes his hand and squeezes it. "Thank you. Thank you, George. You've been so good."

"Please don't even say it," he says. "Just be well. Be okay. For me. I need you, Mum."

"I know. I will be. I promise," she says, holding his hand in hers a moment longer before letting it fall. "I think I'm going to try and sleep now."

"Good." George retreats, stops at the door and turns off the lights by summoning a virtual panel.

"No. Don't. Leave them on," Clara says.

"Okay," he says, putting the lights back up. "I'll be in the other room if you need me."

"Thank you Honey."

He pulls the door shut.

Clara lies with her eyes open staring at the armchair. "Are you a ghost?" she says, finally. "Or some kind of hologram that only I can see?"

Clara says, "If you were going to be haunted by a ghost, why would you be haunted by a ghost of yourself?"

"So you are me. I did wonder. It's surprisingly hard to recognise yourself."

"Yes, I'm you."

"What are you? A recording? A message? Is this one of Mathew's strange tricks? A message from the grave? Are you going to recite his will to me?"

"No, nothing like that. I'm from your past."

"I am hallucinating," she says.

"No, you're not."

Clara pulls a sceptical face, "Then what is going on?"

"I'm here to tell you Mathew is not dead."

"This must be the drugs or I'm going mad," older Clara

puts her hands over her eyes.

"You are not going mad."

"I saw him shot. I was with him when he died!"

Young Clara stands and reaches out to her older self. "You must listen to me. He did die, but he is not lost to you. There is a way you can continue to see him, to be with him, but you must listen to me."

Lestrange says, "George heard you talking and is coming back."

The door opens. George pokes his head around. "Mum? I heard voices."

Older Clara looks at her son and sighs. "Talking to myself," she says.

He says, "You must try and rest."

"I know. I'm sorry."

"Don't be sorry, but you will make yourself ill if you carry on like this. I can't lose both of you. I can't."

Older Clara reaches out her hands to her son. George comes to her and sits on the bed. "You won't, George. I'm so sorry. I know how hard this must have been for you with Hathaway appearing on top of everything else. I don't want to add to things."

George takes her hands and squeezes them. "I need you to get well. Please try and sleep."

She nods. He stands and walks to the door. "Sure you don't want the light off?" he asks.

She shakes her head. "Not yet." She smiles.

George leaves.

Older Clara looks at young Clara and says quietly, "You're still there."

"I want to help you. Me. I don't want to live in a future without Mathew," she says. "There is no need for you to be so sad."

Clara says, "I am grief-stricken. I am drugged up. I am not thinking straight. This cannot be real."

"If you don't believe me, let me show you."

"How?"

"Come with me. I'll take you to see Mathew." She reaches out her hand.

Lestrange flashes them forward to the office building in London. Older Clara barely has a moment to take in her surroundings when she is hurried through the door and into the white corridor.

"These must be the best drugs ever taken," she says to her younger self. "Who is he?" she asks Clara, looking at Lestrange suspiciously.

Clara says, "It's a long story."

"Let's say I'm your guide for today," Lestrange says.

"She has to know," Clara says. "*I* have to know."

"She will."

Along the corridor, they pass through the door leading back into the Darkroom and they find themselves sitting in chairs in a row. Lestrange helps them remove their Skullcaps. Older Clara looks around. "This is an antique!" she says.

"It's only thirty-six years old, relative to your time."

"Still."

Lestrange goes to the door, holding it open for the two Claras. "This way."

"What is this place?" older Clara asks. "It looks a bit like Mathew's old house in London, when he was boy."

"It's Mr. Lestrange's house," young Clara says. "He lives next door to young Mathew."

"Are you telling me we are in the past?"

"We're in 2055," Lestrange says.

"So am I going to meet a young version of Mathew? Is that what this is about?"

They climb the stairs. Lestrange says, "It's your husband you are going to meet again."

Lestrange opens the door to a bedroom where Mathew lies asleep on the bed. Older Clara rushes to him. She sits on the bed.

"He is alive," Lestrange says.

Sure enough, older Clara watches her husband's breath, rising and falling steadily.

"How can this be? He was dead. I'm sure he was. His body was destroyed in the fire in the lab." Her voice breaks.

"We rescued him," Lestrange says, "and brought him here."

"Is he alright?" Clara leans over him. She takes his hand, touches his face. Her hands are shaking. "There's not a mark on him. It's amazing."

"He's in an induced coma right now while his body repairs."

"But he will wake at some point? And speak to me again?"

"Yes," Lestrange says.

"How did you do this?"

Young Clara says, "Mr. Lestrange is a descendent of Hoshi and the Yinglong. He's from the future. He helped me break into my future, your time, to rescue Mathew from his own death."

Lestrange says, "Your younger self here found out about what was going to happen to her in later life and insisted we rescue him," Lestrange says. "You shouldn't think this was my idea."

"But if you can do all of this, why not rescue him in his own time?"

"Do you think the Accountants, the Edenists and the new government would have left Mathew alone had he lived?"

Older Clara turns and looks at Lestrange and says, "No. They would have hunted him down."

Lestrange nods.

Older Clara says, "But he can't stay here."

"No, he can't," Lestrange agrees.

"So where will he go?"

"He can go anywhere but the future. He will be free to choose himself when he wakes. Perhaps he will choose to wander."

"But I will need to go home again?" older Clara says.

"Yes, you will. You have a life to live and important things to do."

"So I will never see him again?"

"I didn't say so. You can see him pretty much any time you want to. When you come here, time stops for you. You can spend hours, weeks, months here and go back to your own time at the precise point you left it."

"How?"

"Through the portal. We'll arrange doors and passageways, places you can find each other safely."

"But not how we were."

"No."

Young Clara says, "But he won't be dead, do you see?"

Older Clara looks at her younger self, her long willowy frame, large hands, thin wrists, long hair, smooth, impossibly young skin. Then she says to Lestrange, "I haven't changed at all, have I?"

Lestrange smiles, "Not one bit."

"What happens when he wakes? I don't want him to be scared."

Lestrange says, "I'm sorry we scared you."

Clara nods, accepting the apology. "You should be here when he wakes. You should tell him what has happened and you'll need to explain to him that he can never go home."

"But I don't know what has happened," older Clara says.

Lestrange goes to the door. "Do you both want to join me downstairs? I can provide refreshments." He says to younger Clara, "I think you have a story to tell your older self."

27 THE ALLOWED LIST

DAY THIRTY-EIGHT: Wednesday 29th December 2055

Craig Buchanan takes Mathew to see his father at night. They both have headlamps, but there is a bright moon and the snow reflects what light there is, making their way easier. The path ahead is clearly visible. Mathew is glad of Craig's presence. The woods cast strange shadows in the moonlight.

"Won't we attract attention doing this?" Mathew asks.

"Possibly. Although, if they are tracking us, they will only see your chip. If they send a drone after us, they will follow us to the cabin and see three hot bodies. Given they aren't looking for your father, it won't mean anything to them. Tomorrow your father will move his base. We've found him somewhere else to go. We thought it best, given the traffic to his current cabin."

Mathew stops in his tracks. "The last thing I want to do is expose him," he says. "If you think there's a risk of that, we should go back."

"He wants to see you, Mathew. He's willing to take the risk."

They trudge on through fresh snowfall from the morning, although now it is still and dry. The smoke from the cabin hails them on the moors and soon they are at Soren's cabin, kicking snow from their boots and taking off their heavy outerwear in the warmth of Soren's cabin. Mathew's father heartily shakes Craig's hand.

"Good to see you," he says. "I have a pot of water boiled for tea."

Soren has found a third chair from somewhere, and they all take seats around the fire. Mathew and Craig explain the situation with the scholarship and with Panacea, warming their hands on hot mugs.

"That's a hard choice, Matty," Soren says, looking gravely at his son.

"I've only just found you again," Mathew says. "I don't want to go."

Soren nods. "I don't especially want you to go either," he says.

"Then I won't go."

"It's your choice. But if you stay, we won't see much of one another for a while anyhow, not as long as Cadmus is here. We'd have to rely on Fitzackerly rigging something for us to be able to chat, the same as we would if you were in London. You'd see a hologram of me in whatever shack Craig here can find for me in the mountains. Maybe you'd get to visit me once in a while, but you know this trip and your last one means I have to move on again."

"I know, I'm sorry."

Soren shakes his head. "I'm not sorry, but it's not something we could do a lot even if you were here. Your grandmother is another matter. But I'm willing to bet how she'd feel about taking the money."

Mathew says, "I've an idea about how I can say sorry about Mum."

Soren drinks his tea looking thoughtfully at Mathew. 'That sounds like the sort of thing Craig and I shouldn't know about until it happens. Is it?"

Mathew dips his head, "Yeah."

"You should do what you think is right. Trust yourself."

DAY THIRTY-NINE: Thursday 30th December 2055

"It's only two years and then I can try and get a place in the Highlands University to continue my studies," Mathew is saying to Ju Shen. They are standing in the lobby of the hall, waiting for Shepcutt and Jain.

"Inverness is over a hundred miles away."

It's better than six hundred. Plus, I won't be tied to campus in the way I'm tied to the classroom in London. I can spend weekends and holidays here."

"You'll never come back here to live," Ju Shen says. "Not permanently. But I'm glad you didn't take the Panacea money."

"I couldn't. Not even for Da…"

She puts her finger on his lips. "Don't say that word. And he most of all didn't want you to take the money."

"I know."

"We are here, all of us, any time you want to come home."

"I know. Thank you."

"I spoke to Gen," she says. "She seems like a nice woman."

"She is."

"This is what you want?"

Mathew nods, "I don't want to leave you and… and all of this, these people, everyone here. If I had a choice, I would stay, but I don't have a choice, not if I want to respect myself."

"Sometimes I wish you and I were both a little less moral," she reaches out and touches his face.

"I don't," he says. "Not at all."

He looks across the lobby and sees Isaac talking to Lea.

"Is he still not talking to you?" Ju asks.

"He is, but only in words of one syllable."

"He's angry now, but he'll come round."

"He's had enough of losing people. I promised I wouldn't leave him."

"You couldn't have known. Besides, you'll be friends forever, you two."

Lea catches Mathew's eye and she comes over, dragging Isaac with her. "Bionic boy has come to apologise for being a grumpy ass," she says.

"No he hasn't!" Isaac says.

"It's okay," Mathew says to Lea. He looks at Isaac, "I'm sorry I have to go," he says.

Isaac looks at his feet and mumbles, "You should have taken the money from that company. I don't see why you didn't."

Lea sighs, "I've explained this, Isaac," she says.

"I still don't understand. You could have stayed. You're choosing not to."

Lea looks at Mathew and pulls an *'I tried'* expression.

Ju Shen says, "How's your eye, Isaac?"

Isaac's face brightens, "It's amazing," he says. "I have infrared vision. I can see at night. And I can see far away things in detail."

Through the window Mathew watches Shepcutt and Jain approach. Craig Buchanan walks out to greet them with Isla. They all turn to Mathew and his grandmother.

"I'm so glad you're coming back to complete your studies," Shepcutt says, beaming. He offers Mathew his hand to shake and Mathew takes it.

"I hope you are going to be better at getting him back to London than the other lot were getting him here," Ju Shen says. "I want hourly reports."

"We have extra security travelling with us, Mrs. Shen. Trust me, Jain and I also want to get back down in one piece and we're not taking any chances." He turns to Mathew, "Do you have luggage you need to take back with you?"

Mathew points at his pile of boxes, stacked against the wall, mostly unpacked since his arrival. Shepcutt calls for some help to get the boxes out to the car. Two burly security guards, come into the lobby and help Jain take the boxes out. Buchanan grabs a box and follows the men out to the car park.

Shepcutt says, "Mathew, you should say your goodbyes. When you are ready, meet us in the car park." The two Hermes Link men turn to leave, shaking hands with Isla as they go.

Isla asks Mathew, "Ready?"

"Yes," he says. "Just about."

They all go out into the cold. There are three large armoured all-terrain vehicles in the car park, shining black, thick-tyred, their windows moulded into the body of the car.

Mathew turns to Lea, "How are we doing?" he says.

"We're all ready to go. Tune in at six." She grins. "I'll miss you."

"I'll miss you too."

"Stay in touch or I'll hack into your home system and fry it."

"In that case…"

She hugs him.

"You too, Isaac," he says, when he is finally released from Lea's formidable grip. "Lea will get you set up to chat on the Blackweb or you can always call me using the Nexus." Isaac is still angry and holds back when Mathew hugs him. "C'mon Isaac. Friends?" But Isaac's face is set. He turns away.

Mathew glances at Lea.

Craig, Isla and Ju Shen are waiting to say goodbye to him.

He shakes Craig's and Isla's hands, thanking them both, and turns to his grandmother.

"I want to hear from you all the way down to London and then I want a daily call once you've settled in," she says.

"You got it."

"I'm proud of you."

"I'm proud of you too."

She kisses him sloppily on his cheek. "Don't you dare wipe it off," she says, watching his hand go up. "It is a special protective kiss. Fends off all known adversaries."

Craig shuts the door on him. He winds down the window, so they can see him. Shepcutt nods to the guards who are standing around the three cars and then gets in to the car in front of Mathew's with Jain. They pull away slowly.

The car is a different model to the Panacea cars he is used to travelling in. Spending some minutes familiarising himself with everything, he works out that this car too has a panic room at the back of the mini-fridge. He is relieved that the two Hermes men decided not to travel with him. Finding a drink, he settles back to a holofilm on the coffee table, watching it absently, waiting for the six o'clock news, occasionally gazing out of his window at the lochs and the mountains as they pass through the countryside.

At three o'clock a strange call comes through on his X-Eyte, booting Charybdis. Two tiny figures appear on the table. It is Lea and Isaac.

Mathew laughs, "I've only just left."

"We know. How's the car?"

"Pretty cool."

"Is there any alcohol in the mini-bar?"

"No. Lots of Coke, though."

"Yeuk," Lea says. "Rots your insides. It's like drain cleaner."

"To what do I owe the honour of this visit?" Mathew asks.

"Did we interrupt something?"

"He'll be watching a film," Isaac says.

"I was."

Lea says, "Sorry to interrupt your important work, but Isaac wants to speak to you. I'm going to go now and give him some privacy. Speak later Mat, after the news."

Lea's tiny figure disappears, leaving Isaac alone. He says, "Lea said I should apologise."

"Lea said?" Mathew says.

"I wanted to apologise. I was an idiot. I didn't want you to go."

"I know. I didn't want to go myself. You do understand why I have to, don't you?"

"Not really, but Lea says she's going to get Oli to explain. I also wanted to say thank you, for everything you did for me."

"Anyone would have done the same."

"No they wouldn't. I will never forget what you did for me. I owe you."

"Don't be crazy."

"I mean it. I hope we'll always be friends."

"Of course we will. And now Lea has shown you how to call me, we can chat whenever you like."

"Can I call you on the Nexus? I'm not sure about this Blackweb stuff."

Mathew laughs, "Sure you can. What's your last name? I'll add it to my allowed list."

"Hathaway," he says. "My name is Hathaway."

28 COMING HOME

DAY FORTY: New Year's Eve December 2055

Clara hits a wrong note and stops playing. This is something that never happens and it makes Gen Lacey turn around. She is standing in the window of her front room, half listening to her student and half watching the road through her voile curtains.

Clara is staring at her hands as if they have betrayed her, as if they are no longer her hands.

"Nervous?" Gen asks.

Clara flushes from her neck to the roots of her hair. "I'm fine," she says brusquely and starts to play again, deliberate, precise, without finesse, but also without error. Her concentration is shot and her thoughts are a muddle. The part of her brain that is playing is the the part that could play with her entire body on fire, which in a way, it is.

She wonders if it makes it better or worse knowing that this boy, who she met only a few weeks ago, but that she already has such strong feelings for, is destined to be her husband, and in some future world, already is. Thus far, her conversations with the remarkable Mr. Lestrange, about her future life with Mathew, have felt abstract. Mathew himself, when he was hundreds of miles away in Elgol, was a dreamlike notion. Today, however, the real flesh and blood boy is returning. He will live in her music teacher's home and she will see him every day.

He is likely to turn up any moment now and she is in turmoil.

Will she be awkward with him? Will she do or say the wrong thing and somehow change the way he feels about her and then change history? Will she even feel the same way about him?

She tries to return her full attention to the music and remember the aim of the lesson. Then just as she starts to feel some equilibrium, just as she manages to pull her head and her heart back to the piano, she hears the car pull up outside.

He is here.

She doesn't know how she gets to the front door or how it opens or if Gen comes with her. As she stands in the front garden, the world spins and darkens at the edges. For a moment she thinks she might pass out. *Why do I feel like this?*

He is getting out of the car. He sees her. It is an extraordinary thing to love a particular face, she thinks. Why that face of all faces? He moves at the same time she does. She registers him dropping his bag on the floor; just let it go.

All the way from Yorkshire, Mathew has been thinking of Clara, ever since he realised she will likely be there when he arrives. He thinks about her last rather curt message and how she seems to have retreated from him. It is not surprising, considering how distracted and distant he has been. But then, he thinks, she's not that kind of person. She, of all people, will understand that he has just been overwhelmed by circumstances. There must have been something else going on for her. Perhaps there has been more trouble with her parents. So he puts aside all worry about whether or not she still likes him and pulls up a image he has captured of her, sitting on her bed with her dog Cassie ,and for the first time in weeks, he relaxes.

By the time they reach the outskirts of London, he is anxious again. Even though they sail through the checks at the M25 cordon, the abundance of army personnel and guns, and the tall fences topped with barbed wire, unsettle him. But more than this, he is worrying about what to do when he sees her. In some ways they are so intimate, those many calls, the sound of her voice late at night, but they have hardly spent any time together in the same room. He has no idea what he is meant to do.

Being on Pickervance Road again is a shock. He thinks, of course, of his mother. Part of him expects her to be there as he arrives. Instead, on the doorstep of her house is Gen, and walking steadily towards him is Clara. Before the car has even pulled up, he is opening the door, ignoring the barked commands of his minders. As he steps onto the pavement, he realises he has a bag in his hand and he drops it where it is because he needs to hold out his arms to the girl rushing into them. He needs to concentrate fully on how soft her skin is against his cheek, how warm and right she feels in his arms. And as he kisses her, he is thinking, *I am home.*

29 EPILOGUE

DAY FORTY: New Year's Eve December 2055

Inside the bay window of the front bedroom of number twenty-one Pickervance Road, two men watch as a teenaged boy gets out of a large black off-road vehicle that has pulled up at the kerb, sandwiched between two others.

One of the men standing in the window is tall, thin, rather gangly with pale skin and dark deep-set eyes. The other man is shorter, Asian in appearance, with greying black hair, a long nose and a body thickening around the waist.

The door of the house the cars have pulled up outside is opened by a middle-aged woman with shoulder length curly brown hair, wearing loose fitting trousers and a long bohemian-looking blouse. She starts to move forward down the path, when a girl flies past her, straight into the arms of the boy.

Two men in suits, get out of another car and walk over to speak briefly to the older woman. They shake her hand and hail goodbye to the boy, who isn't listening, and doesn't stir from the arms of the girl. They get back into their car and leave. The small party on the pavement outside slowly turns and heads into the house and the road is quiet once again.

The pale tall man in the window, whose real name is Atteas, but in this human time goes by the name of August Lestrange, leads the other man, who is Dr Mathew Erlang, former researcher in synthetic biology and artificial intelligence, now amateur time traveller, downstairs.

In Atteas' library, Mathew Erlang browses through the large collection of books. "You say I can go anywhere in the collection?" he asks.

"All except these shelves," Atteas says, standing near the door; he sweeps his hand down the last bookcase. "Especially from here."

"So I can go back from there, but not forwards."

"Exactly."

"I can materialise in these worlds?"

"Yes, of course. You can be a ghost or fully materialise, as real as you are now, as you choose, and we can help with things like establishing an identity, getting you somewhere to stay,"

"And Clara can come and visit me?"

"Wherever you are, she can come for a while. She must always return to her own time, though."

"I understand." Mathew idly takes a book from the shelf. It is about Ida Lovelace.

"An early pioneer," Atteas observes.

"Do I need to leave this time soon?" Mathew asks, leafing through the book.

"Now that you are fully recovered physically, if you wouldn't mind, it would be most convenient if you could move on, yes. I wouldn't want our young neighbour to become suspicious, and get distracted again."

"I can tell you from memory, he is distracted in a different way now. I don't think he'll have the energy to be breaking into your conservatory again."

Attic laughs. "Well that is a relief."

Dr Erlang puts the book back and continues to run his hand along history. "What a lot of history there is," he says. "Where should I go?"

"That is entirely up to you."

THANKS FOR READING!

If you enjoyed reading *The Moon at Noon,* please do leave a review on Amazon and Goodreads. You might not think it matters, but it makes a huge difference.

KEEP IN TOUCH

The Moon at Noon may be the last in the House Next Door trilogy, but it isn't the end of the story. Get the latest on what happens next, news about new books and offers by signing up to my mailing list.

http://juleowen.com/mailing-list/

ACKNOWLEDGMENTS

NOTES

The Moon at Noon and the other books in the *House Next Door* trilogy represent my version of the future, inspired by non-fiction books by Michio Kaku, Martin Rees, K Eric Drexler, George Friedman, Alan Weisman, James Lovelock and James Hansen, amongst others. My full list of sources can be found on my website at http://juleowen.com/futurology-resources

We are now living in the Anthropocene age, the first period in geological history when humans have had a significant impact on the earth's ecosystem. One direct result of this is climate change. We are also living in a time of exponential technological innovation. It is an extraordinary and frightening time to be alive. My stories are my way of coming to terms with this and exploring possible futures. Find out more about the background to my stories here http://juleowen.com/futurology/

WITH THANKS

I think the point when I realised that I needed others help to complete my books was the point when it became possible.

Thanks to my editor Lynda Thornhill for your eye for detail and your enthusiasm for my books.

Thanks especially to my eagle-eyed beta readers, Mauro Rizzi, John MacBain, Peter Bell, Chris Green and Adam Masojada.

Thanks also to Lorna Barker, Emilie MacMullen, René Jaspers, Tommy Nakamura, Akvilė Štuopytė, Caroline Juricic, Mauro Rizzi, Caroline Bertin, Mark Klein, James McCarthy, Lisa Beecham, Peter Jansen, Sophie Salisbury, Henry Blanchard, Pilar Knoke, Nativ Gill, Jonathan Hulse, Christina Hegele, Heather Allen, Lindsay Charman, and Laxmi Hariharan.

I owe a huge debt of gratitude to Mark Speed, who was kind enough to read early versions of this book, edit and offer invaluable feedback. He took me under his wing and has been a constant source of encouragement and useful advice. Mark is the creator of the wonderful Doctor How series, the real story behind the Doctor Who myth. For those of you who like some comedy with their sci-fi, Mark's books are a tonic. The first in the series, *Doctor How and the Illegal Aliens* can be found on Amazon.

Thanks to my Dad for always being there.

Most of all, thanks to Lauren for your endless patience, support and kindness. This book would never have been written without you.

ABOUT THE AUTHOR

Jule Owen was born in the North of England in a little place nestled between Snowdonia, the Irish Sea and the Pennines. She now lives in London, UK, where the weather is warmer, and there are more museums, but she misses the wide open spaces and the good quality water.

Jule spent many years working in online technology, latterly in the video games industry and is fascinated by science, technology and futurology, which she periodically blogs and tweets about.

Her books are her creative response to the exponential growth of technological innovation in the era of climate change, with a bit of magic thrown in.

She can usually be found online and would love to hear from you. Look her up here:

www.juleowen.com
@juleowen

Printed in Great Britain
by Amazon